CALDER STRONG

The Calder Series by Janet Dailey

THIS CALDER RANGE

STANDS A CALDER MAN

THIS CALDER SKY

CALDER BORN, CALDER BRED

CALDER PRIDE

GREEN CALDER GRASS

SHIFTING CALDER WIND

CALDER PROMISE

LONE CALDER STAR

CALDER STORM

SANTA IN MONTANA

The Calder Brand Series

CALDER BRAND

CALDER GRIT

A CALDER AT HEART

CALDER COUNTRY

CALDER STRONG

CALDER STRONG

JANET DAILEY

KENSINGTON PUBLISHING CORP.

kensingtonbooks.com

This book is a work of fiction. Names, characters, businesses, organizations, places, events, and incidents either are the product of the author's imagination or are used fictitiously. Any resemblance to actual persons, living or dead, events, or locales is entirely coincidental.

To the extent that the image or images on the cover of this book depict a person or persons, such person or persons are merely models, and are not intended to portray any character or characters featured in the book.

KENSINGTON BOOKS are published by

Kensington Publishing Corp.
900 Third Avenue
New York, NY 10022

Copyright © 2025 by Revocable Trust Created by Jimmy Dean Dailey and Mary Sue Dailey Dated December 22, 2016

After the passing of Janet Dailey, the Dailey family worked with a close associate of Janet's to continue her literary legacy, using her notes, ideas, and favorite themes to complete her novels and create new ones, inspired by the American men and women she loved to portray.

All rights reserved. No part of this book may be reproduced in any form or by any means without the prior written consent of the Publisher, excepting brief quotes used in reviews.

Without limiting the author's and publisher's exclusive rights, any unauthorized use of this publication to train generative artificial intelligence (AI) technologies is expressly prohibited.

All Kensington titles, imprints, and distributed lines are available at special quantity discounts for bulk purchases for sales promotion, premiums, fund-raising, educational, or institutional use.

Special book excerpts or customized printings can also be created to fit specific needs. For details, write or phone the office of the Kensington Special Sales Manager: Attn. Special Sales Department, Kensington Publishing Corp., 900 Third Avenue, New York, NY 10022. Phone: 1-800-221-2647.

KENSINGTON and the K with book logo Reg. U.S. Pat. & TM Off.

Library of Congress Card Catalogue Number: 2025936255

ISBN: 978-1-4967-4475-3

First Kensington Hardcover Edition: October 2025

ISBN: 978-1-4967-4479-1 (ebook)

10 9 8 7 6 5 4 3 2 1

Printed in the United States of America

The authorized representative in the EU for product safety and compliance
is eucomply OU, Parnu mnt 139b-14, Apt 123
Tallinn, Berlin 11317, hello@eucompliancepartner.com

CALDER STRONG

CHAPTER ONE

Blue Moon, Montana
Early summer, 1929

JOSEPH DOLLARHIDE STOOD IN THE DUST OF THE ROUND PEN, THE sun blazing down on his dark head. Sweat drizzled down his face and glued his denim work shirt to his torso as he focused his attention on saddle-breaking a two-year-old colt.

The colt, a spectacular bay with champion bloodlines, had reached a full height of fifteen hands at the shoulder; but the young horse was still putting on muscle. Like a teenage human, the colt was restless, impulsive, and had a great deal to learn. It would be Joseph's job to teach him.

"Easy, boy," Joseph murmured, stroking the white star on the colt's forehead. "Easy, now. That's it. You're safe here. Everything's going to be fine."

The colt's intelligent, liquid eyes watched his every move, ears shifting to catch every nuanced whisper. The youngster, a registered American quarter horse, had been promised to a wealthy Nevada rancher for a princely sum. The balance of the money was to be paid on delivery, after the colt had been broken Comanche-style by Joseph Dollarhide.

Joseph had taken the colt's training at a gentle pace, building trust over time. Now, as he laid the thick, woolen saddle pad on its back, he hummed the Comanche horse chant he'd learned from his grandfather, Joe Dollarhide. The old man, a master horse trainer, had been gone for years, but in his later life, he'd taught his grandson much of what he knew. Joseph had taken every lesson to heart. Now, at twenty-four, he was still learning from experience, but he was already building a reputation as a great natural trainer.

Joseph had heard the story of how his grandfather's life had been guided by dreams of a blue roan stallion. When a similar dream had come to Joseph a few years ago, he'd taken it as a message that he should follow the same path.

But that didn't mean that the path would be easy. Joseph was reminded of that every time he went home to his family.

A quiver passed through the colt's body as Joseph lifted the saddle and laid it over the pad. Still chanting, he buckled the straps and tightened the cinch. The colt had worn the saddle and a light bridle before. But today, for the first time, he'd be carrying a rider—and he was smart enough to sense that something new was about to happen.

Logan Hunter, who was married to Joseph's aunt, Dr. Kristin Dollarhide, watched from outside the log fence. The Hunter Ranch, with its cattle and pedigreed horses, belonged to him. But he'd offered Joseph a partnership in the horse business if his training could bring in enough cash.

For Joseph, that would be a dream come true. But Joseph's father had other ideas.

Blake Dollarhide was already planning for Joseph, his only son, to step into managing the Dollarhide Ranch and Sawmill. But that day could wait, Joseph told himself. Blake was barely into his fifties. He was in good health, and he liked being the boss. Joseph's full-time help wouldn't be needed for years. Meanwhile, he would have time to pursue his dream.

"That colt looks a mite skittish to me," Logan said. "Do you think he's ready to ride?"

Joseph took a moment to shoo a fly that buzzed around the colt's face. "This boy's got a lot of spunk," he said. "That's not going to change. I'd say he's ready, but I'm expecting some resistance."

As he slipped a boot into the left stirrup, preparing to mount, his grandfather's words echoed in Joseph's mind.

Remember, a horse is a prey animal. If something lands on his back, his instincts tell him he's about to become a meal. So he fights for his life. Your horse has the same fear that saved his ancestors. You can't force it out of him. You can only teach him to trust you—and to believe that whatever happens, you'll keep him safe.

Joseph pushed up in the stirrup, swung his right leg across, and settled into the saddle. At the sudden weight, a shudder passed through the colt's body. He snorted. His legs danced sideways. Then, with a squeal of fury, he exploded straight up and started to buck.

As the colt jumped, twisted, and sunfished like a rodeo bronc, raising clouds of dust, Joseph steeled his resolve. It wouldn't do for the young horse to learn that he could get rid of a rider by bucking him off. He'd be sure to try it again next time. The surest way to teach the rascal a lesson would be to outlast him.

Now, as he fought to stay in the saddle, Joseph could feel the colt tiring. Little by little, his frantic jumps slowed and weakened until, at last, he stood with his head down, his sides lathered and heaving.

With dust clouds settling and Logan cheering from the fence, Joseph eased his battered body to the ground. He had won the battle of wills. Now all that remained was to cool his pupil down, give him a good rubbing with a towel, and take a well-earned break on the ranch house porch with a glass of cold milk and a wedge of Aunt Kristin's apple pie.

He was walking the colt around the pen, feeling proud of his progress, when he heard the faint ringing of the ranch house telephone. He paid it scant attention. As Blue Moon's only doctor, his aunt often got calls from people who needed her services.

Moments later, Kristin burst out of the house. Still wearing her apron and clutching her black medical bag, she raced for the Chevrolet Superior truck she drove on emergency calls. Her auburn hair blew loose. Her pale face wore an expression Joseph had never seen before.

"Joseph!" she shouted. "Come with me now! There's been an accident—a terrible accident!"

Three days later

Joseph gazed down at the two flower-strewn graves, seeing them through a haze of grief. The sky was a blinding blue, the mounded dirt still raw, like an open wound in the skin of the earth. A circling hawk cast a shadow over the graves, its cry a heart stab as Joseph struggled with the shock of what had happened. How could a single split-second decision end two treasured lives and shatter the peace of a family?

The fatal decision had been his father's. Blake Dollarhide had been driving the family's aging Model T down the switchbacks from the house on the bluff to the main road when a deer had bounded into the path of the car. Acting on reflex, Blake had slammed on the brakes and swerved hard right. The front wheels had overshot the crumbling edge of the road. The vehicle had careened down the high embankment and crashed onto the rocks below.

Three members of the Dollarhide family had been inside the car. Blake's wife, Hannah, and their fifteen-year-old daughter, Elsa, had died instantly. Blake had suffered a shattered pelvis and crushed vertebrae. He would live, but the doctors in Miles City had given him little, if any, hope of walking again. The deer, as if it mattered, had been found dead below the road.

After the frantic call, Joseph and Kristin had rushed to the scene of the accident. Blake had been in shock and too badly injured for them to move him. There'd been little they could do except keep him stable until the ambulance arrived from Miles City. The images Joseph had seen that day—the twisted wreckage and the bodies of his mother and sister—would haunt him for the rest of his life.

Confined to a hospital bed, Blake had been unable to see his wife and daughter laid to rest. But other friends and family members had come for the simple service in the small graveyard behind the house. Blake's older daughter, Annie, had arrived by train from Butte with her mining engineer husband, Frank. Pregnant with her first child, she'd wept inconsolably, sobbing over the graves until Frank led her back to the house.

Britta, Hannah's younger sister, was a tower of strength, her plain face showing little emotion. Married to the former sheriff, who now worked from his wheelchair as the foreman of the Hunter Ranch, Britta was expecting her second child—joyous news for the family. But after she'd lost both parents, two brothers, a sister, now another sister and a niece, Joseph had sensed, as she hugged him close, that his beloved aunt was crumbling inside.

There were others who'd come—neighbors, friends, schoolmates of Elsa's, and women who'd stocked the kitchen with casseroles, breads, and desserts. But one family member hadn't shown up, nor had Joseph expected to see him. Mason Dollarhide, Blake's half-brother, had created a permanent rift in the family twenty-five years ago when he'd impregnated an innocent farm girl and left town to avoid a shotgun marriage. It was Blake who'd stepped in, wed young Hannah, and raised her son as his own.

In every way save one, Blake Dollarhide was Joseph's father. But Joseph's striking eyes—jade green, like Mason's—were on display for all to see and know the truth.

Had Mason, who'd inherited the nearby Hollister Ranch from his mother, stayed away out of respect or out of indifference? But that question didn't matter. Hurts ran long and deep in the Dollarhide family. Even if he'd come to the service, Mason might have been tolerated. But he would not have been welcomed.

Others, however, were there. Blue Moon was a close-knit community. At tragic times like this, most quarrels and feuds could be put aside to pay respects to the bereaved family.

"Joseph, I'm truly sorry. What a loss." Chase Calder stood facing Joseph, his hand extended. Tall and broad-shouldered, with dark hair and piercing brown eyes, Chase was barely two years older than Joseph. As boys, they'd been friends. But that was before long-standing family rivalries had driven them apart.

Chase's handshake was firm. After the passing of his father,

Webb, he'd taken control of the biggest ranch in the state of Montana. His ascendancy showed in his bearing, his confidence, and the air of entitlement that came with the Calder name. Like his father and grandfather before him, Chase was Calder strong and Calder rich. He wore his power like a crown.

They exchanged a few polite words. Joseph thanked him for coming and watched him walk away. Their meeting had been cordial enough. But despite Chase's handshake and consoling words, Joseph could be sure of one thing. The rivalry between the Calders and the Dollarhides hadn't changed and probably never would. For years to come, perhaps for the rest of their lives, the two boyhood friends were destined to be rivals.

Midsummer, five weeks later

Joseph stood on the porch of the sprawling log home that had sheltered his family for three generations. Gauzy clouds drifted over the full moon, casting shadows that flowed like water across the yard. Insects chirped and droned in the darkness. Bats darted and dived, catching their prey in midair. From somewhere down the wooded slope, the call of a coyote quivered on the night breeze.

The house was silent, as if the accident had sucked the life of what had once been a home. Hannah and Elsa had been the happy members of the family, chatting, laughing, and singing as they went about their day. Now, memories lurked like ghosts in empty rooms and shadowed corners. Even the air felt dead.

Joseph's hands rested on the porch rail, his calloused fingertips finding the old chisel marks left from the shaping of the wood. Joseph's grandfather had built the house on the crest of a high bluff with a panoramic view of the family empire—the barns, sheds, corrals, and the bunk house, the pastures teeming with white-and-red Hereford cattle, and at the foot of the bluff, the sawmill.

The Dollarhide sawmill had spread into the pastureland like an ever-growing fungus. A convoluted maze of logs, stacked boards, sheds, machinery, and mountains of sawdust, the mill was ugly even by moonlight. But the demand for lumber had contributed greatly to the Dollarhide fortune as well as provided jobs for more than twenty men.

Joseph had grown up hating the scream of saw blades, the gritty air, and the vile yellow sawdust that coated everything, even the sweating men and the huge, gentle draft horses that pulled the logs. As a youngster, he'd vowed that when he grew up to be the boss, he would close the mill, maybe sell it to someone who would cart everything away, and let the land go back to nature. As a man, he knew that wasn't going to happen, especially now that he had no choice. It would be up to him to carry on his father's legacy. The mill was a vital part of that legacy.

Blake Dollarhide had devoted his life to providing for his family, both the present and future generations. Under his stewardship, the Dollarhide holdings had more than tripled in value. But at what cost? Joseph had never known his father to take a vacation or to spend money on any unnecessary pleasure, not even a nice car. He had the money. He could have bought a DeSoto, a Packard, or any other auto that caught his fancy. But he'd insisted that the family's eight-year-old Model T was good enough for a sensible man like him. He had been driving that car when it left the road and crashed.

As if thinking of Blake could summon him, Joseph heard the rumble of wheels crossing the darkened parlor. His father had been home for almost three weeks. A young orderly had been hired to help him around and see to his needs. But despite being in considerable pain, Blake refused to rest. He was pushing his limits, denying his grief, and fighting to prove that he was the man he'd always been. Using his powerful arms and gritting his teeth against the pain, he'd managed to drag himself from the bed to his wheelchair. Now, on his own, he could go anywhere on the main floor of the house, at any hour.

Joseph turned toward the sound, then checked himself. He had learned the hard way not to offer help. Instead, he waited for his father to come to him.

The wheelchair rolled out onto the porch and stopped beside him at the rail. Blake had made it on his own, driving the large wheels forward with his hands. "Shouldn't you be resting, Dad?" Blake asked. "It's after midnight."

"Can't sleep. Too much going on in my head. How about you?"

"The same, I guess." Joseph knew that his father was grieving. But Blake had scarcely mentioned the loss of his wife and daughter, choosing to keep his emotions locked inside. It was his way of being a man, and he expected the same of his son.

"I've been worried about the mill," Blake said. "The men are good workers, but if you don't check the quality of every board that goes on those wagons, things can get slipshod, and the next thing you know, you're losing customers. Are you spending enough time there?"

"I was there most of the morning yesterday." Joseph spoke the truth. "Everything was fine."

"What about that big order for the new warehouse in Miles City? Will the first batch of lumber be ready on time?"

"Yes, everything's on schedule," Joseph said. "I checked on the cattle, too. Coyotes got one of the calves in the upper pasture. I had to fire the cowboy who went to sleep on the job and let it happen. You could use a dog or two up there. I know a man in town who's got some pups for sale."

"I don't want no damn dogs. Just more mouths to feed. And you can't trust 'em. First thing you know, they'll go rogue and start killing stock on their own." The gritty undertone in Blake's voice told Joseph his father was speaking through excruciating pain. But Blake would never own up to that.

This would be no time for Joseph to mention his work with Logan's horses. While his father was in the hospital, he'd stolen enough time to finish breaking the bay colt. But there were more colts waiting and no time to spare. Logan would have to do the work himself. For now, maybe even forever, Joseph's dream would have to wait.

Gazing out past the porch, into the moonlit darkness, Joseph could see across the distant pastures to where a crude dirt road cut across the open country. The road, which from here looked as thin as a pencil line, connected the Dollarhide and Hunter ranches. From there it meandered through a scatter of dirt farms before joining with the road to town.

Something was moving along that road—a distant speck of light that became a pair of headlamps before taking a cutoff and disappearing in the dark.

"Looks like moonshiners," Joseph said. Smuggling illegally brewed liquor was nothing new in these parts. It had been going on since the passage of the Volstead Act in 1919. When one moonshiner died or got arrested, others would show up to take his place. For the most part, law-abiding folks had learned to look the other way.

"Do you think Mason's up to his old tricks?" Blake rarely mentioned his half-brother and their painful past. "You'd think five years in prison would cure a man. But I know for a fact he went back to smuggling after he got out."

"What Mason does is no concern of ours." Joseph and his teenage friends had been caught up in Mason's first bootlegging operation. When their involvement had almost gotten the boys killed, Joseph had cut all ties to his natural father. Mason was married now and had supposedly gone straight. But Joseph would never trust him again.

The two men had fallen silent. Joseph could almost feel the pain in each labored breath his father took. Blake had broken ribs in addition to his spinal injuries. The healing would take time.

Joseph was about to suggest that they go back inside and go to bed when Blake cleared his throat and spoke.

"There's something I've been meaning to say. After the accident, I thought it might be too soon. But I've waited long enough."

"I'm listening." Joseph braced himself for bad news. What else could it be?

"I've spent my life building a legacy for this family," Blake said. "Not just for now, but for future generations of Dollarhides. Now

I've begun to wonder where those generations are going to come from or whether they'll even exist.

"Your mother, rest her sweet soul, was still young. I'd always hoped we might have more children. But now . . ."

The words choked off his throat. Joseph waited for him to recover and go on, even though he could already sense where this conversation was leading.

"Now Elsa's gone, and Annie won't be raising her children on this ranch. Frank's a mining engineer. He can't make a living here. As for me, there's no chance of my marrying again. What woman would have me? And why even think about it, when I can't . . ." He let the words trail off, though his meaning was clear enough.

"Aunt Kristin has two boys," Joseph volunteered.

"They have their own place, damn it. Besides, they don't have the Dollarhide name." He twisted his head to fix Joseph with a stern gaze. "The future of the Dollarhide family is going to depend on you, Joseph."

"Uh, Dad you know—"

"Of course, I know." Blake cut him off almost angrily. "Your children won't be my direct descendants. But they'll be a direct line from Joe Dollarhide. They'll have the name, and the boys will carry it on."

Joseph had sensed that this was coming. Still, he felt as if he'd been struck by a cannonball. At twenty-four, he'd been enjoying a carefree bachelorhood, doing what he pleased, romancing any girl or woman who caught his fancy, bedding the ones who were willing and knew the score. Someday, he'd take a wife, but only when he found the right one. Meanwhile, there was no reason to rush. Now all that was about to change.

"It's time you lived up to your responsibility, Joseph," Blake said. "There are plenty of single girls in Blue Moon. Pick a nice, fertile one, get married, and start filling this empty house with little Dollarhides! That's an order!"

CHAPTER TWO

On Friday, Joseph totaled the past two weeks' payments for lumber deliveries, put $6,255 in cash and checks into his briefcase, and set out for the bank in Miles City.

In the days after the accident, with Blake in the hospital, the ranch had needed a vehicle. The brand new Ford Model A Tudor sedan that Joseph had bought for $500 was still a sore point between father and son. Joseph could've argued that if Blake had been driving that car when the deer jumped in front of him, his wife and daughter might still be alive. But there was nothing to be gained by casting blame. Blake had already cast enough blame on himself.

Price-wise, the Tudor was at the low end of the Ford line. But driving the shiny red auto was pure pleasure. The motor started up without the need of a crank. The forty-horsepower engine gave it a top speed of sixty-five miles per hour, with a three-speed sliding gear and a single speed reverse. The four-wheel mechanical drum brakes could stop on a dime.

The day Joseph had driven his father home from the hospital, Blake, braced and in pain, had complained all the way about the cost of buying a new car when several hundred dollars could have been saved on a used Model T. But Joseph had understood that the real issue wasn't money. It was that Blake had been bypassed in the decision to buy the car. He hadn't even been asked.

For now, Joseph would be walking a tightrope between pleasing his father and carrying out his new responsibilities. Much as he longed to be free again, there could be no turning away from the demands of the ranch and the mill.

Had Chase Calder felt the same when his father died, leaving his son to run the biggest ranch in Montana? No, Chase had stepped into his new role as if born to it—which he was. Chase had been the crown prince of the Calder line from his boyhood. Now he was king.

Joseph felt more like a glorified lackey, in charge of the family enterprises but accountable to his father for every decision.

Now, as he drove down the switchback road from the house, he put out a hand to keep the briefcase from sliding off the seat beside him. He slowed the car as he passed the place where Blake had swerved the Model T and careened over the side. Joseph's first order, the day after the accident, had been to have the crumbling edge shored up with rocks and timbers. Other spots on the road to the bluff were equally at risk. He would need to get a crew on road repair soon, before another tragedy occurred.

After stopping by the sawmill and taking time to check with the foreman on duty, Joseph drove on to the junction with the main road and made a right turn toward town. The week of the accident, the road had been a quagmire of mud. The recent summer hot spell had dried the potholes, ridges, and furrows to the hardness of concrete. The Model A lurched and shuddered over the washboard surface, jarring Joseph's bones.

As far as he knew, the only paved road in fifty miles ran the short distance from downtown Miles City to the railway depot. With so many people driving autos, there'd surely be a demand for more paving. Somebody with the money to invest would be in line to make a fortune.

That wouldn't be him. But while he was in Miles City, he would arrange a bid on getting the bluff road graded and graveled. The cost would probably be more than the ranch could afford. But he couldn't just sit back and wait for another tragedy.

What would Blake say to that idea? It made sense that Joseph's father would approve. But Blake had been hard to read since the accident.

As he drove into Blue Moon, Joseph's thoughts shifted to his plans for the day. He would stop there to fill the Model A's gas tank and check for mail at the post office. After that, he would drive to Miles City and spend his time doing business. That business would include submitting bids for two new lumber contracts. His heart wasn't in the job, but he owed the family his best effort.

Midmorning was the busiest time in Blue Moon—the time when farmers came in for supplies at the Feed and Hardware and their wives came along to shop at the general store. It was a time for greeting friends, exchanging gossip, and looking over the newest goods. Children who trailed after their mothers might get a penny treat.

This was a prosperous time for the small town, which, in its long history, had gone from road stop to boom town to derelict and in recent years had settled into a dowdy sort of permanence. Autos, buggies, and wagons were parked along the main street. Horses drowsed in the sun, swishing flies with their tails and dropping piles of fresh manure in the dust. Ladies kept to the boardwalk, mindful of their shoes.

Jake's Place, a former saloon converted by Prohibition to a restaurant, had been sold to an unknown buyer. A couple of workers were piling unwanted items—cardboard boxes, stained table linens and bedding, broken furniture, charred pans, and other trash—onto a wagon. Jake and his restaurant had been well liked, even with the "nieces" he brought in to wait tables and ply their trade up the back stairs. People agreed that it was a shame to see the roadhouse close, especially because of its tender, juicy steaks, cooked to order. Maybe the new place would have more class, but to most folks, that wouldn't matter as long as the food was good.

The street was crowded. Joseph geared down and slowed the auto to a crawl. A trio of girls in fluttery summer dresses crossed in front of him, giggling and skipping. They appeared to be about fifteen. Too young for him. But the sight of them, so gay and pretty, sparked the memory of his father's order to find a wife.

Joseph was in no hurry to lose his freedom. But Blake wouldn't be fully satisfied until the proper woman was found, married, bedded, and pregnant. At least, Joseph would need to show that he was willing. But marriage was a lifetime commitment. Would finding a woman he could love be asking too much?

He'd lost his virginity at nineteen to a pretty and very willing farm girl named Annabeth Coleman. The romance had lasted a few dizzying weeks. But Joseph had only been looking for a good time. And Annabeth's plan to get pregnant and marry a rancher's son had scared him off. When he'd stopped calling, she'd wed a dirt farmer like her father and disappeared from his life. By now she was probably raising a passel of barefoot kids.

Joseph had barely broken up with Annabeth when he'd fallen hard for the ladylike Lucy Merriweather, a guest of the Calders. He'd never gotten more than a few kisses from the glamorous brunette. But that was just as well. She'd turned out to be a married con artist who'd left a trail of ruined lives behind her. The last he'd heard of Lucy, the woman had been sentenced to prison for fraud and was serving time.

There'd been a few other women over the years, the encounters brief and meaningless. None of the ladies had been the sort Joseph would choose for his future family. So here he was now, without a prospective wife in sight—and no time to look for one. It was all he could do to handle his responsibilities with the ranch and the mill. Blake's wish for a new family would have to wait.

Lost in thought, Joseph barely glimpsed the small child who darted into the street, right in front of his auto. Seeing the flash of her blue pinafore, he slammed on the brakes and leaped out of the car, imagining the worst.

But no, thank heaven, he'd stopped in time. A little girl, about three years old with wheaten braids, stood in front of the car with traffic and people milling around her. She was wailing at the top of her lungs.

"Ma . . . Ma . . ."

Joseph swept her up in his arms, meaning to get her out of the road and find somebody to take her. But being picked up by a stranger only frightened the child more. She squirmed and kicked, her wails rising to high-pitched shrieks.

"Ellie? Oh, my stars, Ellie!" A woman had burst out of the general store and was pushing her way through the crowd. Dressed in faded gingham, her face shadowed by a drooping straw hat, she battled her way to Joseph's side.

"Mama!" The little girl screamed and struggled. Her cries faded to sobs as she saw her mother. Workworn hands, a thin gold band on one finger, reached up to take the child. Joseph exhaled with relief as those hands lifted the little wildcat from his arms.

"Elinor Mosby, you scared me to death!" the woman scolded her daughter as she cradled her close. "I was looking for you everywhere! Why did you go outside?"

"I saw a puppy," the little girl whimpered. "I wanted to pet him. He ran over there." She pointed toward the far side of the street. "Don't be mad at me, Mama."

"I'm not mad. But you can't just go running into the street. You could've been . . ."

Her words trailed off, as if she'd just become aware of Joseph, who was standing a step away. She raised her head, giving him a first look at the face below the broad-brimmed hat.

"Forgive me for ignoring you, sir," she said. "It would be rude of me not to thank you for rescuing my daughter."

He stared down at her, almost forgetting to breathe. How could a man forget that heart-shaped face, framed by tendrils of sun-streaked golden hair? How could he not remember the little cleft in her chin and the violet eyes, their color so deep that in a certain light they appeared almost purple?

Her lips parted. She stepped back, looking as if she were about to turn and flee. Joseph knew she was married. But he couldn't help wanting to delay her, if even for a few seconds.

"Hello, Annabeth," he said. "It's been a while."

"Yes. It has . . . Joseph." Her eyes were as wide and startled as a doe's. Her arms clasped the little girl almost protectively. Joseph hadn't meant to make the woman feel uncomfortable. But clearly she was.

How long had it been since he'd last seen her? Not since before her marriage, Joseph realized. Was it a coincidence that so much time had passed without a word or a glimpse, or had she been avoiding him? In a small town like Blue Moon, that would take some effort.

Joseph hadn't known the man Annabeth married—she was a lively beauty and would've had her choice of suitors. Her clothes and her roughened hands told him she might not have chosen well. But that was none of his business. He could only hope that she was happy.

"I have to go. It was nice seeing you, Joseph." She turned away, her child still clinging to her neck. The street swarmed with onlookers drawn by the near accident. She would have to push her way through.

"Let me help you back to the boardwalk." He guided her with a touch at her elbow, his free arm parting the crowd. The little girl had stopped sniffling and was looking ahead. She raised her small, plump hand and began to wave.

"Mama, I see Daddy and Lucas! They're by the store!" she warbled in her childish voice.

The boardwalk was clearing as people moved on. Waiting outside the general store was a tall man in jeans, a plaid shirt, and a straw Stetson that shadowed his face. Holding his hand was a boy who appeared to be about five years old.

Joseph's gaze was drawn to the boy. Dressed in outgrown overalls, he was dark-haired and slender. He looked nothing like the rosy, blond girl-child in Annabeth's arms. Maybe he resembled his father. But that was none of his concern, Joseph reminded himself. Neither was the fact that the man waiting by the store had made no move to come and assist his wife.

Joseph guided Annabeth around a clump of horse manure. He would see her and her daughter safely to the boardwalk. Then he would get back to his car and be on his way.

The little girl was still waving. "Lucas!" she called. "I saw a puppy!"

The man had not moved from the spot. But a slight lift of his head revealed a chiseled face with sharp cheekbones, a slit of a mouth, and dark, piercing eyes—eyes that were looking straight at Joseph with cold, undisguised hatred.

Joseph's family was well-known. He was used to being recognized. But not like this. Maybe the man knew about his past relationship with Annabeth. But that had ended years ago. It didn't make sense that he'd be jealous.

Suddenly the boy—Lucas—broke free of his father's hand, plunged into the crowded street, and made a beeline for his mother and sister. His face broke into a grin as he reached them.

"What are you doing, Lucas?" Annabeth scolded him, her face lowered. "Stay with your father. We'll be right there."

He tugged at her skirt. "Dad says we can have root beer. Come on, before he gets mad and changes his mind."

Annabeth glanced up with a worried expression. "You can go, Joseph," she said. "We'll be fine now."

"I'll just—"

"No." She cut him off, her voice thready with tension. "Just go, Joseph."

"Who's this man, Mama?" Lucas had turned toward Joseph. He was a handsome boy, long-limbed and athletic, with dark, curly hair and a sprinkling of freckles. Thick lashes veiled his eyes from above.

"He's just a man who was helping us cross the street. Come on, Lucas. Let's go get root beer."

Balancing her daughter with one arm, Annabeth caught Lucas's hand and tugged him toward the store entrance. For an instant, the boy resisted, looking back at Joseph. That was when a shaft of sunlight caught his eyes.

Joseph's throat jerked, cutting off his breath.

Lucas's eyes were the color of fresh spring clover.

There would be no root beer that day. Annabeth's children dragged their feet as they followed their parents to the dusty Model T that was parked in a lot alongside the store. But they knew better than to complain out loud. Their father had changed his mind, and that was that.

Annabeth helped Lucas into the back seat and settled Ellie on her lap for the ride home. Her husband's silence and the grim set of his mouth told her there would be a reckoning later, when they could speak in private.

Silas Mosby backed the auto out of the side lot and swung onto the bumpy, narrow road that led to the dry farms east of town. As he drove, Annabeth stole a sidelong glance at his rigid posture in the driver's seat. She could already sense the storm brewing inside him.

Silas had known she was pregnant when he married her. He'd also known who'd fathered her baby. Before their vows were exchanged, Silas had made her promise that she would never speak of the man in his, or the child's, presence.

"I'm willing to raise your baby, Annabeth," he'd told her. "Especially if it's a boy. We can always use another pair of hands on the farm. But when I slip my mother's ring on your finger, you'll become a Mosby, and so will your baby. There'll be no mention of the Dollarhide name. Your child will know me as its father. And that rich bastard who took advantage of an innocent girl can burn in hell."

At the memory of her so-called innocence, Annabeth's mouth twitched in a bitter, secret smile. She had loved Joseph to the depths of her sixteen-year-old heart. She had *wanted* him to get her pregnant.

She had done what it took to catch him off guard, hoping to marry into the Dollarhide family, just as Joseph's mother had done. But by the time she discovered that the first part of her plan had succeeded, her chance was gone. Joseph was off pursuing that witch, Lucy Merriweather. And much as she wanted him, Annabeth knew that if Joseph were forced to marry her, he would hate her for trapping him. She would never have his heart.

Finding another man to wed her had been easy enough. Older than Annabeth by a decade, hardworking, and handsome in a rawboned way, Silas had his own farm and was looking for a wife. At the time, he'd appeared to be an ideal choice. Only later had Annabeth discovered the dark side of his nature.

But at least he was a man of his word. Over the past four years, going on five, Silas had treated Lucas as his own, even though the boy was the green-eyed, golden-skinned image of Joseph Dollarhide.

Ellie had fallen asleep, her pale lashes lying feather soft against her rosy cheeks. She was Silas's child—fair-haired, gray-eyed, and headstrong. Silas had hoped for more sons to continue his own lineage. That so far Annabeth had given him just one child, a girl, had to be a stinging disappointment. But Annabeth loved her daughter—almost as much as she loved the boy she still thought of as Joseph's son.

"Who was that man helping you, Mama?" Lucas's voice piped up from the back seat.

Silas's knuckles whitened on the steering wheel.

"Who was he?" Lucas demanded again.

"Nobody," Annabeth replied. "Nobody at all."

Numb with shock, Joseph watched the family of four disappear around the corner of the store. Were his eyes playing tricks? He could believe that he'd seen Annabeth and exchanged a few words with her. But that boy—a boy whose appearance and age suggested the unthinkable . . .

No, it wasn't possible. After all this time, surely he would have known—or Annabeth would have told him. What he'd seen of the boy was nothing but a fleeting impression, too brief to be real.

The blast of an auto horn reminded him that he'd left his car in the middle of the street and it was blocking traffic. He rushed to start the engine and move it down the block, where he parked in front of the garage, next to the gasoline pump. His thoughts churned as he waited for the attendant to fill the tank. He had to forget what he'd seen—or imagined he'd seen. Otherwise, he would drive himself to distraction. Even if the boy had been real, what could he do? He had no right to interfere with another man's family. Almost angrily, Joseph forced the thought aside.

After he'd paid for the fuel and moved the car, he stopped by the post office. There was nothing in the mail but bills and invoices, most of them related to the lumber business. He tucked them into his briefcase, to be opened later.

He was about to leave the post office when he noticed a hand-decorated flyer thumbtacked to the notice board—a reminder of Blue Moon's annual Independence Day celebration, which would be held next week. There would be a parade, a picnic with games, and a dance in the evening.

The sawmill would be shut down to give the workers a holiday. Joseph wasn't much for parades—especially this year, when he might be tempted to scan the crowd for Annabeth's green-eyed son. But he should probably go to the dance, as he had in other years. At least it would give Blake the impression that he was scouting for a bride. He might even have a good time.

The drive to Miles City, which Joseph had made countless times, would take about an hour. The weather-beaten road passed through open country dotted with patches of scrub and forest and occasional farms. Traffic was light, the weather bright and clear. There was nothing to keep his thoughts from straying into the forbidden past.

Had he loved Annabeth? He'd liked her a lot, that was for sure. She was smart for a farm kid and prettier than any of the town girls. And there was a raw honesty about her—she'd grown up working with animals and had even delivered two of her younger brothers. She'd been a virgin when they started seeing each other—she'd said so and he knew how to tell. But even the first time, sex had come as naturally to her as breathing.

At nineteen, Joseph had been driven by raging teenage lust. But love? He'd been too young to know the meaning of the word. He only knew that he couldn't get enough of her willing body.

He'd been aware of how babies were made, and he'd known enough to pull out before he finished. He'd done that every time—except for once, he recalled, when she'd wrapped his hips in her strong legs and held him inside her until he'd lost control. Annabeth had done it on purpose, with clear intent. She'd even confessed her plan.

That had been the last time he'd been with her.

A couple of months later, after he'd discovered Lucy and fallen under her spell, he'd seen Annabeth at the Harvest Dance with another boy. The sight of her, twirling on the dance floor in a slim-waisted blue dress, had reassured him that she must not be pregnant. It appeared that he'd been wrong.

She could have told him, damn it. If the baby was half his, hadn't he deserved a say in its future?

But what kind of husband and father would he have been—nineteen years old, with no more sense of responsibility than a jackrabbit?

Annabeth might have realized that. Besides, Joseph could imagine how he'd hurt her, dropping her for a more sophisticated girl. He could hardly blame her for turning to another man. Still . . .

The Ford's chassis shuddered as the right front wheel lurched into a washtub-sized pothole and settled with a sickening thud. Joseph cursed as he switched off the engine, climbed hastily out of the car, and walked around to the other side. Blast it, he should have been watching the road instead of wallowing in old memories.

The Ford was tilted at a rakish angle toward the wheel, which had sunk almost to the hub. Joseph crouched low enough to peer underneath. If the axle was broken or the auto otherwise seriously damaged, he could be hours getting it to Miles City and more time, even days, waiting for repairs. He wouldn't know for sure until he could get the vehicle back on level ground.

Through the sifting dust, he could see the axle resting on the edge of the hole. It appeared to be in one piece, and the wheel didn't seem to be bent, but he wouldn't know for sure until he could get a better look.

Pushing or pulling the car out of the hole would be impossible without help. If the engine had enough torque, backing out the way the wheel had gone in made the most sense. But the hole had been washed out where last month's rains had found a weak spot.

Its edges were steep all the way around. Even behind, there was no slope for the wheel to climb.

Joseph kept a few tools in the trunk for emergencies. Among them was a short-handled shovel. If he could dig away the rear edge and enlarge the hole, he might be able to back the wheel out onto the level surface of the road.

With a sigh, he rolled up the sleeves of his white shirt, found the shovel in the trunk, and started digging. The dirt was a gravelly mix that crumbled into the hole as soon as the ground was broken, filling up the space around the wheel. If Joseph couldn't clear it out, he'd be no better off than before.

He kept on shoveling, loosening the packed earth on the surface and scooping the dirt and gravel out of the hole. Progress was slow, with the overhead sun beating down like a blacksmith's hammer. Sweat poured off his body, soaked his clothes, and streamed down his face. He unbuttoned his dirty shirt and tossed it on the hood of the car. Even working in his singlet, he was hot.

Joseph had paused a moment to rest his back and wipe his face with his handkerchief when a tingling of awareness warned him that he was being watched.

There was no sound except the call of a passing crow, no movement except the wind that stirred the dusty leaves of the serviceberries growing along the roadside. But the subtle feeling was unmistakable. Was he about to be robbed? The loaded pistol Joseph kept under the seat of the auto was out of reach. The only weapon at hand was the shovel. Gripping it, he turned and spoke.

"Hello?"

There was no response.

"I know you're there. Show yourself." Maybe the unknown presence was harmless, even afraid, Joseph reasoned. It could even be a child.

Keeping the shovel close, he lowered himself to a crouch. "Come on out," he coaxed. "I won't hurt you."

The only answer was the mocking call of the crow.

Joseph usually trusted his instincts, but this time he could be wrong. He stood still, waiting for a sound, a movement. Maybe some animal was watching from the bushes. Or maybe his imagination was working overtime.

A farm truck, pulling a wagonload of hay, stirred up clouds of dust as it passed on the road. Joseph waved, but the driver paid him no attention. As the dust settled around him, Joseph shrugged and went back to the task of freeing the wheel.

The drone of an airplane overhead caused Joseph to look up. That would be Chase Calder flying home to his ranch. Webb Calder had built an airfield and paid for his son's flying lessons. Now Chase could fly to any place he needed to go—something Joseph could only dream of. But thinking about that now would only worsen his mood.

After another half an hour of work, the ramp was taking shape. The loose gravel had been piled into a high mound on one side of the hole, leaving a clear space for the wheel. Joseph's skin, hair, and clothes were smeared with dirt and soaked with perspiration. He ached in every joint and muscle. Getting back on the road would be worth the effort, he told himself. But only if his plan worked.

After a few more minutes of shoveling, he was ready. He pulled on his shirt, stowed the shovel in the trunk, and walked around to the driver's side of the car. The vehicle was tilted, with the left front wheel resting lightly on the ground. But both rear wheels looked solidly grounded.

The driver's side door was ajar. Had he left it that way when he jumped out of the car? Never mind. He could only hope the wheel was sound and the engine would do its job.

In the driver's seat, he started the engine, shifted into reverse, and pressed the gas pedal. The engine roared as the rear wheels dug into the earth, spitting dirt and rocks. Joseph's heart sank as he began to smell heat. But then the wheels found purchase. Slowly, the car began backing up, the right side lifting as the wheel moved up the ramp and onto solid ground.

Joseph allowed himself a deep breath. Everything appeared to be all right. He could drive into Miles City and leave the Ford to be checked by a mechanic while he took the lumber payments to the bank.

He glanced at the passenger seat where he'd left his briefcase with the money. Not seeing it, he checked the floor and the space under the seat where it might have slid. A sick sensation crept over him as the certainty grew.

The briefcase was gone.

CHAPTER THREE

"*I* saw the way he looked at you—and the way he looked at the boy." Silas's voice was as harsh as a slap. "What did he say to you?"

Backed against the kitchen table, Annabeth willed herself not to shrink away from him. Silas's rages could be terrifying, but she'd done nothing wrong and she had her pride.

"I asked you what he said." Silas took a step closer, looming over her.

"He said hello, or something to that effect," Annabeth replied in a level voice. "That was all."

"And what did you say to him?"

"I thanked him for saving Ellie. She could've been hit, you know. Somebody said that she ran right in front of the car."

"And why weren't you watching her? Maybe your eyes were somewhere else."

Annabeth ignored the innuendo. "She was right next to me, holding my skirt. Then she saw a puppy outside, and she was off like a shot. I was looking for her when I heard the squeal of brakes. My heart stopped. But she was all right."

Not that she owed her husband an explanation, Annabeth thought. Most of the time, Silas paid no more attention to his daughter than he did to the ranch dog. He'd never wanted a girl.

Glancing out through the kitchen window, Annabeth could see her children in the yard, throwing a stick for Freckles, the collie mix. She always kept a sharp eye on them. They were bold, inquisitive, and precious beyond words. And here on the ranch, there were plenty of dangers.

"What about the boy?" Silas's gaze drilled into her. "Did the bastard see him?"

Annabeth forced herself to meet his eyes. "How would I know what he saw? Lucas was curious enough to ask about him, but you heard my answer, Silas. I said he was nobody. Stop making this into something it isn't."

"Nobody?" His powerful hand gripped her arm. "I saw the way you were looking at *nobody*. And I saw the way he was looking at you."

"You saw nothing. There was nothing to see. Let go of me, Silas. Let me go to my children."

"They're *our* children, and don't you forget it." His grip on her arm bruised her flesh. "And I'd better not catch that man coming around my family. If I do, so help me, God, I'll tie him down, sharpen my knife, and make damn sure he never ruins another woman."

In Miles City, Joseph left the Ford at a mechanic's shop and walked up the street to the sheriff's office. He probably looked like a homeless bum, but he walked with a purposeful stride. He was a Dollarhide, and he wasn't about to be humiliated by a petty criminal.

The portly, graying deputy heard his story. "Did you see anybody?" he asked.

"No. And I didn't hear anybody, either. But I had the feeling someone was watching me. Whoever it was, I figure they must've been hiding in the bushes next to that big pothole, waiting for an accident to happen. When they grabbed my briefcase, they struck gold. The checks might not do them any good, but there was almost eight hundred dollars cash in that briefcase."

"We'll want a description of the briefcase and everything in it. If you're lucky, it'll show up in some alley with the checks still inside. But don't bet on it. We're dealing with a clever thief, most likely a professional."

"Keep me informed." Joseph stood up to leave. "The sneaky sonofabitch is going to find out he picked the wrong man to rob."

Without taking time to clean up, Joseph went to the bank next. No one questioned his appearance. The Dollarhides were important customers. Closeted with the manager, he recounted what had happened and warned him to be on the lookout for the checks. They weren't endorsed, thank goodness, but there was still a chance the thief might forge the signature and try to cash them.

Outside the bank, in the shade of the awning, he debated what to do next. He'd planned to deliver the bid for a second new warehouse, but the document he'd prepared was in the stolen briefcase. And the paperwork he needed to draw up a new one was back at the ranch.

The day was blistering hot, and his muscles were beginning to stiffen. He felt like a fugitive from a chain gang and probably smelled like one, too. He could always check into the Olive Hotel, order a change of clothes from the nearby haberdashery, and enjoy a cleansing shower and a meal in the dining room before spending the night in town.

Or he could just write off the day and go home. One thing he mustn't do was wait around doing nothing. His thoughts were too apt to stray onto forbidden paths, to a violet-eyed woman and the green-eyed boy he could never claim.

He'd be better off pondering what to do about the stolen money and how he was going to handle the problem with his father.

He would check on the auto. If it was fit to drive, he would leave town at once. If it needed more extensive repairs than he'd hoped, he would get a hotel room, clean up, and make an evening of it. There was a new Buster Keaton picture playing at the cinema. He could go after dinner and give himself a rare treat.

Keeping an eye out for a thief with his briefcase, he walked back to the mechanic's shop. The Ford was ready to go. "We checked her over, cleaned out the wheel, tightened a few bolts, and shined her up pretty," the owner said. "She's as good as new."

Joseph thanked the man, paid him an extra tip from the money in his wallet, and took the vehicle. He was on the road out of town when a rumbling sensation in the pit of his stomach reminded him that his only meal of the day had been hastily gulped morning coffee. He was running on empty, and home was more than an hour away.

Lunch at the hotel would take time and also be bad for appearances. But the snack bar at the railroad station sold sandwiches and sodas. That should be enough to slake his hunger for the drive back to the ranch.

As he parked behind the station house and climbed out of the car, a shrill whistle blasted the air. Bell clanging, rods pumping, and steam hissing from the wheels, the Northern Pacific train rolled up to the platform.

The sight and sound of the train stirred a vague yearning in Joseph. How would it feel to leave his old life, climb aboard, and ride as far as it would carry him—across the prairie to the big eastern cities, all the way to the ocean, where anything, anyplace, was possible? He had grown up reading books about travel and adventure—Africa, India, China, and so many other exotic places he would never see. Unless another war called him away, he would live out his life here, in this remote corner of Montana, bound by family duty to his father, the ranch, and that accursed sawmill.

And when he married, any sons he had would likely do the same. He thought about Chase Calder, who was also bound by tradition. All the Calder land and money in the world couldn't buy his freedom. But maybe Chase didn't care. Maybe the life he had was the only life he wanted.

The train wouldn't be here for long. Most of the passengers and cargo were bound for points east. A middle-aged couple waited on the platform with their luggage. Before boarding the passenger car, they stepped aside to let a slender young woman make her way down the steps. Two husky workers were picking up a bag of mail and unloading a large, leather-bound trunk from the baggage car. Minutes later, with a call of "All aboard" and a blast of the whistle, the steam-driven wheels began to churn. The train pulled away from the platform, picked up speed, and vanished down the track, leaving two people alone on the platform—Joseph and the young woman.

Hunger forgotten, he studied her with furtive glances. She was dark haired, fair skinned, and strikingly pretty. Her navy blue traveling suit and prim straw bonnet spoke of modest means but refined taste.

Every inch a lady. The timeworn phrase rose in Joseph's mind as he watched her from a discreet distance. She glanced around uncertainly, as if looking for help. Her gaze found Joseph, then shifted away, as if dismissing him on sight. He could hardly blame her. He looked like a tramp—hardly someone a lady should trust.

As minutes passed and no one else showed up, she grew visibly impatient, pacing as she gazed up and down the platform. At last, squaring her shoulders, she walked directly to where Joseph stood. In her hand, she held a dollar bill.

"Excuse me, sir," she said, extending the bill. "I'm in need of a taxi to take me and my trunk to Blue Moon. If you'll find me one, this money is yours."

"Keep your money," Joseph said. "I have a car and I'll be going to Blue Moon. You're welcome to ride with me."

She hesitated, eyeing him as if he were a slice of spoiled meat. "I really don't think—"

"I understand." Joseph brushed a dirt smudge off his sleeve. "My apologies for the way I look. I had to deal with an emergency on the road. My car's around back. Joseph Dollarhide's the name. My family has a ranch outside Blue Moon. The station attendant will vouch for me."

She glanced toward the station house, as if she planned to go inside and ask. But then she shrugged. "All right, Mr. Dollarhide, if you're sure my trunk will fit in your car."

"We'll make it fit." Joseph fetched a cart from a line outside the station house and loaded the heavy trunk on it. "Follow me, Miss—"

"It's Miss Rutledge. Francine Rutledge. I've been hired as the new schoolteacher in Blue Moon."

"Right this way, Miss Rutledge." As he wheeled the cart around the station house to his car, Joseph felt his spirits rise. Until now, the day had been a long chain of disasters. But maybe his luck was about to change.

Annabeth bent over the rows of her garden, pulling weeds and checking the progress of her vegetable crop. The carrots, turnips, and beets, on which she depended for winter storage, were doing poorly, the tops wilted and scraggly. Looking down the row, she could see the mound of freshly dug earth that told her the reason. Blasted gopher! She would have to set a trap for it—or for them, since there could be a whole family of the varmints tunneling under the ground to feast on her precious vegetables.

Straightening, she brushed the dirt off her hands. Her thumbs massaged the small of her back. She didn't mind hard work—she'd been helping on her family's farm since she wasn't much older than Ellie, peeling potatoes and plucking birds in the kitchen, milking cows, hoeing weeds, and minding her younger siblings. Her parents were gone now, their property passed on to Annabeth's two brothers, who'd sold it and departed for greener pastures. The three girls, including Annabeth, had married and started families of their own. The last of Annabeth's siblings had moved away three years ago, leaving her alone in Blue Moon.

Annabeth had once hoped for a better life. She'd read every book she could find, kept herself clean, and practiced ladylike manners. When she'd wed Silas, she'd treasured the hope of a happy marriage and a loving home. Too late, she discovered that she'd bought into a life like her mother's, married to a cold, controlling man who treated her like property.

Her hope now was for her children—fearless little Ellie and thoughtful Lucas, who was growing to look more like his natural father every day.

Looking across the yard, she could see them on the porch steps, sharing a tattered picture book that Annabeth had saved from her childhood. She'd started teaching Lucas to read. He knew his letters and numbers and could write his name. But Silas was already pushing to start the almost five-year-old boy working on the farm.

"A farmer's got no use for book learning," he'd told her yesterday. "Books can't teach him to plant a field, hitch a wagon, or butcher a hog. They'll only fill his head with useless ideas. Start him working young, and he'll know his place as a man."

Annabeth had controlled her temper, knowing that to speak up would only trigger a tongue-lashing. She knew exactly what her husband meant. He was raising a farmhand—not the blood heir he was still hoping for. Meanwhile, he'd be damned if he'd let her turn the boy into a Dollarhide.

She was about to go back to her gardening when Silas came out of the house. His dark blond hair was slicked down and combed. He'd changed out of his work overalls and wore denim pants with a clean shirt.

"Don't wait up for me," he said, stepping around the children. "I'll be playing cards with the boys, so I might be late getting home."

"All right." At first, when these late nights had started, she'd suspected Silas of seeing another woman. But over time, she'd overheard enough to know that he was involved in some kind of business with his friends. He hadn't given her the details, and she'd known better than to ask him, but he'd dropped hints about making a lot of money—not that she'd seen any of it. Annabeth sensed that the activity was illegal. She feared he might be arrested, but short of worrying, there was little she could do.

As he came down the steps, she moved out of his way. But he caught her waist, pulled her to him, and kissed her possessively. "When I come home, I'd better find you waiting for me—in bed," he muttered.

"Just be careful." She kept her voice level as he released her.

"I mean it, Annabeth. That's my ring you're wearing. If you ever betray me, so help me, I'll know, and I'll make you pay." Leaving the words to hang, he strode to the car and drove away.

Annabeth watched him go. She had never been unfaithful to

Silas, nor had she wanted to be. But he would never let her forget that she'd carried another man's child in her body or that he had saved her from dishonor. He had endless small ways of reminding her that she was damaged goods, unworthy of trust or respect. Her failure to give him a son only made matters worse.

What if she had told Joseph about the baby? His family would have forced him to wed her—she had little doubt of that. But at nineteen, he would have felt trapped and he would have come to despise her for it. For the sake of her children, she could bear Silas's contempt. But Joseph's? That would have broken her heart.

She turned back toward the house, where her children waited to hear the story she'd promised to read them after Silas left. Her life was far from perfect, but she had Joseph's son and her bright, bold, little Ellie. They were her blessings, her shining stars. For now, that would have to be enough.

On the drive back to Blue Moon, Joseph had resolved to keep his eyes on the road. But he couldn't resist stealing a few quick looks at his companion. Every glance was a new discovery—her profile with the slightly turned-up nose; the tendrils of dark brown hair that framed her face, lying damp against her porcelain skin; and the intriguing little mole at the corner of her mouth. Her hands were small, the nails bitten to the quick. She smelled faintly of lilacs. He breathed her in.

"Tell me about Blue Moon," she said. "How did the town get such a funny name?"

"That's an interesting story." Joseph steered around a bundle of firewood that had likely fallen off a truck. "Back in the late 1800s, it was just a rest stop on the road—there was a saloon as I recall, with feed and water for horses. The place was so isolated, folks declared that travelers would only stop there once in a blue moon. As the town grew, the name stuck."

Her laughter was musical. "What's the place like now? I read about the teaching job in a Kansas City newspaper and accepted the offer long-distance. Evidently, I was the only person who applied."

"So you've never been to Blue Moon?"

"Never. Should I be worried?"

"There's nothing to worry about. But as a city girl, don't expect to be impressed. It's an ordinary small town, surrounded by farms and ranches. Not much going on in the way of excitement. But the people are neighborly. They'll treat you well, especially since you'll be teaching their children. You can expect to be invited for a lot of Sunday dinners." He risked a sidelong look to see her studying him from under the lush black fringe of her eyelashes. Emboldened, he decided to take a chance.

"The big Independence Day celebration is coming up on Thursday," he said. "There'll be a children's parade, a patriotic program, and a baseball game. You'd have a chance to meet some of your students and their families. Then at night, there'll be a dance with a live band. It's the big event of the summer. If you'd like to go, I'd be honored to escort you."

Her silence was a beat too long. "Let me think about it," she said. "I'll need some time to get settled. But maybe by the holiday, I'll be ready. Can I let you know?"

"Sure." Joseph turned his full attention back to the road. A few more minutes and they'd be passing through the outskirts of Blue Moon. After letting Miss Francine Rutledge and her trunk off at the school, with its adjoining small house, he would drive home to face his father. He still wasn't sure how much to tell Blake about the stolen money. It might be wise to hold the news for a few days in the hope that the thief might be caught and some of it recovered.

"What can you tell me about the Calders?" Francine asked.

"Why? What do you want to know?" Her question had caught him off guard.

She tucked a stray lock of hair under her hat. "I'm just curious. Even in Kansas City, I read news articles about the Calder family and that huge cattle ranch."

"If you've read the news articles, then you know about as much as I can tell you." The Calders weren't exactly Joseph's favorite subject.

"I remember reading about Webb Calder's death—so sudden and so tragic. I understand that his son is running the ranch now. But I don't recall his name. What is it?"

"Chase."

"Oh, that's right. Chase. Chase Calder. Does he have a family? A wife?"

"From what I know of Chase, he's married to his ranch."

Joseph sensed where this conversation was leading. He had just met this fascinating creature, and he already had a rival for her affections. Time would tell whether Chase would even be interested. But if it came to that, Joseph wasn't afraid of some healthy competition—not even from the boss of the Triple C.

The school was coming up on the right. Francine had told him that the school board was expecting her and the house would be unlocked, with the lights and water turned on. Joseph would only need to help unload the trunk and make sure everything was in order.

"They even promised clean sheets on the bed and some food in the kitchen," Francine said as he drove up to the house. "Let's hope the good people of Blue Moon are true to their word."

"They will be. In a little backwater town like Blue Moon, good teachers are hard to come by. You'll be welcomed with open arms."

So what was an attractive, confident young woman who could probably get hired anywhere doing in Blue Moon? Joseph pondered the question as he dragged the heavy trunk into the house and pushed it against a wall in the bedroom. Maybe he already had his answer. She'd given it to him when she'd asked about Chase Calder.

But that wouldn't stop him from trying to change her mind.

After checking the house, seeing Francine settled, and reminding her about the dance, Joseph got into his vehicle and drove back to the main road. Francine had been a pleasant distraction, but he needed to shift his thoughts to the serious problem of the stolen money.

For now, he decided, he would spare his father the news of the theft. Between grief and his disability, Blake was dealing with all a man could bear. He didn't need one more blow. But if he started asking questions, Joseph would have no choice except to tell the truth.

Ahead, he could see a heavy truck with a trailer parked outside the roadhouse. He slowed the car for a better look. Workmen were unloading crates and pieces of furniture—tables, chairs, a dresser, a bed. It appeared that the new owner of Jake's Place was moving in. The citizens of Blue Moon would be abuzz with curiosity about the new business and its proprietor.

For a moment, Joseph was tempted to stop, ask a few questions, maybe even meet the new owner. But that would mean putting off his return home, and he'd procrastinated long enough. His father—and his other duties—would be waiting for him.

A breeze had come up, stirring the dust that rose behind his car's wheels. As he passed the former roadhouse, he glimpsed a figure standing on the front stoop—a shapely woman in a dark dress, her features hidden by a Chinese parasol, held low. Could she be the new owner?

Dismissing the question, he drove out of town and headed south toward the cutoff for the ranch. Now that he was alone once more, his thoughts began to wander forbidden paths.

Somewhere on the flatland east of town, where dirt farmers eked out a subsistence from the used-up soil, the son he could never claim was living his childhood. His life was bound to be hard. Would he have enough food to eat, shoes on his feet, and a coat to keep him warm? Would he have a doctor if he got sick? Would he have the book learning he needed to make his way in the world?

And what about the stern-looking man who was raising him? Would he treat the boy as his own? Would he be a good husband to gentle Annabeth?

Joseph had no right to ask those questions. Even though the true answers might break his heart, there'd be nothing he could do. He could only try to forget what he'd seen today.

Lucas. His lips formed the name, then let it fade, unspoken, on the hot summer wind.

* * *

The woman known as Lola De Marco closed her parasol and stepped back into the shadows of the cluttered dining room. Boxes, crates, and pieces of furniture rose around her like the ruins of an ancient kingdom. She'd had the rooms cleaned out ahead of her arrival, but many hours of work remained before the place would be ready to open for business.

She'd kept Jake's name for the restaurant. She'd also hired Smitty, Jake's former cook, at a generous raise in salary so her customers could expect the same good food. But she was planning other, less visible changes—changes that promised to make her a wealthy woman. These would take time and money.

Her ex-husband's secret stash, which she'd found after he went to prison, had given her enough money to buy this place. But her funds were running low. She needed to get more cash coming in, and soon.

She stepped aside to make way for two husky workers carrying a mattress destined for the second floor, where she planned to live for now. Her quarters wouldn't be fancy, but she'd known far worse in the recent past.

She'd hired several men for the move through an agency in Deer Lodge that found jobs for ex-convicts. Two of them would be staying on to help her get the restaurant set up for business—and maybe as permanent help if they proved their worth. The others would be paid and dismissed.

Maneuvering around a heap of secondhand chairs, she walked to the front of the dining room. The windows had been covered with brown wrapping paper to block curious gazes. Now she peeled back a corner and peered out through the dusty pane at the street. There were more autos on Main Street and more power lines overhead. Otherwise, Blue Moon hadn't changed much in the past five years. Same businesses, same little working-class houses with laundry flapping from clotheslines and children playing in the yards.

As she recalled, most of the people were rubes, which suited Lola fine. Only two families made the place worthy of notice—the Calders and the Dollarhides.

Lola hadn't missed the sight of Joseph Dollarhide driving past in that red Model A Ford. When she'd known him before, he'd been nineteen years old, on the cusp of manhood. They'd spent some pleasant times together, even exchanged a few chaste kisses before their budding romance ended badly. Now he'd grown into a fine-looking man, but those days were over—water under the bridge, as folks were fond of saying.

After replacing the paper, Lola turned away from the window. Two workers had just carried a mirrored dresser through the door. The heavy piece, meant for her upstairs bedroom, would have to be carried up the steep, narrow stairs. The men had left it in the middle of the floor while they went for more help.

The mirror had been covered with a protective cloth. Now the cloth had slipped to one side, exposing part of the frame and the glass. As Lola reached to pull the cloth back into place, the mirror caught a shadowed reflection of her face.

The impulse to turn away never left her, even though Lola forced herself to keep looking. Four years ago, in the women's wing of the Montana State Penitentiary, a fellow prisoner had savaged her face with a broken bottle. The prison doctor had stopped the bleeding and saved her damaged eye. But he could do nothing about the scars that made a relief map of her once exquisite face—ugly scars she would carry for the rest of her life.

If Joseph had seen her face today, he would not have recognized the pretty girl he'd courted. Lola had changed her name and the style of her clothes. Her dark mahogany hair was now dyed coal black. That she looked like the wicked witch in a children's fairy tale was a reality she'd come to accept.

Lucy Merriweather no longer existed. Her beauty was gone forever. Now, for Lola, only two things mattered—money and power. Those, at least, were within her reach.

CHAPTER FOUR

On Thursday, July 4, the town of Blue Moon was decked out for its annual celebration. Swaths of red, white, and blue bunting festooned the store fronts and hung from lines strung above the street. In the field beyond the school, a stage had been set up on the baseball diamond for the patriotic program. Blankets had been laid out to save spots for family picnics.

Children, dressed in their Sunday best and carrying miniature flags, clustered at the top of Main Street, waiting to line up for the parade. They would lead the procession, with an older boy—usually the sixth-grade honor student—carrying a larger flag on a pole.

A three-man brass-and-drum ensemble, playing John Philip Sousa marches, would follow the children. Four floats—three from businesses in the town and one from the American Legion Auxiliary—would bring up the rear.

The sawmill was closed for the day, and most of the stock hands had been given time off after morning chores. Joseph had offered to drive his father to the celebration, but Blake's response had been an angry refusal.

Joseph had understood his pain. Hannah and Elsa had loved Independence Day. They would have risen before dawn to prepare a lavish lunch of fried chicken, potato salad, and apple pie, to be enjoyed while the family viewed the baseball game. Last year, Elsa had been excited about watching a boy on the home team—her first crush. The boy, whose name Joseph couldn't recall, hadn't even come to her funeral service.

After leaving Blake at home with Oliver, his caregiver, Joseph had driven into town alone. He'd never cared about the parade or the program, but he'd hoped to see Francine Rutledge again and remind her about the dance.

He parked the Ford on a side street and strolled back to the parade route. People were already lining up along Main Street. The parade would be a short one, barely worth the time, but it was a tradition that drew the people in Blue Moon together. Parents, especially, looked forward to seeing their children march proudly down the street, two abreast, waving their little flags. And the war veterans, riding on the last bunting-draped float, always drew a round of applause.

Joseph scanned the crowd. There was no sign of Francine. Maybe she didn't feel ready to step out and meet the townspeople. He thought about going to her house and offering to escort her, then decided against it. Intruding on her privacy wouldn't win him any points.

At the end of the street, volunteers were herding the children, like so many ducklings, into a double line, pairing each small child with an older one. Joseph tore his gaze away. To search the group for a certain dark-haired boy would go against every promise he'd made himself—against all decency and common sense.

Even thinking of Lucas as his son would be wrong. Joseph knew that. But as the parade music began and the procession moved down the street toward him, flags waving, he stood rooted to the spot. Half in hope, half in dread, he scanned the face of each young boy who marched past him.

Lucas wasn't here.

Neither was his family, Joseph realized as his gaze swept over the crowd.

As the last of the children moved down the street, Joseph took a ragged breath. Until now, he hadn't realized how much he'd wanted to see the boy. All the more reason to keep his distance.

But as he turned to walk back to the car, he couldn't help wondering why Lucas and his family hadn't come to the parade.

Was it because of him?

He remembered the look of hatred Annabeth's husband had given him. Did the man know—or even suspect—who might have fathered his wife's baby? That would explain a lot of things—why Joseph hadn't seen Annabeth or the boy in years and why the family wasn't here today.

But that was none of his business. Annabeth had chosen to keep her child a secret from him and wed another man. He had no right to interfere with her choice or even to question it. The kindest thing he could do, for her and for the boy, would be to forget he'd ever set eyes on them.

He had almost reached his car when he heard a voice behind him.

"Joseph! Joseph, wait!"

He turned to see Francine hurrying to catch up with him. Flushed and breathless in an airy mauve dress, she looked ravishing enough to stun a man's heart.

"I was hoping to find you," she said, stopping beside him. "If your invitation is still good, I'd love to have you show me around Blue Moon. But, of course, if you're about to leave . . ."

She glanced at the car, then looked up at him with twinkling brown eyes.

"I'm not going anywhere," Joseph spoke hastily. "I'd be happy to show you around. Not that there's much for a city girl like you to see, even today."

"Nonsense." Laughing, she linked her arm through his. The subtle fragrance of lilacs crept into his senses. "Blue Moon looks like a lovely little town. And being with you will make it easier for me to meet people."

Blessing his good fortune, Joseph guided her back to Main Street, where the American Legion Auxiliary float was passing the final corner of the parade route. As the last notes of John Philip Sousa faded, people began to disperse, most of them going to the patriotic program at the ball field. Some older boys were lighting firecrackers in front of the Feed and Hardware Store. The sharp scent of cordite drifted on the air.

"Come on." Joseph tightened his arm against hers. "Allow me to show you a real, old-fashioned, small-town Fourth of July celebration."

"I want to go to the parade, Mama!" Ellie's wails had diminished to hiccups, but tears were still streaming from her pretty, blue eyes. "You said we could. You said I could wear my new dress."

"Hush, baby." Heartsick, Annabeth wiped her daughter's runny nose and sponged her face with a damp cloth. "I know what I said, but your father has to work. We can have a good time here. You'll see. We'll make cookies, and I'll read you a story."

"I don't want cookies! I don't want a story!" Ellie stomped her feet. Her small hands doubled into fists. "I want to go to the parade."

Freckles, the collie mix, looked up at her with worried eyes. Ellie was his favorite person, the one he followed and protected. He whined, his tail making anxious thumps on the planks of the porch.

"The parade is over, Ellie." Lucas was the calm, reasonable child. "It's too late to go now."

"We can still go. We can get hot dogs and see fireworks."

"You heard your mother." Silas had come around the house to stand at the foot of the porch steps. "I've got to check the big field for potato beetles. If they get a start, we could lose the whole crop."

"I don't care! I want to go! Can't you take us, Mama? You promised."

"You know your mother doesn't drive," Silas said. "Now stop whining or you'll get a spanking to remember."

"Come on, Ellie." Annabeth swept her daughter up in her arms. "You're tired. It's time for your nap."

"No . . ." Ellie's protests faded as Annabeth carried her into the house and down the hall. Her head rested against her mother's shoulder. "Mama, can I take my nap on your bed?" she asked.

"Do you promise you'll lie still and go to sleep?"

"Uh-huh. I promise." Ellie could be sweet when she chose.

"All right. If you're good, you can help me make cookies later.

Here we are. Let's get your shoes off." Annabeth sat on the edge of the bed with Ellie on her lap and unlaced the little girl's shoes, which were getting too small for her growing feet.

New shoes cost money. Silas would complain, but Annabeth could deal with that, just as she dealt with isolation, hard work, and a cold, controlling husband who'd burned the few beloved books she owned because he didn't believe women should waste time reading. She had her beautiful children. They made up for all the rest.

"Sing to me, Mama." Ellie lay back on the pillow, gazing up at her mother with those angelic blue eyes. If she hadn't married Silas, this precious child wouldn't exist, Annabeth reminded herself. Surely, the life she had was meant to be.

"Go to sleep, my baby," she sang softly. "Close your drowsy eyes . . . Angels up in heaven, peeking at my baby from the skies . . ."

By the time she'd sung the old lullaby twice, Ellie's eyes had closed. Annabeth rose from the bed, tiptoed out of the room, and closed the door behind her, leaving it slightly ajar. She returned to the porch to find Silas waiting alone.

"Where's Lucas?" she asked.

"He's putting on his work clothes," Silas said. "I'm taking him with me to check the potato field and pull off any beetles or grubs we see on the plants. It can be hot, dirty work, but it's time he got used to it."

"Oh, no, Silas!" Annabeth thought of the blistering sun, the dust and the vermin, the snakes and spiders that could be lurking among the plants with no protection for childish hands. And the field was large. Checking every plant would take several days. She would offer to take her son's place, but that would mean leaving her children alone.

"Please, Silas, he's so young. Can't this wait?"

"Waiting will only make him lazy. He's ready, Annabeth. You should have seen his chest puff out when I told him he was old enough to do a man's work."

"He doesn't understand. He's barely five. Give him time."

"That's enough out of you. I'm the head of this family. I make the decisions."

"Yes, you do." Something snapped in Annabeth. She knew what to expect, but she couldn't remain silent.

"Nothing matters except what you want. That field could have waited until tomorrow. Instead, you chose to disappoint your children—after I promised them. And I know why. You were punishing me by punishing them—and all for nothing."

His expression darkened. His eyes seemed to blaze as he loomed over her. "I'm not punishing anybody, woman. I'm protecting my family and keeping you from temptation. You know he'll be there."

Annabeth stood her ground. "You're flailing at shadows, Silas. There's nothing there. We met him by accident. And now, because of him, you've ruined the day for your children. Stop behaving like a jealous fool. And stop punishing Lucas. He can't help being who he is."

His hand shot out. She was braced when it struck the side of her face, setting off lights behind her eyes. Her head was still clearing when she heard a small voice from somewhere behind her.

"I'm ready to work, Dad. Let's go."

Lucas stood in the doorway, wearing his ragged overalls and a straw hat that came down to his eyebrows. How much had he heard? What had he seen?

She knew her boy. Whatever he'd witnessed, he would likely keep it to himself. But the hurt would fester inside him like a wound. And she didn't know how to protect him from more.

Without a word, Silas ushered Lucas down the steps and around the house. Moments later they were headed out to the potato field, side by side, both of them carrying buckets. Silas also carried a shovel. She would have to trust him to take care of the boy. Silas wasn't a bad man, but from her childhood, Annabeth remembered the father who'd raised him, a harsh man who drove his son mercilessly. Silas knew of no other way, she told herself.

Struggling to master her emotions, Annabeth went back into the house. There was no sound from the bedroom. With luck, Ellie would sleep for at least half an hour. That would give her time to burn off her frustration by cleaning the kitchen. She would start with the cupboards, then do the floor.

After filling a pail and getting the mop and scrub brush, she went to work. She'd be tired when she was finished, but she could warm up some stew for lunch. After that, maybe Ellie would settle for making sugar cookies.

By the time she'd finished wiping down the cupboards and scrubbed the floor, Ellie had yet to appear. Maybe it was time to wake her. Otherwise, she might not sleep tonight.

Annabeth dried her hands on her apron and walked down the hall to the bedroom she shared with Silas. The door she'd left ajar was now closed. When she opened it, her heart lurched.

The bed was empty. Ellie was gone.

The coverlet and pillow were cool to the touch. And Ellie's shoes were missing from the rug. The little scamp must've put them on, crept through the parlor while her mother was busy in the kitchen, and slipped outside.

Heart in her throat, Annabeth raced out onto the front porch. Ellie was nowhere in sight. Only after she'd checked the yard and both sides of the house did she realize the dog was missing as well. If Ellie had run away, Freckles would have followed her.

And there was just one place Ellie would want to go.

With her gaze intent on the dusty ground, Annabeth searched until she found the small shoe prints and the fresh dog tracks alongside. Ellie had ridden in the car enough to know the way to town. What her young mind wouldn't understand was the effort it would take to walk there. And she had no idea of the danger—thorny scrub, coyotes, snakes, even the searing sun. Annabeth couldn't be sure how long her daughter had been gone, but the little girl could already be in peril.

Annabeth began to run.

Joseph had spent the better part of an hour with Francine. They'd seen the very end of the parade and sat on a blanket at the ball field to watch the patriotic program, with its speeches and musical numbers, including an off-key soprano rendition of "America the Beautiful," a baton twirling demonstration, and a tableau of teenage girls wearing the colors of the flag. He could imagine what she thought of the small-town production. But he'd enjoyed her charming laugh, clear and pure, like the tinkle of a glass chime. He'd treated her to a hot dog for lunch, since the new restaurant had yet to open. After that, he'd seen her to her door, where she'd promised to let him escort her to the dance.

Now, Joseph had started the Ford and headed for home, planning to spend the afternoon with his father. This would be a difficult day for Blake, haunted as he was by memories of a time that would never come again. He seemed to be aging every day, with little interest in anything beyond the mill and the ranch. Maybe Joseph could draw him into a game of chess, something he'd once enjoyed, or better yet, help him release his grief by talking. Joseph was grieving, too. Sharing could be a step toward healing. But he knew better than to expect too much.

Main Street was clogged with traffic—mostly families who'd come for the parade and program but weren't staying. Faced with joining the mob of autos, buggies, and wagons, he decided to take the back road, which led east out of town.

Joseph knew the road well. After a few miles, it forked. One branch kept on east, winding past the dirt farms to the ranches beyond. That was the road Joseph's Aunt Kristin took to her medical office in town. It was also the route most commonly used for late-night moonshine smuggling. The other branch swung south, all the way to the lumber mill. The Dollarhides paid for access, along with a crew to keep the surface maintained for the heavy lumber wagons and log trucks that traveled that way.

Today the road was almost empty. The day was clear, the crops still green from the early summer's rain. A flock of blackbirds rose like a swirling cloud from a corn field and vanished into the sky.

From where the roads forked, Joseph could make out what appeared to be a distant farm—a low house and unpainted barn, some outbuildings, and a windmill. Could that place, or one like it, be where Annabeth was raising his son? Did he have a happy life there?

But that line of thought couldn't be allowed. Young Lucas was no more his son than he, Joseph, was the son of Mason Dollarhide. It took more than a bloodline to make a man a father. It took years of sacrifice, responsibility, and patience. Even love, the kind of love Blake had given him.

Annabeth's husband had married her and was raising Lucas as his own. Joseph's only contribution had happened in a careless moment on a moonlit night. Beyond that, he had no right to the boy.

Lost in thought, he had let the Ford slow. Now he gunned the engine and swung the car onto the south road. Why was he moping about something he could never have? He'd just met a delightful young woman, and he'd be escorting her to the dance tonight. That was something to celebrate.

Joseph had gone another quarter mile when he spotted something on the expanse of scrub land that bordered the road on both sides—a flash of blue, perhaps a hundred yards away. He braked to a stop. Shading his eyes, he studied it through the open window. Maybe it was nothing—a bird or a piece of clothing blown off somebody's wash line. But his instincts told him he'd be wise to investigate. He climbed out of the car and started toward it.

He'd covered about half the distance when he heard a dog barking—an urgent, almost frantic sound. Shading his eyes again, he could see the dog in a small clearing—middle-sized, with a shaggy brown-and-white coat. He could make out the spot of blue as well. It didn't appear to be moving.

Joseph broke into a sprint, dodging clumps of sage, cheat grass, and thistle. A jackrabbit burst out of hiding and bounded away. Through a screen of sagebrush, the blue object had taken the shape of a huddled child.

Seized by dread, Joseph plunged through the brush. Now, half-muffled by the barking dog, he could also hear the sound of sobbing. He broke into a sweat of relief. *Thank God!*

His throat jerked as he recognized Annabeth's little girl. She lay on her side in her blue pinafore, her legs drawn up against her body. One shoe was missing, along with its stocking. The other was trailing its laces. Her face was stained with crusted tears and dust.

She was whimpering in pain. As he came closer, Joseph could see why. She'd stumbled into a clump of thistle weeds. One leg and her bare foot were covered with tiny stickers.

As a boy, Joseph had fallen afoul of thistles more than once. The pain was miserable. He muttered a curse, knowing how the poor child must be suffering and how anything he could do for her here was going to hurt worse.

The dog stood guard over her, its lips curled in warning. But when Joseph spoke to it, the shaggy creature seemed to understand that he was here to help. It moved away and sat down nearby, its worried eyes on its young mistress.

"Ellie." He knelt beside her and spoke softly, not wanting to frighten her. "Do you remember me from town?"

She nodded, grimacing. "I got stickers. They hurt . . . bad."

"I know. I've had stickers before. I'm here to help if I can. Where's your mother?"

"Home. I wanted to see the parade. I lost my shoe." She shifted her leg, bringing a yelp and another surge of tears.

The sun was blistering hot. She was probably dehydrated as well as in pain. "You must be thirsty. Don't try to move. I'm going to get you some water."

Joseph kept a canteen in the back of his car. He'd found it and was just closing the trunk when he saw a distant figure racing through the scrub. A woman in a dress and apron, her fair hair fallen loose. That would be the mother. His pulse quickened. Annabeth.

The dog began to bark again as Joseph knelt and helped the little girl drink. She gulped the water. "Careful, not too much at first," he murmured, willing himself not to think about the woman who would soon be here. "Your mother's coming, Ellie. You'll be all right."

Annabeth's pulse raced with her feet as she followed the sound of barking. Thorns and thistles, grown hip high, raked her arms and tore at her skirt. Heedless, she plunged ahead. Nothing mattered but finding Ellie and getting her safely home.

Looking over the screen of brush, toward the road, she could see a flash of red. As she came closer, it became a Ford Model A. Anxiety tightened a knot in her chest. She knew who had a car like that, and she knew he lived nearby. It had to be Joseph. But right now even that wasn't her first concern. She had to get to her daughter, and it could be that Joseph had found her.

The dog came through the thicket, his shaggy coat matted with burrs. Whining and tugging at her skirt, he pulled her past the brush into a small clearing. There, she saw Joseph supporting Ellie with one arm while she sipped water from a canteen.

"Ellie, what—?"

The words died in her throat as she saw her daughter's leg and her bare foot, the flesh already inflamed.

"Mama." Ellie turned a tear-stained face toward her. "I've got stickers."

Annabeth dropped to her knees beside the little girl. As a child, she'd gotten a few thistle spines in her legs, but this was the worst she'd ever seen.

"Don't be scared, love," she said. "I know it hurts. We just have to find a way to get them out and get you home."

"I found her like this a few minutes ago," Joseph said. "When I got stickers as a boy, my mother used to soak me in Epsom salts and pick them out with tweezers. But I don't know how you're going to carry her home without hurting her."

Strange, the two of them talking face-to-face like this. Even after so many years it felt natural. But right now that wasn't important. Annabeth had to help her child. She searched her memory.

"I saw my father do this once. If you've got a knife, or even a card from a deck, we might be able to scrape some of the spines off with the edge. At least enough to get her home, where I can get them out with tweezers."

"I've got a pocketknife." Joseph pulled the folded knife out of his pocket and snapped open the blade.

"No!" Ellie shrank away from him. "Don't let him cut me, Mama."

"Nobody's going to cut you, Ellie," Annabeth said. "We're just going to scrape some of the stickers off."

"Will it hurt?"

"Some. But you're a brave girl."

"You do it. All right, Mama?"

"All right." With a silent prayer, Annabeth nodded and took the knife from Joseph. There was no way this wasn't going to be painful. "My friend here will need to hold you. All right?"

The little girl nodded. Joseph eased her onto his lap and secured her with one arm. "I can tell you're a brave girl, Ellie," he said. "But if it hurts too much, or if I hold you too tightly, you say so. Okay?"

"Okay." At least Ellie seemed to trust him.

As Annabeth wetted the blade and wiped it on her skirt, she struggled to picture how her father had held the card at a square angle and used it like a razor to scrape the spines from her brother's leg. Her brother had howled with pain, and he'd been older than Ellie. But something had to be done.

Annabeth clasped the handle of the pocketknife and took a deep breath. She would have to be perfectly steady to keep the sharp blade from cutting Ellie's fragile skin. "Hold her," she said to Joseph.

At the first stroke of the blade, Ellie sucked in her breath but didn't cry out. Perspiration soaked Annabeth's body as she scraped away at the tiny spines, taking care not to press on the blade. Some of the looser spines came out. Others were so deeply embedded they would have to be soaked and tweezed.

The dog looked on, whining softly as if feeling his little mistress's pain. Ellie whimpered but didn't cry out. Annabeth could hear Joseph singing softly to her as he cradled her against his body.

"This old man, he played one. He played knick knack on my thumb . . ."

Time seemed to stand still as Annabeth worked. In reality, only a few minutes passed before she'd covered the surface of Ellie's leg and foot. She released a long breath and folded the knife.

"That's all I can do," she said. "Now I need to get her home, soak her in a warm bath, and tweeze the rest of the stickers out."

Joseph passed Ellie into her arms. The little girl finally released her tears. Sobs shook her body. Annabeth held her close, mindful of her leg. "My brave girl," she whispered.

"My aunt is a doctor," Joseph said. "Her ranch isn't far. I can take you there."

"No!" The word sprang to Annabeth's lips. "I'm aware of who your aunt is. But I can't ask you to drive us there. I'll take care of Ellie at home."

"But a doctor might have something to help—"

"No. Please don't ask me to explain."

He studied her, his expression puzzled, then knowing. "Your husband." It wasn't a question.

She looked away, breaking contact with his piercing eyes. "I said, don't ask me. Silas has his reasons for being the way he is."

"Fine. But you can't carry Ellie home in her condition. I'll drive you."

Annabeth was about to refuse when she realized he was right. Ellie was in misery, and the farm was more than a mile away. Trying to carry the child, with her leg so sore that she could barely stand to have it touched, would be torture.

Slowly, she nodded. "You'll let me off where I tell you?"

"Of course. But my God, Annabeth, what kind of—?"

"Not another word." She cut him off. "Silas is a good man, but you have to know him. If you did, you'd understand."

They walked to the road, where Joseph had left the car. He might have carried Ellie, but the little girl's arms were wrapped so tightly around her mother's neck that it seemed no power on earth could make her let go. As he helped them into the car, he saw a tear trickle down Annabeth's cheek. He willed his emotions to freeze. Caring about this woman and her children was the most reckless thing he could do.

The dog came trotting out of the brush with the mate to Ellie's shoe in its mouth. Joseph took the shoe and let the beast jump into the back seat—burrs, dusty paws, and all.

He took the left branch of the road back to the farm. Annabeth sat beside him, silent as she cradled Ellie on her lap. Joseph knew better than to ask her about Lucas or about her marriage. The less he knew, the better. They would not—could not—meet again.

After letting her off at a discreet distance from the house, he cut back by another route and headed for the ranch. Forcing thoughts of Annabeth and her family to the back of his mind, he imagined the coming dance, whirling Francine around the floor with her lovely face smiling up at him. His father would be interested in hearing about the charming new schoolteacher.

Nearing home, he checked on the closed sawmill, drove up the switchback road, and parked behind the house. In the parlor, he found his father waiting for him. The expression on his haggard face put Joseph on instant alert.

"What is it, Dad?" he asked. "Is something wrong?"

"You tell me," Blake said. "This morning I got a telephone call from the sheriff in Miles City. He wanted you to know that the thief who stole your briefcase and the money in it has been arrested. You can call him back. But first you owe me an explanation. What in hell's name is going on?"

CHAPTER FIVE

As HE DROVE DOWN THE SWITCHBACK ROAD, ON HIS WAY TO THE dance, Joseph willed his thoughts to focus on the good time ahead. But memories and worries roiled in his mind like clouds before a thunderstorm.

He'd telephoned the sheriff in Miles City and arranged to see the prisoner the next day. The thief had been caught when he tried to cash one of the checks with a forged endorsement. Alerted ahead of time, the bank staff had detained him and called the sheriff. The remaining checks and the briefcase were safe. But, as he'd feared, the cash—almost $800—was gone.

Blake had been furious at Joseph for keeping the theft a secret from him. "I may be sentenced for life to this chair, but I built this ranch into what it is, and I'm still the boss," he'd stormed. "I don't need protecting, and I'll be damned if I'll let my son treat me like a . . ." He'd choked on the last word. "Like a *cripple*!"

Joseph had taken the tongue-lashing as a lesson. Tomorrow morning, before leaving for Miles City, he would take time to inspect the cattle operation, oversee the startup of the mill, and report back to his father. Joseph was capable of running the Dollarhide enterprises. One day he probably would. But Blake was still the man in charge. For the foreseeable future, it would be Joseph's job to follow his orders and pay him the respect he deserved.

For now, as son and heir, that was his duty. His own needs, including time with his beloved horses, would have to wait.

The day was ending in a glorious blaze of sunset. Ribbons of mauve and flame streaked across a sky of deepening violet, the same soft hue as Annabeth's eyes.

Joseph had vowed not to think of her again, but now the memories flooded through him like a spring thaw. Annabeth had been a girl of sixteen when he'd known her before. Now her strength in the face of a hard life made her seem older than he was. That strength lent her a soul-deep beauty.

He buried her image in memory, the only place where it belonged.

By the time Joseph turned onto the main road, headed for Blue Moon, the sky was already darkening into twilight. The dance would just be starting. He could see the lights and hear the music through the block as he drove to the schoolhouse to pick up Francine. His pulse danced with anticipation. When he walked her onto the dance floor and took her in his arms, he would be the envy of every man in town.

Annabeth was getting up from the supper table when Silas sprang his surprise. "Fix your hair and put on a pretty dress," he said. "My sister's agreed to watch the kids at her place while we go to the dance tonight."

"But . . ." The word trailed off as she thought of Ellie, who was free of stickers but still sore and peevish, and Lucas, who was so exhausted he could barely eat his supper.

Earlier, knowing Ellie was liable to talk, she had told Silas about meeting Joseph. Silas's reaction had been a cold glare. "I'd have run him off with a shotgun," he'd muttered before turning away.

Now, he'd brought up the dance, which wasn't like him at all. Was he planning some kind of showdown?

The children were still at the table, watching their parents in wide-eyed silence. They were old enough to understand at least part of what was being said.

"How can I leave the children tonight, Silas?" Annabeth protested. "Look at them. They need to be in bed, and I need to be here in case they need anything."

"They can sleep at Nancy's place," Silas said. "I thought you'd be happy. A regular woman would enjoy a night out with her husband."

"As I would, on any other night. But the children—"

He exhaled, his breath hissing out through the narrow gap between his front teeth. "The children always come first with you, don't they? Maybe you should give some thought to your husband. I've given you a home, Annabeth. And I've given you respectability. You know that sonofabitch would never have married you. You'd have been branded a fallen woman with a bastard baby."

Hot fury, fueled with shame, surged through Annabeth's body. She fought the urge to lash out at him. The children were watching. Whatever the cost to her pride, she had to make peace.

Annabeth began clearing the table, stacking the dishes on the counter to be washed when she had time to heat water. "All right, Silas, as long as we don't stay too late, I'll go to the dance with you. I'll need time to change."

"Fine. We can drop off the kids on the way." He rolled a cigarette and settled in a chair to smoke. "Take your time getting ready. I want everyone who sees my beautiful wife to be jealous of me."

Silas rarely gave her compliments. The remark was so unlike him that Annabeth felt gooseflesh creep over her skin. Yes, he had some kind of plan in mind. She could only hope it would be harmless.

The open-air dance hall in the square was strung with electric lights and crepe-paper streamers. The four-piece band, hired out of Miles City, alternated popular numbers like the turkey trot and the black bottom with traditional waltzes, two-steps, and tangos—something for everyone.

As Joseph presented his tickets at the entrance table, heads were already swiveling toward him and his date. Francine was a vision in an apricot silk gown that floated around her as she moved. Tiny pearl drops gleamed her ears, matching the long strand that hung almost to her waist. Other girls and ladies glanced down at their own feeble finery and sighed. It was as if a swan had glided in among a flock of barnyard geese.

"Oh, my," she whispered to Joseph. "I do believe I've overdressed."

"Nonsense. You're perfect," Joseph said, although privately, he conceded that her beauty would probably make her some enemies among the women.

As they waited for the next set to start, his eyes scanned the crowd of dancers and watchers. Several of his mill workers and cowhands were there with their girls. And he saw a few old friends. Neither of his aunts were there. Kristin had never been much for dancing, and Britta's husband, the former sheriff, was confined to a wheelchair—a tragic accident in which Joseph had played a part.

Joseph's jaw tightened as an earlier night replayed in his memory—a dance, exactly five years ago. Lucy Merriweather, with whom he'd been infatuated, had convinced Joseph she needed money to get away from Webb Calder's sexual advances—a claim that turned out to be a lie. Joseph had taken two hundred dollars from his father's cashbox and brought it to the dance for her. A short time later, Lucy was seen running off with the money and her lover. When sheriff Jake Calhoun had tried to stop them, the man had fired his pistol. The bullet had severed Jake's spine and almost claimed his life.

In his mind's eye, Joseph could still see Jake sprawled on the ground in a pool of blood, Britta bending over him, and Lucy fleeing with the shooter in his car. The scene would haunt him for the rest of his days.

"Joseph, where have you gone off to?" Francine was tugging at his sleeve. "The music is starting—a foxtrot. Come on. We came to dance."

With a smile and a murmured apology, Joseph led her onto the dance floor. She was pure enchantment in his arms, weightless on her feet, her dress flowing around her, her eyes gazing up at him with a twinkle of mischief. The subtle fragrance of lilacs crept through his senses. Francine Rutledge was everything a man could wish for. He would be a fool not to make her his.

The music ended, leaving Joseph hungry to hold her again in another dance. He was standing next to her, imagining how their first kiss would feel, when a voice at his shoulder shocked him back to reality.

"Well, Joseph, are you going to introduce me to the new lady in town?"

Chase Calder stood next to him. His words were addressed to Joseph, but Chase was looking down at Francine like a bear at a pot of honey.

Biting back a curse, Joseph introduced the pair. He was aware of Chase's reputation with women. When a pretty female took his fancy, she'd be treated like a princess—until Chase grew tired of the game and turned away, leaving one more broken heart behind.

Only one girl had broken Chase's heart—fiery young Maggie O'Rourke, daughter of a dirt poor family with a ranch in the foothills. Chase had been crazy for her. But the romance had ended when Webb Calder hanged Maggie's father, Angus, for stealing cattle. Maggie's brother, Culley, had avenged his father's death by hanging Webb's prize stallion from a rope in the Calder stable. Maggie had been hustled off to live with her late mother's relatives in California. Chase's heart had healed and turned to stone.

It would be useless to warn Francine about Chase, Joseph told himself. She would only think he was jealous, which was true. But that didn't mean he was giving up. This woman was worth fighting for, and he wasn't about to back off. Not even for the high and mighty Chase Calder.

"Joseph, would you mind if I borrowed your lady for a dance?" Chase asked.

Hell, yes, he minded. But good manners demanded that he be gracious. "Francine is her own woman," Joseph said. "Suppose you ask her."

In the next moment, the music had started, and the pair of

dirty linen. Tonight, hers had been hung out for all to see. A man's misbehavior could be easily excused and often was. But a woman's reputation, once stained, would never be clean again.

She burned to say those things, to shout them into the ears of her uncaring husband. But she'd learned the hard way that speaking up would only get her a deluge of accusations, threats, and other punishments. Better to freeze her emotions, keep her head down, and find joy in raising her children. Annabeth was already counting the minutes until she could hold them and take them home.

It came as a blessed relief to see the lights of the farmhouse where Silas's sister, Nancy, lived. A decade older than Silas, she'd married young, raised four children, and lost her husband two years ago. A tall, grim, solitary woman, she ran the small farm mostly by herself. Nancy was no friend to Annabeth, but at least she could be trusted with the children.

Silas drove the auto through the gate and up to his sister's house. "I'll be going out again after we get home," he said, speaking as if the fiasco at the dance had never happened. "Nothing to concern you. And don't bother waiting up."

"I understand," she said.

The porch light had come on. He cast her a stern look. "This business between us isn't over, Annabeth. But we'll put it aside for now. I've got other things on my mind." He opened the driver's door and climbed out. "Stay here while I get the kids."

Alone for the moment, Annabeth allowed herself to breathe deeply. She'd been through worse. She would deal with the pain and survive. But what about Joseph? What had he been thinking, rushing to her rescue with no thought for himself?

His interference had only made the situation worse. Tongues would be wagging all over town, how Joseph Dollarhide had flung himself between a man and his wife and gotten bloodied for it.

By rights, she should be angry with Joseph. But the thought that he would expose himself to danger and scandal to protect her stirred an ache so sweet that it brought tears to her eyes.

A few tears were all she could allow herself. Silas was her hus-

backward. Snorting like a bull, Silas waded in to finish him. He was bigger than Joseph and clearly a brawler. Joseph was faster, and he'd beaten bullies before, but the thought of Silas slapping Annabeth made him angry. And anger made him reckless.

Joseph's fists rained punches against the big man's work-hardened body. Hitting him was like smashing his fists against a brick wall. Silas's blows were fewer, but they landed with bruising force. People were coming outside from the dance. Hands and arms pulled Joseph back. Others were doing the same to Silas.

Annabeth was on her feet, her face florid where Silas had slapped her. Shaking off restraining hands, Silas turned toward his wife. "Stay away from him, you hear?" he said. "If you have anything to do with the man, so help me, you'll never see your children again." He opened the car door. "Get in."

As the Model T started up and drove away, Joseph became aware of the people surrounding him. Francine stood next to Chase. Her unsympathetic gaze took in Joseph's swelling eye, bruised jaw, and nose dripping blood onto his clothes. She shook her head and turned to her companion. "Please take me home, Chase," she said.

As the pair walked away in the direction of Chase's car, a shadowed figure drifted along the fringes of the crowd. Through a veil of black Spanish lace, Lola De Marco watched Francine slip a hand through the crook of Chase's arm. Her grotesquely scarred features twisted in a satisfied smile. *Perfect.* So far, things were working out just as she'd planned.

Annabeth was quiet on the drive back to the farm. With her face still burning from Silas's slap, she stared down at her clasped hands. Beneath the prison of her silence, she seethed. Part of her wanted to rail at him, to demand why he'd chosen to humiliate her in public when she'd done nothing but accept help—the only help at hand—for her little girl. The embarrassment had been far worse than the physical pain. She'd never believed in the airing of

Stopping in a spot that gave Joseph a direct view, Silas took his wife in his arms. His feet barely moved to the music as he drew her hard against him, molding her body to his. His hands roamed up and down over her curves, making a show of caressing her through the thin fabric of her dress and slip. When he glanced at Joseph, his mocking look seemed to say, *See, she's my woman. I can do anything I want with her—things you can only do in your dreams.*

Some people cast startled glances at the pair. Others were visibly trying not to look. Annabeth's face was crimson, its expression rigid as she endured the humiliation—as punishing to her as it was to Joseph. But there was worse to come. Silas kissed her, his hands sliding down to cup her buttocks through her dress. Only then did Annabeth snap.

"That's enough, Silas!" she hissed, pushing away from him. "I'm going to the car. Take me home. Now." She walked off the floor and out of the dance hall, into the moonlit parking lot.

The surprise that flashed across Silas's face darkened to fury as he strode after her. With no time to weigh the consequences, Joseph followed.

He caught up to find Annabeth struggling with Silas next to a car. His big hand clasped her wrist. The other hand was raised to strike. "Make a fool of me, will you?" he muttered. "You're my wife. I'll teach you not to shame me in public."

Annabeth was twisting and pulling to get away. But when the flat-handed blow struck her hard enough to send her head jerking sideways, the fight went out of her. She gasped. Her knees buckled. But Silas kept his grip on her. His free hand shot up to strike her again.

"That's enough!" Joseph seized Silas's upraised arm from behind, pulling him off-balance. Recovering, Silas shoved Annabeth aside and wheeled to face him. Hatred gleamed in his eyes as he swung.

Joseph dodged the first blow. But a second punch from the opposite fist struck his jaw hard enough to send him staggering

them were moving around the floor to a sensual tango. After looking for another partner and finding no one available, Joseph stood seething as he watched them. They made a striking couple, with Chase turning on the charm and Francine beaming up at him, her head cocked like a pretty little bird's.

The music was nearing its end when Joseph happened to glance toward the ticket table. His mouth went dry as the raw-boned man he remembered from the incident in town walked in with Annabeth on his arm.

Dressed in the same blue frock she'd worn at the dance five years ago and with her golden hair brushed loose, Annabeth looked softly beautiful. But even from where he stood, Joseph could sense the strain in her. Clearly, it hadn't been her idea to come here.

Her husband—Silas, she'd called him—was eyeing the crowd like a hawk scanning for prey. Had he learned about his wife's encounter with Joseph earlier in the day? Was he here for a showdown?

Joseph pretended to ignore the pair. He was here to impress a choice lady, not quarrel over an old flame. If Silas wanted trouble, he would have to find it somewhere else.

The music had ended. Couples were circulating on the dance floor. According to custom, Chase would be expected to return his partner to her escort. But Chase had never been one to play by the rules. He and Francine were still together on the dance floor.

Joseph knew better than to stride out among the dancers and demand her return. That would embarrass Francine and make him look like a fool. All he could do, with no other partner in sight, was stand on the sidelines and seethe.

The band had begun to play again—a slow waltz, the kind of tender, romantic music that urged couples to hold each other close. Chase and Francine were swaying together as if lost in a dream. Joseph stifled a groan. Then he saw Silas leading Annabeth onto the floor.

band, promised in holy matrimony. He had threatened to take her children. If pressed hard enough, he would do it. He would do it because he could. There was only one way to remedy the situation.

She would never see Joseph again.

Two nights later

The O'Rourke Ranch, situated in the eastern foothills above the Calder spread, had never been much to look at. Now, with no one left of the family but Culley, the wild-eyed son, the place had gone to ruin. The cattle were scattered and gone, the outbuildings fallen in, the clapboard house barely holding together.

But none of that mattered anymore. The only thing of worth was inside the cave that burrowed back into the hillside behind a screen of scraggly box elder trees.

The moon was high when Silas Mosby parked the Model T behind a dilapidated shed, climbed out of the car, and trekked up the hill toward the trees. The night was alive with sound. Insects chirred in clumps of untended scrub. A rabbit, caught by a predator, squealed in the darkness. The wind that rustled the leaves carried the sickly sweet aroma of fermenting mash downhill to Silas's nostrils.

Under the lip of the hillside cave, lit by kerosene lamps, Culley O'Rourke and Buck Haskell were working an illegal still. Fermented corn mash simmered over a fire in a five-gallon copper vessel called an alembic. A series of tubes and containers collected the alcoholic vapor and distilled it into liquid. With the addition of some glycerin, bitters, and other flavorings, it became moonshine—and really good moonshine was liquid gold.

Buck, a husky, good-looking cowboy who worked for the Calders, gave Silas a grin. "You're just in time, partner," he said. "We've got a new batch of white lightning, bottled, crated, and ready to go."

"It damned well better be," Silas said. "I've got a customer waiting for delivery. She'll be mighty sore if she has to wait."

"Are you talking about the new owner of Jake's Place?" Buck

shook his head. "I've never met the woman, but I hear she's ugly enough to stop a runaway freight train."

"She might've been a looker till she got her face carved up," Silas said. "But who cares, as long as her cash is good?"

"Does she plan to bring any girls in?" Buck's grin widened. "Those so-called nieces of Jake's looked like they'd been rode hard and put away wet, but at least they were available."

"That's none of my business," Silas said. "You'll have to ask her yourself."

Buck laughed. "Aren't you the gloomy one tonight? What is it? Woman troubles?"

"Don't ask."

"Hell, Silas," Buck teased. "If I was married to that pretty little gal of yours, I'd never stop smiling."

"Then you don't know the half of it. Shut your face, Buck, and get me my cargo. I've got a delivery to make."

Culley O'Rourke came out of the back of the cave, lugging two crates of filled mason jars packed in straw. Pale and scrawny, with black hair hanging over his eyes and down his back, he didn't look strong enough to carry the heavy burden. But he managed it with ease. This was the man who'd hanged a 1,200-pound horse by hoisting a rope over a rafter in Webb Calder's barn. His guilt had never been proven, but Silas knew the truth of it.

"There's two more of these," Culley said. "Buck can help you carry them down to the car."

Silas waited while Culley brought out the other crates. The three men had been partners for more than a year. Culley and Buck had been boyhood friends. Silas was a neighbor they'd known and trusted.

Smuggling illegal liquor was rampant in this part of Montana. People who knew the ropes were making good money. One night, after a late-night card game on Culley's ranch, the three had decided to get into the business. They didn't have the money or the connections to import smuggled Canadian liquor, but good homemade moonshine was selling for twenty dollars a gallon to folks who couldn't buy the real thing.

Silas and Buck had put up the cash for the still. Culley's contribution had been his land, a failed ranch that no one, including the law, had any reason to visit.

Moonshine whiskey was being brewed in homes, barns, and backwoods hideouts all over the country. Every time federal agents seized a still, others would crop up to take its place. Most of the liquor from these stills was barely drinkable. The partners had agreed that theirs would have to be better than the competition's.

Thanks to their quality copper equipment and ingredients, word soon got around that they made a good, reliable product. Soon they had as many orders as they could fill, most from homes and ranches but some from speakeasys as far away as Miles City.

Culley tended the still. Buck, who had a telephone in his cabin on the Calder Ranch, brought in supplies and contacted customers. Silas made deliveries and collected payment, which was divided among the three partners.

Silas had already amassed a nice nest egg, money that he'd hidden in the potato cellar on his farm. He was still deciding how he was going to spend it and whether his plans would include Annabeth and the children, who were mostly a burden. Either way, he didn't intend to be a farmer forever.

The crates of bottled moonshine were heavy. Silas hoisted two. Buck lifted the others and followed him through the trees and down the hill. There, they stowed the crates in the hollowed-out space under the rear seat. For larger deliveries, they used Culley's old farm truck, piled with hay to camouflage the cargo. But Silas's Model T would do for tonight.

Buck prepared to mount the horse he'd ridden here. "Keep a sharp eye out," he cautioned Silas. "I've heard the feds will be on the prowl. They've got orders to clean out small-time operations like ours."

Silas spat in the dust. "I don't know why they bother with us. This isn't Chicago. We're filling a need and not hurting anybody."

"Maybe not. But every moonshiner and bootlegger those boys shut down gets them more gold stars from J. Edgar Hoover. So just be careful. That's what I'm telling you. And there's more. I've heard a rumor that a gang from Chicago is moving into this part of Montana to corner the market, and they don't play nice. They're genuine gangsters, not small-timers like us. They'd steal your cargo and shoot you just to get you out of the way."

"I'll keep that in mind." Silas cranked the starter, climbed into the driver's seat, and headed for the back road to town. He'd been craving a newer vehicle, but the old Model T, no different from hundreds of others in the county, was less likely to be noticed, stopped, or remembered.

Truth be told, he enjoyed these late-night runs. The element of danger made his blood race. While it lasted, he could even make believe he was living a different life, free from the drudgery of the farm and the disappointment of his family—a son who was another man's bastard, a useless girl who would grow up to be a useless woman, and a wife who was about as passionate as warm milk.

Annabeth was pretty enough, but pretty didn't count for much in the dark. Even after he'd finished with her, Silas sensed that something was missing. Damn it, he wanted more from a woman than submission. At least she should try harder to give him babies—sons that a man could claim and be proud of.

Blue Moon was dark and quiet at this hour. A single lamp glowed in the window of the Feed and Hardware Store, another in the sheriff's office above the jail. Jake's Place, under its new ownership, was at the far end of Main Street. Silas doused his headlights, then, guided by moonlight, drove in by way of the back street. As he parked behind the building and switched off the engine, a door opened at the top of the outside stairway to the second floor.

Veiled in a black lace mantilla over a satin robe, the woman called Lola glided down the stairs. Silas stood watching her. She had a fluid, almost serpentine way of moving that intrigued him. He'd seen her face and heard the rumor that she'd been in prison, but he knew better than to ask questions about her past or her scars.

"How much did you bring?" Her voice was gravelly, as if her throat had been slashed along with her face.

"Four crates. That was the order."

She fished in the deep *V* of her robe and brought out a wad of bills. They felt warm when he took them from her hand. "You can count them," she said.

"I would trust you. But I owe it to my partners to count everything." He leafed through the bills, mostly twenties and tens. Their scent was faintly musky and exotic, the way he imagined her body might smell. "All there," he said. "Where do you want the crates? In the cellar?"

"Yes. Where you left the others."

The outside door to the basement opened under the stairs, the way all but hidden by a tangle of hip-high weeds. Lola unlocked the door and held it while Silas carried two crates inside. A single bare bulb, hanging on a wire strung from upstairs, cast a glow over a space that was surprisingly large.

Some changes had been made in the week since Silas had last seen it. A stage curtain had been hung to conceal the storage area, where unused furniture was stacked, including a dusty yellow velvet chaise longue, along with kitchen items and crates of moonshine. On the other side of the curtain, space had been cleared for two folding tables with chairs and a bar improvised from a wide plank and two large barrels. It didn't take a fool to recognize a crude speakeasy.

"It doesn't look like much yet." Lola spoke as if reading his mind. "But give me a few weeks and it'll be first class. Meanwhile, my customers will have a place to gamble and get what they want to drink."

Buck had mentioned girls. Silas wondered if whores were going to be part of Lola's operation. Maybe that was what the yellow chaise longue was intended for.

"When will you be in business down here?" he asked.

"Soon. I'm still learning how to dilute the whiskey with fruit juice for the drinks—cocktails, to give them a fancy name. I'll charge more for the straight stuff." She stood close to him—close enough to make him aware that she was naked under the robe. His body stirred in response. Her face might be ruined, but there was nothing wrong with her voluptuous figure.

Silas went out for the other two crates, brought them in, set them down, and closed the door behind him. After a moment's hesitation, he slid the bolt into place.

Lola reached up and pulled the string that hung from the light socket. As the room plunged into darkness, her satin robe swished to the floor.

The scent of her perfume swam in Silas's senses as he unbuckled his belt and took her in his arms.

CHAPTER SIX

JOSEPH'S PLAN TO DRIVE TO MILES CITY HAD BEEN DELAYED BY A broken circular saw blade at the mill. The steel teeth had struck an old ax head in a log, buried in the tree as it grew. The impact had twisted the big blade and stripped the gears, shooting shards of wood in all directions. One of the mill's best men had nearly lost an arm. He would recover but would need weeks to rest and heal. Joseph had ordered replacement parts from a company in Detroit. Until the parts arrived, production would need to be shifted to a smaller saw, the delivery schedule changed, and impatient, sometimes angry customers notified.

Three stressful days had passed before Joseph could be spared to confront the thief who'd stolen his briefcase. Raw from worries at the mill, he welcomed the distraction of a drive out of town. The morning was clear, the sunlight a golden haze on the ripening wheat fields to the west of the road. In the marshland, red-winged blackbirds called and flitted among the cattails.

The hour was early. In Blue Moon, the stores and businesses were just opening. Shoppers were hurrying to get their errands done before the heat set in. There was no activity in the small house that adjoined the school. Joseph hadn't seen Francine since the dance. It wouldn't hurt to stop by and make sure she was all right—if she was still speaking to him. But there'd be time for that later, maybe on the way home. Right now he had unfinished business in Miles City.

He was more concerned about Annabeth, especially after the way her husband had abused her at the dance. Did Silas hit Lucas and little Ellie, too? The thought sickened Joseph. But there was nothing he could do. Any attempt at interference would only make things worse for her and her little family.

The auto carried him out of town and into the open country. When he saw the deep pothole ahead, he slowed down and gave it a wide berth. How much nerve and stealth would it take for a thief to steal something out of a car with the owner a few feet away. Joseph had little doubt that he was dealing with a master criminal who deserved a long sentence behind bars.

In Miles City, he drove to the sheriff's office and parked out front. The sheriff was expecting him.

"We've got your briefcase with the checks inside, including the one that the thief tried to cash," he told Joseph. "After you leave here, you'll want to take them to the bank."

"What about the prisoner?" Joseph asked. "What's going to happen to him?"

"His trial's set for next week. We'll need you to testify, so plan to be here. Since he couldn't make bail, he's cooling his heels behind bars."

"Does he have a record? Any other crimes he's wanted for?"

"Not that we can find on short notice," the sheriff said. "You can see him if you'd like."

"Yes, I'd like that very much."

"You can even talk with him if you want. Maybe you can get more out of him than I've been able to."

Joseph followed the sheriff down a dim corridor to the jail at the rear of the building. There were four cells, three of them empty. As Joseph's eyes adjusted to the dim light, he could make out a small figure in an oversized black-and-white jail uniform huddled on a bunk against the concrete wall.

The sheriff stepped close to the bars. "Hey, Forrest, wake up. You've got a visitor."

Two skinny arms unfolded into sight, followed by a shaggy head of dirty blond hair above a sunburned face.

"Go to hell." The voice was a boy's, just beginning to change.

"Good lord, he's just a kid," Joseph muttered.

"He's a thief," the sheriff said. "He stole from you, and he needs to be taught a lesson. Stand up, boy, or I'll come in there and make you wish you had."

The black-and-white bundle rolled off the bunk and stood. The pant legs were so long that they covered his feet and pooled on the floor. The boy appeared to be about thirteen, or maybe older and small for his age. He stood a few feet back from the bars, a defiant scowl on his face.

"Mind your manners, boy," the sheriff said. "This is Mr. Joseph Dollarhide. He's the man you robbed."

"I know. Not the name, just him." He eyed Joseph, his chin thrust in a show of bravado.

Joseph turned to the sheriff. "Can you leave me with him? I'd like to take some time."

"Take all the time you want. I'll be out front. But watch him. He's as sly as a little weasel."

As the sheriff left, the boy stood in place, sizing Joseph up. It was plain to see that he'd come from a hard life—untrimmed, tangled hair, a bruise on his face. What Joseph could see of his body was mostly skin and bones.

"Are they treating you all right here?" Joseph asked.

"What do you think? At least I get fed."

"Forrest. Is that your first name or your last name?"

"Forrest McCoy. Or McCoy Forrest. Take your pick. I don't give a damn what you call me."

"All right, Forrest. How old are you?"

"Sixteen." The kid was clearly lying, but Joseph would let that go for now.

"I have some questions for you, Forrest. If you know what's good for you, you'll give me straight answers."

Forrest shrugged.

"I'll start with an easy question," Joseph said. "I'd like to know how you managed to steal my briefcase out of my car while I was right there."

The boy shrugged again. "I've always been good at sneaking. Back home, I could sneak up on a rabbit and twist its neck 'fore it even knew I was there. Folks called it my gift. Your car was easy. I grabbed the first thing I saw. Got lucky, I guess. Before I got stupid and tried to cash a check."

"You mentioned back home. Where was that?"

"Kentucky."

"And where are your parents?"

"Dead. Our granny took care of us—me and my big brother, Cam—for a while. When she died, we got sent to an orphanage." He was opening up. Joseph let him talk.

"That orphanage—it was awful. Ain't no words bad enough for what they did to us there. First chance we got, we snuck out and hopped a train, hid in a freight car. It took us to Chicago. Biggest place I ever saw. We stole some food and caught another one. We talked about maybe goin' all the way to California." Forrest paused and wiped his nose on his sleeve. "Say, I can talk better if you get me some soda pop."

"I'll see what I can do. We're not finished."

Joseph walked back down the hall. He found the sheriff at his desk going over some paperwork.

"So are you getting anything out of the kid?" the sheriff asked.

"Only that he's had a rough life. Have you got any cold sodas? He's talked himself dry."

"Working his con on you already, I see," he said. "Don't let the little hooligan fool you. He's bad to the bone."

"Sodas?"

"Ice chest is in the corner. You'll find some root beer in there. Opener's hanging on a nail. You'll see it. God, I hate prohibition. What I wouldn't give for a cold beer. The real thing, not that homemade swill."

Joseph found a bottle of root beer, pried off the cap, and took it back to Forrest. The boy was standing where Joseph had left him. He held out his hand.

"Only if you promise to tell me why you stole my briefcase."

"I was getting there. Give me the soda. *Please.*" The last word was tinged with sarcasm. Joseph passed the bottle through the bars. It occurred to him that the kid could break the glass bottle and use it as a weapon later. But that wouldn't be very smart. And this boy, Joseph sensed, was at least clever.

Forrest tilted the bottle to his mouth, finished it in a few gulps, and passed it back to Joseph. "Thanks, I like it cold," he said.

"So, what about the rest of your story?"

Forrest sank onto the edge of the bunk, which was nothing more than a frame strung with ropes for support. There was no mattress or blanket. "Like I said, Cam and me, we were on the train. It was slowing down for Miles City when some men got into the car. Bad men, if you know what I mean. We had to jump. I was okay, but Cam twisted his knee. He could walk, but he couldn't run.

"We needed food to keep going. There was a farm across a field. We made it there and asked at the house. The lady told us to go away or she'd sic the dog on us.

"We left, but we were starving. We waited till dark, and I snuck into the chicken coop and stole some eggs. We were so hungry, we sucked 'em out of the shells and ate 'em raw.

"Cam was too tired to walk anymore, so we bedded down in a windbreak at the edge of the field. We slept till daylight, when we heard the dog barking and the farmer cussing. We took off, figured he just wanted us to go. But the man had a gun. I heard the shot from behind. Cam went down. He was hit bad.

"I couldn't leave him. I put up my hands and begged the farmer to help my brother. The man just grinned and said, 'Have you got any money? I can save him, but you'll have to pay me first.'

"The road wasn't far. I ran all the way. But when I tried to wave down a car and ask for help, nobody stopped for me.

"Then I saw you hit that big hole in the road. When you got out, I was going to ask you for money, but I could tell you were in a bad mood. I was afraid you'd say no. Then I looked in your car and saw what was there."

"So you took it."

"I ran back to the farmer with the cash. He met me partway. I couldn't see Cam. But when I held out the money—I hadn't even counted it—he took it all. Then he laughed. He told me that my brother was already dead, and if I didn't get out of there, he'd shoot me, too."

Joseph exhaled. "That's quite a story. Is it true?"

"Every word, I swear to God."

"Did you tell the sheriff?"

"He didn't believe me. He said that a boy like me would usually be sent to reform school. But because I'd committed grand larceny, I'd probably be sentenced to the big prison at Deer Lodge." The boy's voice cracked. He appeared genuinely afraid.

Conflicted, Joseph turned without a word and walked away. What was he thinking? The boy had robbed him and come up with a story so gut-wrenching that it was scarcely believable.

Did Forrest deserve a second chance, or was he a clever con artist who'd take every advantage he could?

"I see he got to you," the sheriff said. "Don't say I didn't warn you. The kid has a real talent."

"Did you really tell him he was going to Deer Lodge?" Joseph asked.

"Only to scare him. But he'll be facing time in reform school, probably till he's eighteen. There's a chance it could straighten him out, but most kids come out of that place worse than they went in."

Joseph put the soda bottle in a box for empties. "What if I declined to press charges? What would happen then?"

"You'd sign some papers, and the kid would go his merry way, probably to commit more crimes. I wouldn't recommend it. The little thief needs to learn his lesson."

"What about probation—lasting until he worked off the money he stole?"

"Under your supervision? Good luck with that. He'd probably be gone the first time you turned your back."

"Then his probation would be cancelled. He'd be a fugitive. My question is, If I decided to, could I arrange it?"

"Maybe. You'd have to talk to the judge. But he'll probably think you're out of your mind."

"Maybe so. But I was one of the lucky kids, born into a good family with resources. If the story Forrest told me is even half true, the boy hasn't had a decent break in his life. What about his brother's death? Did you look into that?"

"I did. The body was taken to the morgue and buried. The farmer claimed he was defending his property against robbers. He denied that there was ever any money involved."

"A likely story," Joseph said.

"Take your pick. The judge's office is in the courthouse. He'll give you the same advice as you got from me."

"I'll give it some thought," Joseph said. But something told him he had already made up his mind.

Two hours later, after visiting the bank, talking to the judge, and signing the paperwork, Joseph found himself in his car, driving back to Blue Moon with Forrest in the passenger seat.

The boy had been given a shower and haircut at the jail. Joseph had bought him a set of work clothes, boots, and extra underthings. Joseph's frugal mother had saved most of her son's outgrown clothes. They were still in good condition. Forrest could wear the ones that fit.

Forrest sat quietly, hands fidgeting in his lap. Joseph couldn't blame him for appearing nervous. After his time at the orphanage and in the jail, the boy could be expecting anything.

"Do you know where we are, Forrest?" Joseph asked.

Forrest shook his head. Behind bars, he'd been almost cocky. Now, alone with a man he barely knew, all his defenses were up. The goings-on at the orphanage could have been as evil as the boy implied.

"We're coming to a town called Blue Moon," Joseph said. "My family's ranch is south of there. We have cattle and a sawmill. It's a nice place. You'll be working there until the money you stole is paid off."

"What kind of work?"

"Whatever we ask you to do. Don't expect things to be easy. But if you work hard and behave, you'll be treated fairly. If you lie, try to run away, or take anything that isn't yours, you'll be sent straight back to jail. Understand?"

"I reckon I do." His tone made it clear that he was still suspicious. They were coming into Blue Moon now. Joseph had heard from his workers that the new Jake's Place was open and the food was as tasty as before. The boy would be hungry. A good meal might ease his fears.

Joseph parked the car in the empty lot next to the restaurant. The lunch hour was over. When he ushered Forrest inside, he found most of the tables empty. An old man sat at the counter eating a sandwich. A couple of cowhands who worked for the Calders were finishing their meals at a corner table. Joseph recognized Buck Haskell, a former boyhood friend. The other cowboy was a stranger.

The two men got up from the table. They passed Joseph on their way out. Buck gave him a polite nod. Their friendship had ended years ago, on the night when they'd fallen into the crossfire between bootleggers and federal agents. Buck had turned tail, leaving Joseph to face the deadly danger alone.

Forrest turned to watch them walk out. "Are those real cowboys?" he whispered.

"As real as they come. Those two even smell like real cowboys," Joseph said. "You sound surprised. Don't they have cowboys in Kentucky?"

"Not where I come from. But I saw a cowboy movie once. Granny took me and Cam. Tom Mix was in it. He could shoot and ride a horse and throw a rope like you wouldn't believe."

"We have cowboys on the ranch," Joseph said. "They work hard, taking care of the cattle and their horses. It's a tough job, not much like the movies."

"Could I learn to be a cowboy?"

"Not right away," Joseph said. "Maybe later. But first you'll need to prove you're strong enough and can be trusted around cattle and horses. That's going to take time."

"How much time?"

A plain young woman in an apron had come out of the kitchen.

Joseph remembered her from when Jake had owned the place, although she hadn't been one of the "nieces" who'd been known to ply their trade in the upstairs rooms.

She greeted Joseph and Forrest with a smile, showed them to a table, gave them menus, and hurried back to the kitchen. Joseph scanned his menu, which hadn't changed much since Jake was running the place. "I already know what I want," he said. "What looks good to you, Forrest?"

The boy studied the menu, his eyebrows knotting in a scowl of concentration. Finally, he sighed. "Sorry, but I need help. Could you read this for me?"

"You can't read?"

He shook his head, dabbing at a tear with his sleeve. "Granny couldn't read. And nobody at the orphanage gave us any learning. They just put us to work—mostly in the fields, in the laundry, and in the kitchen. I know numbers, and I can write my name. I copied the name on that check I took to the bank, the one that got me caught. But I can't read *this*." His grip tightened on the paper menu as if he wanted to crumple it in his fist.

"Goodness, we'll have to do something about that."

The musical voice from behind Joseph made his reflexes jump. Startled, he swung around in his chair to find Francine standing there, wearing a sky blue dress and a smile that was like sunlight breaking through clouds. "Did I hear this young man right, Joseph? I'll have some time on my hands before school starts in the fall. If he wants to learn, I'd be happy to give him some reading lessons."

Questions swarmed in Joseph's mind. What was she doing here? Had she seen him go into the restaurant? And why was she being so nice after the way he'd embarrassed her at the dance? What had happened with Chase?

Joseph found his voice. "Please join us for lunch, Francine. My treat. You can get to know my friend Forrest, here, and maybe talk to him about reading lessons if he's interested." He handed her his menu and turned to the boy. "I'd recommend the hot beef sandwich with gravy, Forrest. That's what I'm having."

"Thank you, Joseph." Francine took a seat and adjusted her skirt. "I'll have the same."

After the girl in the apron had taken their order and left, Joseph made formal introductions. He hesitated, wondering how to explain Forrest's presence to Francine. She was a proper lady. Would she still be willing to teach the boy if she knew he was a criminal?

"Tell me about yourself, Forrest." She sipped the sweetened tea she'd ordered. "I heard you mention that you'd been in an orphanage. How did you meet Joseph? Are you a relative?"

"No, ma'am, Mr. Dollarhide is my boss. I'll be working for him on the ranch."

"Working on the ranch? But you're so young, Forrest. What kind of work will you be doing?"

"Whatever he tells me to. Mr. Dollarhide said the work would be hard. But anything's better than jail."

Francine's delicate brows shot upward. "Jail? Heavens, Joseph, what's he talking about?"

Joseph sighed. He'd hoped to avoid this revelation, but he should have known better. "Ask Forrest. He's done a pretty good job of explaining so far. He might as well tell you the rest."

Francine listened raptly as the boy recounted his odyssey from the orphanage to the Miles City jail. Watching her, Joseph saw her expression transform from distaste to pity to compassion. By the time he'd come to Joseph's part in his release, the apron girl had come out of the kitchen with plates of tender roast beef sliced over toast, with gravy and mashed potatoes.

As if fearful that he might be dreaming, Forrest used his fork to dip a morsel of meat in the gravy. He tasted it cautiously. "Oh, my gosh," he said, and set to devouring his food like a starving puppy. This was the boy who'd been hungry enough to suck raw eggs. And jail food probably hadn't been much better. Forrest hadn't said much about losing his brother. That hurt would be a long time healing. With luck, he would find that time on the ranch.

Francine met Joseph's gaze across the table. She was smiling. "You're a good man, Joseph," she said. "I almost misjudged you at the dance. But I realized later you were protecting a woman who was being mistreated. And now you've taken on this boy who stole your money..."

She shook her head, her voice breaking slightly. "I'd be happy to give Forrest some reading lessons. I can tell he's a bright boy. He's bound to learn fast. But you'll need to bring him to my place. Shall we say twice a week? Or is that asking too much of you?"

"We can work it out. I hope you'll let me pay you for your time."

She shook her head. "I wouldn't think of it, Joseph. If I can help this young man on his way to a better life, that's pay enough for me."

Forrest had cleaned his plate. With a smile, Francine passed him her half-finished lunch. He muttered his thanks and started on the leftover meat and potatoes, probably the best meal he'd enjoyed in years.

She stood. Remembering his manners, he stood with her. As they waited for the boy to finish, Joseph filled his eyes with her. To him, she had never looked more beautiful, standing across the table in a dress that set off her brown eyes. Perhaps it was because she had just shown him her kind heart. Whatever the reason, Joseph sensed that he was falling for her. He hadn't felt this way about a woman since the treacherous Lucy Merriweather had reeled him in with her lies. But he'd been a boy of nineteen then. He was a man now, old enough to know his own mind and his own heart.

Hearing the sound of footsteps behind him, Joseph assumed that it was the girl bringing the bill. He had just opened his wallet when an odd, throaty voice spoke.

"No charge for new customers, Mr. Dollarhide. Lunch is on me today."

He turned to find a startling woman standing behind him. Dressed in a peasant blouse and embroidered skirt, with a lace shawl over her head, she might have been a beauty once. But her face had been cruelly and utterly destroyed. Puckered scars crisscrossed her features, pulling them into a grotesque mask that was framed by waves of coal black hair.

Joseph willed himself not to look startled or turn his gaze away. He knew who she was. By now, almost everyone in town did. He stood to greet the woman.

"So you're the new owner," he said. "My compliments on the food. It's as good as ever."

"Thank you." She offered a hand, which he took. Her grip was as strong as a man's. "Francine here is already a regular. She's told me all about you. You can call me Lola. Everybody does." Her gaze fell on Forrest, who was still finishing his second plate. "And who is this young man?"

"This is Forrest, who's too hungry to remember his manners, if he has any. I'll make sure he knows better by the next time we come in."

"So, there *will* be a next time, yes?" She spoke with an accent he couldn't place. With that black hair, could she be Spanish? Maybe Portuguese or even Romany? He could swear he'd never met the woman. With that face, he certainly wouldn't forget. But something about her tugged at his memory. What was it? A look? A gesture?

He pondered the idea for a few seconds, then dismissed it.

"Bring your family and friends," she said. "Think of this place as your second home."

"I'll do that," Joseph said. "But please allow me to pay for our meals."

"No . . . no. Only come again soon."

"Then at least let me tip the girl who served us." He handed her a dollar bill.

"Of course. I'll see that she gets this." Her mouth twitched in a semblance of a smile.

Francine pushed back her chair and stood, brushing off her skirt. "I'll be going now. No need to see me home, Joseph. It's only a short walk. Let me know about the lessons. Until school starts, my time is free."

They walked to the door, and he held it open for her. As she walked past him, the fragrance of lilacs lingered in the air.

Back in the car, Joseph and Forrest headed for the ranch. By the time they'd passed through the outskirts of town, Forrest had fallen asleep like the tired child he was, his head lolling against the side window.

Joseph had questioned his decision to take the boy. But now his doubts had flown. So far, Forrest had been well-behaved. And because they'd stopped for lunch, he could look forward to seeing more of Francine.

This morning, he'd set out for Miles City with no idea how the trip would end. And the day wasn't over. Life had a way of throwing surprises, both good and bad. For now, he would take the good and enjoy it.

The bad surprises would come soon enough. Somehow, they always did.

CHAPTER SEVEN

THREE DAYS HAD PASSED SINCE JOSEPH'S FATEFUL TRIP TO MILES CITY. So far, Forrest seemed to be doing all right. Joseph had him working around the house—cleaning, helping in the kitchen, weeding the yard and garden, and raking the chicken coop. Next week he would introduce the boy to the horses and start him cleaning the tack and shoveling out the stalls.

Forrest slept on a mat in the storeroom and took his meals in the kitchen with the cook, a crusty former cowpuncher called Patches. The boy was never locked up or guarded, but Joseph had no worries about his running away. The young fugitive had fair treatment, good food, and the lure of becoming a cowboy—and he had nowhere else to go.

Blake had grumbled about having a thief under his roof and admonished Joseph to keep the cashbox locked away. But he hadn't gone so far as to have Forrest thrown out. Joseph could only hope that, over time, his father might warm to the boy. It could be good for Blake, having a young person around. But meanwhile, Forrest was staying out of his way.

Now it was past midnight. The great log house was quiet inside except for the creak of settling timbers and the steady tick of the mantel clock.

Joseph had lain awake for hours, hearing the cry of a great horned owl in the ancient ponderosa pine outside his window, the brush of windblown branches against the glass, and the scampering sound of a small animal running across the roof. Finally, too restless to sleep, he'd rolled out of bed, pulled on his clothes, and gone through the motions of checking the house.

Blake had been known to pull himself into his wheelchair and roam the main floor at all hours. Tonight Joseph found him in bed, snoring in deep sleep. Forrest was asleep in the room where supplies for the house were stacked in boxes and burlap bags. He had rearranged some of them to surround the space where he slumbered on his bedroll, curled like an exhausted puppy. Tomorrow he was due for his first reading lesson with Francine. Joseph was looking forward to the lesson as well. Any excuse to spend time with Francine was worth the effort.

No one else was in the house. Patches lived in a cabin out back. Oliver, the young orderly, had judged Blake fit to care for himself with help from the household. He had returned to his duties at the hospital.

Go back to bed, Joseph told himself. But he knew he wouldn't sleep. Not with the restless churning inside him, the questions, the worries, and the premonition that something was about to happen—something unforeseen and life-changing.

Needing to move, he wandered outside and around the house. The family graveyard was laid out in a grove of pines and surrounded by a low, wrought iron fence. As he paused outside the gate, the night wind stirred his hair and carried the aroma of fresh-cut sawdust from the mill below the bluff. The shrill cry of a nighthawk pierced the darkness. Joseph glimpsed the white bars on its wings as the bird darted after insects.

There were only four graves inside the fence, although plenty of room had been left for more. Two of them were older—Joe Dollarhide and his beloved Sarah. The other two were so fresh that the headstones were still on order. An ache tightened like an iron band around Joseph's heart. He missed his mother, Hannah, and his lively young sister, Elsa. And in a way, he'd lost his father, too. Blake's life, as he'd known it, had ended with that terrible accident. Blake was already talking about how, when his time came, he would lie in the earth beside them.

Not all the Dollarhides would end up here. Blake's sister, Kristin, would want to be buried with her family on their ranch. As for Mason, Blake's half-brother and Joseph's biological father, that wild, law-breaking rebel had inherited his mother's ranch and settled down with a wife and young daughter to become a solid citizen.

Joseph had no love for Mason. But there was no way he could deny the man—not when, every time he looked in a mirror, Mason's green eyes looked back at him. And now there was Lucas, with those same eyes.

Joseph had sworn that he would never be like Mason, but now he'd done the same thing—fathered a child by an innocent girl and left her to marry another man. Was he like Mason in other ways? Was that why being tied to his duties at the ranch and the sawmill felt like a lifelong prison sentence?

Turning away from the graves, Joseph rounded the side of the house and climbed the front steps to the porch. With his thoughts churning, he leaned on the log railing and gazed out into the darkness, which was faintly lit by the waning moon.

From here, he could see as far as the town. At this hour, there was no sign of life. In the ten years since the Volstead Act had shut down the saloon, there was no reason to keep the lights on. The only activity Joseph could see was a vehicle moving along the back road—a distant dot of light.

Moonshiners again, most likely. Joseph had sampled moonshine whiskey. In his opinion, it wasn't much better than horse piss. But some people craved alcohol enough to tolerate the taste and put down their money. The good stuff, bootleg liquor smuggled in from Canada, was scarce around here, especially now that the feds had rooted out the big operations such as Al Capone's. But moonshiners were as numerous as cockroaches in a cheap boarding house and about as hard to catch.

Joseph's eyes followed the distant dot of light. The vehicle was traveling at a cautious pace along the bumpy back road. Its slow speed was a sign that it was loaded with breakable cargo—most likely bottled moonshine whiskey. Was it going to a customer in Blue Moon, or would it turn onto the main road and head for Miles City?

Suddenly, another set of headlights appeared, coming from the opposite direction and moving fast. Were the federal agents closing in—or was the second vehicle just returning from a late-night errand? Leaning against the porch rail, Joseph watched, waiting to see what would happen.

When Silas saw the distant speck of light moving toward him, his pulse lurched. Maybe it was nothing—some farmer returning from a visit to a lady friend. But no, Silas reasoned, he couldn't be that lucky. This was trouble.

Without waiting to find out more, he doused his headlights, swung the truck around in a cloud of dust, stomped on the gas, and headed up the back road that led to the Dollarhide mill. He could hear the crates sliding and clinking as the wheels bounced over the ruts. He'd been on his way to Miles City with an extra heavy payload in the back of the truck. He'd probably broken some bottles already. But if he got caught, he'd lose it all—all that and more.

Glancing back, he saw that the dot of light had become two headlights. Whoever was following him, they were coming fast and getting closer. Buck had warned him that the feds were on the prowl. But he'd also mentioned the Chicago gang that was out to take over the eastern Montana moonshine business by wiping out the competition. It didn't make sense to Silas that they'd bother with small-timers like him, but maybe they had some bigger plan in mind. Right now that didn't matter.

Whoever it was, they had a faster vehicle than Culley's old hay truck. But Silas knew the network of back roads and lanes like he knew the palm of his hand—and in his favor, a bank of clouds had blown in to cover the moon. His one chance of escape lay in cutting off on a side road and losing his pursuers in the dark.

Behind him, the headlights were getting closer. The first turn-off, strewn with rocks and potholes, lay just ahead. He couldn't see it, but he knew it was there. With a muttered oath, he swung the wheel hard left.

Silas felt the crunch as the front axle high centered on an imbedded boulder. Pushed by the rear wheels, it crashed down the other side. Had he broken something on the undercarriage? No matter, he had to keep going. He gunned the engine. The truck surged ahead, jarring its way over the road's pitted surface. He could no longer see the headlights. Maybe he was going to make it. Maybe he was going to be all right.

From somewhere behind him, he heard the deadly rat-a-tat of a Thompson submachine gun. The first volley shredded the rear tires. The second shattered the truck's back window and tore into the passenger seat. There were more shots, but after the next one, Silas neither heard nor felt them. He was slumped over the steering wheel, blood dripping from bullet wounds in his side and the back of his head.

Distant but clear, the rattle of gunfire rang through the quiet night. Joseph recognized the report of a Thompson submachine gun, the so-called tommy gun favored by mobsters.

From where he stood, he could no longer see the first vehicle. The driver may have turned off the headlights. But the lights of the second vehicle had stopped moving. Joseph could see nothing more. Was he witnessing an arrest, maybe even a murder, or was this an innocent event, overblown by his imagination?

After stopping for a few minutes, the second vehicle swung around and headed back the way it had come, toward the main road out of town. Joseph watched it until it vanished from sight. There was still no sign of the first one.

It was time he turned in and got some sleep, Joseph told himself. But curiosity was eating him alive. He wouldn't be able to rest until he knew what had happened out there on that dark road.

Taking his keys and a flashlight, he went out to the car. There was a loaded pistol in the glove box. He would keep it handy—not that it would be much protection against a submachine gun if the shooters were close by. Maybe he was taking a foolish chance. But the thought didn't stop him.

After turning on the headlights, he started the engine and drove down the switchbacks, past the closed sawmill, and onto the back road used for mill deliveries.

The clouds had cleared the face of the moon, illuminating a landscape of sagebrush and scrubby juniper. A coyote streaked through the headlights' beam and vanished like a ghost. A flying insect spattered against the windshield. Joseph kept driving. Here he was no longer on Dollarhide property. The land was mostly public, but his family paid to use the access road for the mill.

So far, there'd been no sign of the first vehicle he'd seen. He was about to turn around and go home when his eyes caught the gleam of light on metal. There it was, pulled off to the right on an old side road that led to a dry water hole.

The old flatbed farm truck looked as if it had been used for target practice, although it would take only seconds for a submachine gun to riddle the chassis with holes. The tires had been shot out, the windows blown. The empty bed and the ground were scattered with hay. So far, Joseph could see no sign of the driver.

Since there was no sign of life, Joseph left the pistol in the glove box of his car. With the flashlight, he walked over to the disabled truck and peered through the shattered side window. His breath caught as he saw the man slumped over the steering wheel, his head and clothes thickly mottled with blood.

The man would have to be dead, Joseph thought. A good twenty minutes had passed since he'd heard the gunfire. Even if this man had survived the shooting, he would have bled out by now.

The wise course of action would be to leave him, go home, and phone the sheriff. But first, Joseph needed to make sure the man was beyond help.

Reaching past the broken glass, he slid a hand under the side of the man's jaw and down to his throat. His flesh was warm, the pulse a barely discernable flutter against Joseph's fingertips. He was alive. Barely.

Joseph forced his thoughts into a plan. Get him out of the car, stop the bleeding, and get him to the nearest source of help. He cursed under his breath. Why hadn't he brought any first aid supplies in the car? He would have to make do, any way he could.

"Sir, can you hear me?" he asked. "I'm here to help you."

There was no response.

After opening the door, Joseph leaned over the man and directed the light to the bloodied back of his head. Taking care, he fingered the wound. It appeared to be a scalp crease that hadn't penetrated the skull. Otherwise, the fellow most likely would be dead. But the wound was serious enough. And his blood-soaked clothes told Joseph that the bullets had done more critical damage to his body. Dragging him out of the car could worsen the blood loss, but it had to be done.

After turning off the flashlight and jamming it into his hip pocket, Joseph seized the man by the shoulders and eased him out from behind the wheel. He was tall and muscular, a leaden weight in Joseph's arms. As Joseph pulled him away from the open door, the man's body straightened. Joseph could see blood oozing from a wound, above the hip, toward the left side, that was soaking through his clothes.

Joseph backed him off until his booted legs fell free of the car and dropped with a thud. Sweat drizzled down Joseph's face as he cradled the bleeding head with one arm and eased the upper body to the ground.

By now, his shirt was smeared with blood. His arms ached from hauling the heavy body out of the car. Getting it into the back seat of the Model A would be another struggle. Maybe by then the moonshiner—which he undoubtedly was—would be awake.

Joseph pulled the flashlight out of his pocket, switched it on, and directed the beam at the man's face.

The flashlight froze in his hand as the circle of light fell on lean, chiseled features, a long jaw, and a twist to the mouth. This was the man who'd shamed Annabeth at the dance and slapped her face. This was the man Joseph had fought.

He was looking at Silas Mosby.

Joseph couldn't stop the thought from crossing his mind. He could walk away and leave the man to die. He'd be doing Annabeth a favor. She'd have the farm and could no doubt find a better husband.

But maybe she loved this man. Maybe Ellie and Lucas loved him and needed their father. In any case, it wasn't Joseph's place to judge or play God. Whatever it took to save this man, he had to give it his all.

Joseph pulled away the hem of the bloodied shirt and loosened the trousers to uncover the bullet wound—an oozing, thumb-sized hole above the crest of the hip. Except for the fact that Mosby was alive, there was no way to know where the bullet had gone or whether it had hit any vital organs. For now, he could only stop the bleeding and try to get some help.

"You'd better not die on me, you sonofabitch," Joseph muttered, leaning over him. "I don't want to be the one who has to tell your wife she's a widow."

With nothing else at hand to stanch the wound, Joseph yanked off his flannel shirt. Using his pocketknife, he ripped off the shirttail and folded it into a thick pad, which he pressed onto the wound. Then, with effort, he worked the shirtsleeves around the body and tied them in a knot over the pad. When he pulled the knot tight, he felt a reflexive twitch and heard a low groan. Mosby could be coming around.

He would need water. Joseph kept a canvas water bag in the car. He found it, along with a bandana he'd tossed on the seat and forgotten. It would do for binding the head wound.

Kneeling, he supported Mosby's head and tied the bandana around it. He kept the pressure as tight as he could. Head wounds, even superficial ones, tended to bleed heavily. Joseph could hope the injury was no more than the scalp gash it appeared to be. But the blood loss was still a worry.

Steadying Mosby's head, he splashed the blood from his face and tilted the mouth of the water bag to his lips, just enough to wet them. "Drink it," he muttered. "I'll be damned if you're going to die on my watch."

Mosby's eyelids twitched and opened. He accepted the water

and took a swallow. "Not too much. You don't want to choke," Joseph warned. "That's it."

He took the water away. Only then did Mosby's eyes widen in recognition. "You . . . bastard." Every syllable was laced with pain and hatred. "What're you doing here?"

"I'm trying to save your life, you fool. Now shut up before I change my mind."

"The truck . . . ?"

"Shot to pieces by the goons who took your cargo. You're shot up, too. Got a big hole in your side." Joseph gave him more water. "I've got to get you in my car. Can you walk if I help you?"

Gritting his teeth, Mosby struggled to sit up. He was a strong man, but he groaned with pain as Joseph braced him to stand and hobble to the car. He purpled the air with curses as he was laid on the rear seat, half-curled on his side with the wound on top. The blood was already soaking through the makeshift dressing.

"Where . . . where're you taking me?" he asked.

"To a doctor. My aunt is close. You know her ranch."

"No!" He grunted with pain. "A doctor has to notify the law. I'll go to . . . prison. No doctor. Take me home."

"You've got a bullet in you. If it doesn't come out, you'll die from the infection. You need a doctor." Joseph climbed into the driver's seat and started the engine.

"No—please, God, no doctor," Mosby pleaded. "My wife can do it."

"Your wife isn't a doctor."

"She doctors the animals on our farm. Does a damn good job of it . . ." His voice trailed off into a gasp of pain as the car began to move.

Joseph thought of Annabeth and the awful weight of responsibility he would be placing on her. "But she doesn't have the medicine, the tools, or the experience to save you. You could die if I take you home. And your wife would have to live with that."

Mosby swore as a rear wheel crunched through a low spot in the road. "Hell, her and the kids would be better off having me dead than in prison. But I'm not going to die, Dollarhide. I'm not leaving her and that bastard boy for you to take."

The word that the man had applied to Lucas hit Joseph like a gut blow. He'd hoped, at least, that the son he couldn't claim would be valued and loved.

"That brat is never going to amount to anything." Mosby's words continued through what had to be a haze of excruciating pain. "I've tried to make a man of him. But he's got no spine. The little whiner's going to grow up licking the shit off other men's boots."

Joseph struggled to keep his temper in check. Mosby was trying to break him. He couldn't give the lying skunk the satisfaction—no more than he could force him to accept treatment from a doctor.

"Shut up, Mosby." Joseph kept his voice level. "Any more of that talk and I'll throw you out of the car. You can die on the road."

"Just take me home . . . Drag me onto the porch and clear the hell out. I'm not letting you in my house or anywhere near my . . . wife." His voice faded with the last words.

"All right, if you say so, I'll take you home. What happens after that is on you." Joseph doubted the words even as he spoke. How could he leave Annabeth alone to deal with her critically wounded husband? What would she do if he were to die?

He waited for a reply. But from the back seat, there was nothing but silence. When he slowed the car and glanced around, he saw that Mosby was still breathing, but his eyes were closed. Hopefully, he'd passed out.

Now would be the time to get him to the doctor. But Mosby had been right about one thing. Joseph recalled his aunt mentioning that doctors were obligated to report gunshot wounds to the authorities. For Dr. Kristin Dollarhide Hunter, saving the man's life would mean sending him to prison for trafficking in moonshine. Even if Joseph asked her to, she couldn't make an exception.

Joseph had reached the turnoff to the Mosby farm. He hesitated, thinking of Annabeth and her children, and the consequences of his next action—including the stain of being connected to a criminal. There were no good choices here.

Decision made, he swung the car onto the lane that would lead him to the house.

* * *

Annabeth lay alone in the double bed she shared with her husband. After a long day of housework, tending her children, making bread, updating the farm accounts, milking the cows, delivering a breeched calf, and cooking supper, she was exhausted. But on these late nights when Silas was out, she never slept. And tonight he was out later than usual.

She liked to pretend she didn't know what he was up to. But she was no fool. She knew who his friends were, and every instinct told her they weren't just playing cards.

Earlier, she'd checked on her children. They were fast asleep in the next room, safe in their shared bed. Ellie slept curled like a kitten with her thumb in her mouth, which seemed to comfort her. Lucas lay on his back with his hands resting on the patchwork quilt. Today his father had taken him to the potato field again. The boy had lost his oversized gloves and had to pick through the foliage for bugs with his bare hands. The sight of his bleeding fingers had nearly broken Annabeth's heart. Silas's only comment had been, "That'll teach the little bastard not to lose expensive gloves."

Annabeth had doctored his hands with her homemade salve. But they needed time to heal. Tomorrow she wouldn't allow him to be taken to the field. Silas might rail at her, maybe even hit her. But she would stand firm. Lucas would not be working without suitable gloves that fit his hands.

A frantic pounding on the front door broke into her thoughts. She kept the door locked at night, but Silas had a key. This had to be somebody else—although it was strange that the dog hadn't barked.

She tossed back the covers and swung her legs off the bed. With Silas's robe thrown over her thin nightgown, she closed the children's door and hurried into the front room. The pounding on the door continued, along with a muffled voice calling her name. Silas's loaded shotgun hung on a rack by the door. She snatched it down before answering.

"Who's there?"

"Annabeth, it's Joseph!" Her throat tightened as she recognized his voice. "Your husband's been shot! Open the door!"

She put the gun aside, turned on the light, and flung open the door. Joseph stood in the glow of the porch light. His white singlet, his arms, and his hands were smeared with blood.

Her husband's limp body lay half-draped across his shoulders. Silas's head and midsection were wrapped in blood-soaked rags.

"He's got a bullet in his side." Joseph crossed the threshold, staggering under Silas's two-hundred-pound weight. "It's got to come out. We'll need him on the table." He drew a harsh breath. "You'll want to get a sheet—then some kind of sharp tool, and something for bandages."

Annabeth's knees had almost given way at the sight of so much blood. But this was no time for weakness. Even questions could wait. She dashed to the linen cupboard, found a clean sheet, and spread it over the kitchen table. Without being asked, she lifted Silas's legs, supporting them as Joseph lowered his head and upper body to the tabletop. Then she filled a dishpan with water, set it on an open burner, and added several coal chunks and kindling sticks to the firebox in the cookstove. It never hurt to have hot water on hand.

Turning back to her husband, she found a clean kitchen rag, wet it at the sink, and began sponging the blood from his face. His eyes were closed, his skin deathly pale. Only the rasp of his labored breathing and the faint throb of a pulse at his throat told her he was alive. The bandana around his head was stiff with drying blood. Caution told her to leave it in place.

Joseph had washed with soap at the sink and was peeling away the bloody wrapping from around Silas's waist. His hands were sure and careful. His face revealed nothing.

"Tell me what happened, Joseph," she demanded. "Did the two of you fight again? Did you shoot him?"

A look of shock flashed across his face. "You know I wouldn't do that to your family," he said. "He was ambushed on the back road. I saw the lights, heard the shots, and decided to investigate. I found him like this, in the truck. It was shot full of holes.

"He was talking for a while on the way here. I wanted to take him to the doctor. But he wouldn't hear of it. He claimed that a doctor would have to report him, and he'd be sent to prison."

Annabeth listened in silence as the picture came together. It was just as she'd suspected. Silas, the fool, must've been smuggling moonshine for his friends. A rival gang had cut him down and probably taken his cargo. Blast the man. How long had he been doing this? How long had he been lying to her?

Joseph's gaze locked with hers across Silas's unconscious body. "He told me that you'd doctored animals. He said you could get the bullet out. Can you do it?"

She shook her head, a sick fear taking root in her stomach. "I've stitched up a few barbed wire cuts and delivered some calves. But no, nothing like this. Heaven help me, Joseph, what made him think I could do this? What if I kill him?" She gazed down at her shaking hands.

"He told me to leave him on the porch and go," Joseph said. "But I couldn't do that to you. I've never probed for a bullet, but I watched my aunt do it once, so I know what has to be done. Our best chance of saving him is with the two of us working together. All right?"

"Yes." The fear was still there, but this was her responsibility. She couldn't ask Joseph to do it alone.

"You'll need something to push into the wound and lift the bullet out. I don't suppose you've got forceps."

"No." She thought fast. "But this might work." Opening a drawer, she took out a long-handled dessert spoon, narrow at the scoop end. "I don't have anything better."

He studied it and nodded. "Let's hope it will work. My aunt would clean it with carbolic acid. I don't suppose—"

"No, I had some, but I used the last of it in the barn, delivering a calf. This will have to do." Annabeth dropped the spoon into the bubbling water to sterilize it. While they waited, she found a worn bedsheet and began tearing it into strips, forcing her hands to the task. Her heart was racing, but this was no time to be nervous. "What about his head?" she asked, eyeing the blood crusted bandana. "It looks bad."

"It felt like a scalp wound. We'll know for sure when we clean it. For now, that'll have to wait." He opened his pocketknife and began cutting away the makeshift bandage to expose the ugly hip wound. Pausing, he met her gaze.

"Getting that bullet out is going to hurt like hell," he said. "He's unconscious now, but the pain could bring him around. If it does, he'll be wild. You won't be strong enough to hold him. You'll need to get the bullet while I hold him steady. Can you do that?"

"I'll have to, won't I?" Annabeth forced her hands to keep busy. She knew enough to wrap a cloth around a flat knife, which would be used to thrust between his teeth.

She gazed down at the man who had married her, loved her, lied to her, and abused her—the father of her children, in name, at least. Now it would be up to her to save his life. If her skill wasn't up to the task, he could die. But she mustn't think about that now. "I'm ready," she said.

Joseph worked the wrapped knife between Silas's teeth and moved around the table to make room for her. "You'll want to find the bullet with your finger first," he said. "That way you'll know which way to probe with the spoon."

Steeling herself, Annabeth studied the wound, trying to judge the best angle. She was about to begin when she heard a small voice behind her.

"What are you doing, Mama? What's the matter with Dad?"

It was Lucas.

CHAPTER EIGHT

Joseph was bending over Mosby, reaching for his shoulders to hold him steady. At the sound of that small, anxious voice, his hands froze in midmotion. In his concern for the injured man, he'd scarcely thought about Annabeth's children and how near they would be.

And now, here was Lucas, worried about the man he called his dad. Joseph felt something twist inside him—the pain of having lost what he'd never known. Despite his best intentions, he couldn't take his eyes off the boy.

"He's bleeding, Mama." Lucas spoke again, his eyes wide with fear. "What happened to him?" He gave Joseph a startled glance. "Who is this man?"

"Your father had a very bad accident with a gun, Lucas." Annabeth's voice was calm and steady. "This kind man brought him home and stayed to help me take care of him."

"Is my dad going to die?" Lucas directed the question at Joseph.

Joseph swallowed the lump in his throat. He wanted to reassure the boy, but it wasn't his place to promise anything. "I won't lie to you, Lucas. He's hurt pretty bad. But he's strong, and we're taking good care of him."

"I need you for something important," Annabeth said to her son. "Go back to your room and take care of your sister. Keep her in bed with the door closed. If she wakes up and hears something, tell her not to be scared. Maybe you can tell her one of your stories. Can you do that?"

"Uh-huh." He nodded.

"Can you be very, very brave?"

"I'll try." Lucas looked as if he was about to cry but was struggling not to show it. Joseph couldn't hold back an unexpected surge of love.

"That's my good boy," Annabeth said. "Now run along."

With a last worried look, Lucas walked back down the hall to the bedroom.

"You've raised a fine son." No sooner were the words spoken than Joseph regretted them. Annabeth's stricken look told him that this was neither the time nor the place.

She raised her chin and tightened her jaw, the picture of determination. "Let's get this done," she said. "Are you ready?"

"Ready." He placed his hands on Silas Mosby. The man was solid muscle. Joseph had felt his brute strength at the dance. If Mosby woke up fighting, he'd be hard to hold down. But it was Annabeth who had the more challenging task.

Her index finger slid into the bullet wound. Joseph's hands pressed Mosby's body hard against the table. He could see the concentration in Annabeth's face as she probed deeper, then deeper, almost as far as her finger could reach. Mosby twitched and jerked but didn't wake up.

"I think I can feel the bullet," Annabeth whispered. "My finger's touching something solid."

"You're sure it's not a bone fragment? The bullet went in close to his hip."

"Yes. It's smooth—it gives a little. I'm sure."

She withdrew her finger, washed her hands in the sink, and used a pair of forks like tongs to fish the spoon out of the hot water. She tested it to make sure it wasn't hot enough to burn, then turned back to the table.

The spoon went in at a slant, carefully and slowly. Joseph knew she'd been nervous earlier, but now her hands were steady, her mouth set in a firm line. In the years when they were young, he'd assumed that he knew everything about her. But he'd never imagined how strong she could be.

As the spoon probed deeper, Mosby's body went rigid. His jaws clenched on the wrapped knife between his teeth. His eyes were closed, but he was coming around, feeling the kind of pain that could make a strong man scream. Joseph tightened his grip.

"I'm touching it with the spoon," she said. "I'll have to work the spoon under the bullet to lift it out. That's going to hurt even worse than going in."

"Go ahead. I've got him," Joseph said. "The bullet could've taken a scrap of his shirt going in. Make sure you get that, too."

Mosby was beginning to twitch. A whimper stirred in his throat. Joseph tightened his grip. Too bad they didn't have any liquor, not even moonshine, to dull his senses.

Perspiration beaded Annabeth's face as she worked the spoon deeper. Her breath came hard with the effort of keeping her hands steady.

Mosby groaned. Joseph fought to hold him still. "Don't move," he said. "Your wife is digging that bullet out of you. You don't want to make her slip."

Mosby's eyes opened. As he blinked his vision into focus, his expression changed from confusion to blazing hatred. His angry grunts were muffled by the wrapped knife between his jaws. He might have reached up and pulled it out, but Joseph's grip pinned his hands to the table.

"Keep still if you want to live!" Joseph muttered, close to his ear. "You have a beautiful wife and children who love you. You've got no business catting around the country, breaking the law and getting yourself shot. They deserve better than that. They deserve the best of you."

Mosby paid him no attention. Out of his head with pain and fury, he began to buck and kick. Joseph used his full weight to pin his upper body down, but it wasn't enough. Mosby was still thrashing to get free.

So far, Annabeth had managed to keep the spoon in place. But Joseph could see that she was struggling to hold it steady. The pain had to be driving her husband wild, but if she didn't finish what she'd started, the infection would kill him.

She cast Joseph a desperate look. Then her eyes narrowed, her mouth tightened into a resolute line, and she shoved the spoon deeper. Moseby's muffled scream shattered the air. It went on for what seemed like minutes as his wife twisted the spoon and pulled it out of the wound. Joseph heard something hard drop to the floor and roll away, followed by the clatter of the falling spoon. "I got it," Annabeth said in an unsteady voice. "It's out—the cloth bit, too."

Mosby was no longer screaming. He had fainted again.

Annabeth pressed a wad of cotton bandages against the wound to stop the bleeding. "I'll do that," Joseph said, moving around the table to her side. "You've done enough. Get off your feet."

"No, it's all right. I—" She swayed, slumping against him. He reached out to steady her. And suddenly, he was holding her, cradling her in his arms.

Her curves fit his body, just as they had in the old days when they were hot-blooded young fools. Life had wrenched them apart, and there could be no going back. But right now, holding her felt like something they both needed. He rocked her gently, one hand stroking her hair. A single sob rose in her throat, but that was all. Joseph knew that she was too strong and too proud to cry on his shoulder.

Time stood still for a moment. Then she stirred and pushed away from him. He saw that her robe, hands, and arms were splattered with blood. "My children," she said. "They'll be terrified. I need to go to them."

"Go on. I'll get him bandaged and cleaned up. Then I'll help you get him to bed."

"I'm going to wash and change. Then I'll be with my children. If you need me before I come back, knock on the door," she said.

Mosby was still unconscious. Left alone with him, Joseph went to work, cleaning around the bullet wound, applying a fresh dressing, and wrapping it tight. Annabeth's husband was not out of danger. He'd survived the bullet wound, but the risk of a slow, miserable death from infection was still grave. Joseph thought of his family. There had to be something more he could do. Just one thing came to mind.

The head wound could have used some stitches, but the crease in Mosby's scalp hadn't penetrated the bone. The fool was lucky. A finger's breadth deeper, and the shot would have killed him. As it was, the bullet had probably knocked him out.

Joseph had finished wrapping Mosby's head and was washing up in the sink when Annabeth reappeared, looking exhausted and wearing a faded housedress. She carried a threadbare flannel work shirt that she thrust toward him. "Take it. You'll need something to wear home."

Thanking her, he dried his hands, stripped off the blood-soaked singlet, and accepted the shirt. It was Silas's, of course, but this was no time to be choosy. He was grateful for the soft, clean fabric on his skin. He wouldn't be going straight home yet, but there was no need to tell her that.

She looked down at her husband, the overhead light casting her face in shadow. "How is he?"

"As well as could be expected. He's going to need fluids when he wakes up. Water, or even coffee. Are you ready to move him?"

"The bed's turned down. I laid out an extra sheet."

"Bring the sheet in here. We'll use it to carry him."

Stripped to his drawers and shifted onto the clean, doubled sheet, Silas was lifted off the table and carried hammock-style down the hall toward the bedroom. With Joseph at the head and Annabeth bringing up the rear, they moved with slow, shuffling steps, doing their best not to jar him. But he was already beginning to twitch and moan. By the time they lowered him to the bed, he was thrashing with his legs and muttering half-coherent curses.

As Annabeth laid the covers over him, she sent Joseph an urgent look. "You need to go. I don't want you around when he wakes up. That will just agitate him. If you're gone, he might not even remember you were here—or he might believe he was hallucinating."

"Will you be okay?" It was a useless question. She was right. He needed to leave.

"I'll be fine. Don't worry about the mess in the kitchen. Just go."

Joseph tore himself away and headed out to his car, leaving Annabeth with her husband and her children. He had no business staying or interfering in her life, not even to help her.

He would back off and leave her alone. But there was one more thing he needed to do.

A few minutes after Joseph left, Silas woke up. Annabeth was bending over him, adjusting his covers, when he opened his eyes. Her heart seemed to freeze as he stared directly up at her. His mouth shaped words. "What happened?"

"You were shot. What do you remember?"

His forehead furrowed below the bandage that wrapped his head. "I don't know . . . hurts like hell. You say I got shot."

"In the side. I dug out the bullet myself. Another bullet creased your head." She was talking too fast. She willed herself to calm down. "You've lost a lot of blood. I'll get you some water."

"Water, hell. Get me something for the pain. There's some moonshine in the car."

So, the truth was just as she'd suspected. Not that it mattered anymore. "The car is gone. You must've left it with your friends. The truck you were driving was shot full of holes," she said. "The moonshine's gone, too. I'll get you some water."

She fled to the kitchen. The blood-soaked sheet still covered the table. The sight of it would upset the children if they happened to get up. She took a moment to strip it off, wad it into a ball along with Joseph's singlet, and stuff them both into the trash barrel on the back porch. After giving the table a quick wiping with a damp cloth, she filled a cup with water and carried it back down the hall to the bedroom.

So far, it appeared that Silas was going to live. Infection was the worry now. But Silas was strong, and he had her to care for him. She could only hope for the best and thank fate, or the angels, that Joseph had come along to save him.

What surprised her was the anger she felt—more anger, even, than relief. She wanted to rail at him—How could he do this to his family? He should have been at home with the people who loved and needed him, not lying to his wife, galivanting around in the dark, risking arrest and worse.

He drank the water she gave him but demanded something stronger, which she didn't have. Back in the kitchen, she brewed some chamomile tea. While the tea was steeping, she went down the hall to check on the children.

She opened the door softly and tiptoed to their bedside. Thankfully, both of them appeared to be asleep. But as she turned to go, Lucas opened his eyes. "How's Dad?" he asked in a whisper.

"A little better. We got the bullet out and put him to bed."

"Is that man still here?"

"No. He's gone." Annabeth stroked his thick, silky hair, so like Joseph's. "You're my good boy, Lucas. Close your eyes and go to sleep now. I'll be close by, taking care of your . . . father." She choked on the word. Lucas's father had been here. Now he was gone. And that was the way of things. The only way.

Joseph drove through the gate of the Hunter Ranch and pulled up to the house. The place was dark except for the front porch light and a faint glow from the kitchen at the back of the house. Maybe his aunt had gone out on an emergency. But no, her truck, which doubled as an ambulance, was parked in the driveway. She would be at home.

He rang the doorbell. Showing up in the middle of the night wouldn't be the most considerate thing to do, but this was an emergency.

Mere seconds passed before Kristin opened the door. Tousle-haired and hastily wrapped in her bathrobe, she ushered Joseph inside. "What is it, Joseph? Is Blake all right?" she demanded.

"Yes, he's fine, as far as I know." Joseph took a deep breath. "Aunt Kristin, a man I know was shot tonight. We got the bullet out. I don't think it hit anything vital, but I need something for the pain and infection."

"Why didn't you bring him here?" Her sharp gaze suggested she'd already guessed the reason.

"I wanted to. But he wouldn't hear of it. He said you'd have to report him to the law."

She shook her head. "Joseph, what have you gotten yourself into? Come on inside. Logan's been up with a sick mare. He's making coffee. You look like you could use some, too."

"I really don't have much time," Joseph said.

"Come on. I'm not giving you anything until I know what's happening. We can talk at the table."

She ushered him into her spacious kitchen. The light was on. Her husband, dressed in work clothes, was percolating coffee on the electric stove. The warm, fresh aroma filled the room.

"Sit, Joseph." Kristin pointed to a chair on the far side of the table. She took a seat facing him. Logan filled three mugs with steaming coffee. He passed one to his wife and one to Joseph.

"How's the mare?" Joseph asked.

"Better. Something finally came out the other end, and she's nibbling on her feed. But I still need to keep an eye on her. Sorry I can't stay. We've missed you, Joseph." Logan took his mug and went out the back door.

Kristin studied Joseph across the table. "The truth. And you know better than to lie or leave anything out. Are you in trouble?"

"No. God's truth."

"But a man was shot. Is he a friend of yours?"

Joseph shook his head. "I barely know him. A neighbor. He was running moonshine. Somebody shot up his vehicle. They took his cargo and left him for dead. I saw the lights and heard the shots from the house." Joseph took a sip of his coffee. It was still steaming, but he swallowed it and felt the wet heat moving down his throat. "I found him, did what I could to revive him, and drove him to his place."

"Who took the bullet out? Was it you?"

"No. I held him, but it was his wife—an old-time friend of mine—who dug the bullet out. She did it with a spoon—sterilized with boiling water. But as I told you, she didn't have anything for the pain, and he could still die from the infection. That's why I'm here."

She studied him over the rim of her mug, her gaze deep and knowing. "An old-time friend, you say? Are you talking about Annabeth Mosby?"

Joseph's expression froze—a dead giveaway. Why had he mentioned that Annabeth was an old friend? "How do you know her?" he asked.

"I delivered Annabeth's first baby," Kristin said. "Her sister-in-law called me. The baby was breech, and Annabeth was in trouble. It was touch and go for a while, but she finally gave birth to a beautiful boy."

Joseph stared at her, words failing to come.

"Yes, Joseph, I've known all along," she said. "I knew she'd been your girl before she married that farmer. And when that little boy came out into my hands, I remembered holding you after you were born. He looked just like you."

"And you didn't tell me?"

"What good would that have done? She was married. You were better off not knowing—and now you do. Have you seen the boy?"

"Yes. He's . . ." Joseph shook his head. He could think of no words to describe the miracle that was his son. With emotion threatening to overcome him, he changed the subject.

"So you'll give me the medicine Annabeth's husband needs? And you won't report him?"

"I don't have to report him if I didn't see him." She pushed back her chair and stood. "Stay here and finish your coffee while I get you what you need."

She disappeared down the hall and came back with a glass jug and two small bottles, which she placed on the table. "Aspirin for fever. And laudanum's the strongest thing for pain. The jug is carbolic acid. Use it to clean everything that touches that wound. Wet his dressings in it and hope for the best. There's no guarantee it'll do enough to save him, but for now, there's nothing better."

She put the medicines in a paper bag. "Just the other day I read an item in a medical journal. A Doctor Fleming in England has found a common mold—penicillium, it's called—that stops bacteria from growing. Maybe someday, in the future, it can be used to save lives. But right now, carbolic is all we have."

He took the bag from her. "Thanks. I've got to go."

"You're a good man, Joseph." She gave him a brief hug. "I know you'll do the right thing."

He left her and raced out to his car.

Annabeth sat on a hard wooden chair, watching her husband drift in and out of consciousness. A worry-filled hour had passed since Joseph had dressed his wounds and helped her move him to the bed. Had the bleeding stopped? Was infection already setting in? How serious was the head wound?

Worse, even, than the uncertainty was the total helplessness she felt.

She'd done everything she could for him. When he was awake, she'd given him water and the chamomile tea, which he'd spat out because he hated the taste. He'd cursed her in the most vile language she'd ever heard. But Annabeth had forgiven him because she knew he must be out of his head and in terrible pain.

So far, he hadn't mentioned Joseph. But his memory could return at any time. Could he accept the fact that Joseph had saved his life? Or would that only deepen his hatred?

A light knock on the door interrupted Annabeth's musings. At this hour, it could only mean trouble. Maybe the sheriff had heard about the shooting or someone had found Silas's borrowed truck. Annabeth waited, hoping the person outside would give up and leave. She'd turned off all the lights except a small lamp beside Silas's bed. But the knock came again, not loud but persistent.

Silas appeared to be dozing. Annabeth left the bedroom and shut the door behind her. After a quick check on her sleeping children, she walked through the darkened living room, took the shotgun down from its rack, and cracked open the front door.

She gasped as Joseph slipped out of the shadows. "What are

you doing here?" she whispered. "You need to leave before somebody wakes up."

"I'll only be a minute. I brought you something." As she stepped out onto the porch and closed the door, she saw that he was holding a jug and a paper bag. "Carbolic acid. The doctor says you're to clean around the wounds and soak the dressings with it—the sooner the better, even if you have to wake him. You'll find aspirin and laudanum in the bag. The directions are on the labels. Do you know how to use them?"

"Yes, I think so." Annabeth remembered her mother nursing an injured brother, years ago on her family's farm. But one thing Joseph had mentioned alarmed her. "You say you went to the doctor? What did you tell her?"

"Only what I had to. Don't worry, she won't report him. How is Silas?"

"In a lot of pain, dozing on and off. These medicines you brought could save him. Thank you, Joseph. I owe you. And my children will owe you, too, for saving their father's life."

The last words slipped out before Annabeth could think to stop them. The last thing she wanted was to hurt Joseph when he'd done so much for her, but it was too late to take them back. "I'm sorry, Joseph," she whispered.

He set the jug and the bag on a nearby chair. His arms reached out and drew her close. She came without resistance, fitting against the familiar contours of his body. How natural it seemed, being close to him like this. How safe and protected she felt. But even then, she knew it was wrong.

His lips nibbled a line of kisses along her hairline. "Why didn't you tell me about Lucas, Annabeth?" he murmured. "You know that I would have married you."

"You were only nineteen," she said. "And I knew you didn't love me. If we'd married, you'd have come to hate me for taking your freedom. That hate would have destroyed us both. It was easier to find a man who was ready to be a father. If only Silas—"

Annabeth broke off. She'd already said too much.

"I know." His arms tightened, bringing her close again. "I know how he talked about Lucas and what he called him. If ever you need me to—"

"No." She drew back and laid a finger against his lips. "Whatever happens, I can't lose my children—my beautiful boy and my sweet little Ellie. They're my life, my everything. You heard Silas threaten to take them away if I saw you again. He would do that—and he could—just to punish me. You shouldn't even be here."

"I understand," he said. "Believe me, I would never put you or your children at risk. But know this, Annabeth. If things had been different—"

"Don't." Annabeth could feel her resistance crumbling. She fought a surge of rising need. "What's past is past. Don't talk about what can't ever be."

"Let me finish. Then I'll go," he said. "I would have cared for you and our son. And that won't change. I'll always be there for you and for him."

"You can't be there, Joseph."

"I know. But if you ever need me—"

"Stop it!" Consumed by a reckless yearning, she stretched on tiptoe and blocked his words with her lips. Joseph's body stiffened in surprise. Then, with a low moan, he caught her close, holding her as if he could bind her soul to his. Annabeth could feel his heart pounding against her own. She wanted him in all the ways a woman could want a man. But the kiss he returned was not a kiss of possession. It was a tender, bittersweet kiss of farewell.

Releasing her, he stepped back. "Goodbye, Annabeth," he said.

Left without words, Annabeth watched him stride out to his car and drive away. As the taillights faded into darkness, she squared her shoulders, turned, and went back into the house. It was time to forget him—and to bury the memory that surfaced every time she looked at their son.

At least Joseph hadn't said he loved her. That would have shattered her heart.

Francine lay back against the pillows, a corner of the sheet pulled down to expose one perfect breast. She smiled, her body simmering with sexual satisfaction as she stretched slowly, with a little purring sound. "It's early yet," she said. "The sun won't be up for a couple of hours. Are you sure you won't come back to bed?"

"Greedy little vixen, aren't you?" By the light of a single lilac-scented candle, Chase Calder hunted for the drawers and trousers he'd dropped on the floor. "It's been fun, lady, but I've got a ranch to run. By the time I get back to the Triple C, the workday will be starting."

If we were married, you wouldn't have to drive to town anymore. I'd be right there, in your bed, whenever you wanted me.

Francine knew better than to voice the thought aloud. It was too soon for that. If she wanted to be Mrs. Chase Calder, she would have to play her cards with exquisite timing.

"Just for a few minutes," she teased. "I want to send you home with something to remember me by." She pulled back the sheet and beckoned, a sly smile on her face.

"Cuss it, woman, save it for next time." Chase pulled up his drawers and stepped into his trousers. His shirt was slung over the bedpost. "There's a time for fun and a time for work. I've had my fun. Now I need to get back to work."

My name is Francine. Not Lady. Not Woman. Francine.

Again, she didn't say the words aloud.

With a sigh, she sat up, clutching the sheet over her breasts. She remembered what Joseph had told her in the car, when she'd asked if Chase was single. He'd replied that Chase was married to his ranch.

She was beginning to believe it. But she wasn't ready to give up. Not by a long shot. Chase Calder needed a wife and an heir. She was ready and willing to supply both. And the Calder name would be its own reward.

He left without kissing her goodbye. Francine knew that his car was parked down the block, behind the gas station, and that the vehicle he'd driven was an older Model T, not the shiny new Packard he usually drove to town. She understood he was protecting her reputation as well as his own. Still, it hurt that he'd chosen to keep their relationship secret.

Maybe she'd made a fatal mistake, letting him in her bed.

Too restless to sleep, she tossed the covers aside, got out of bed, and slipped on her robe. The telephone was installed in her small sitting room. She sank onto the sofa, curled her feet beneath her, and made a call to her sister. A sleepy voice answered on the second ring.

"He just left," Francine said.

"How did it go?"

Francine sighed. "About the way you warned me it would. He only wants one thing."

"Blast it, girl, I told you not to sleep with him. Dangle the bait, drive him crazy, and a man will do anything for it—even marry you. Give him what he wants, and it's all over. You should have listened to me."

"Yes, I suppose I should have." Francine had known better. But resisting Chase had been like holding back a charging bull. She'd given in, and she'd enjoyed every delicious minute of it.

"This isn't just any man we're talking about," her sister said. "This is Chase Calder, the richest rancher in the state of Montana, the man you came here to marry. So what are you going to do now? Maybe try to get pregnant?"

"He wears a rubber."

There was a hiss of breath on the other end of the phone. "You little fool! You were holding an ace, and you played it for a useless thrill!"

"There's always Joseph. I know he likes me," Francine said.

"Joseph is a good man, and he'll be rich when he takes over from his father. Any woman he marries will be lucky. But a Dollarhide is not a Calder, with his power and his political connections. We could use those connections and that influence. That's why I had you apply for the teaching job. If you settle for anything less than the Calder name, we'll miss our chance."

"I'm not planning to settle. I'm thinking that I can use Joseph to make Chase jealous. If he sees that another man wants me, that should bring him to heel."

"Good luck with that. I rescued you from that St. Joseph

brothel and brought you here for a reason. I can always cut you loose and send you back. Remember that the next time you're tempted to make a fool of yourself."

The call ended with an angry click.

Francine hung up the phone, rose from the sofa, and began to pace. She had to make this plan work. She couldn't let her sister put her back on the street.

Tomorrow, Joseph would be bringing the boy around for a reading lesson. She would prepare herself to charm him. And she wouldn't cut him loose. Not yet. Joseph was handsome, decent, and the heir to a fortune of his own. If she couldn't manage to become Mrs. Chase Calder, becoming Mrs. Dollarhide would be a nice consolation prize. And there'd be nothing her sister could do about it.

CHAPTER NINE

A WEEK HAD PASSED SINCE THE SHOOTING ON THE BACK ROAD. Silas's body had responded to the medicines and to Annabeth's faithful tending. He was still weak and sore, but his wounds had closed and were healing with no sign of infection.

By now, he was out of bed for much of the day, prowling the house, complaining, cursing his confinement, and snarling at the children when they made too much noise or got in his way.

Annabeth, who'd taken on the outside chores as well as her usual cooking, childcare, and other household duties, was run ragged. Silas had even charged her with tending the potato field, a losing battle that the ugly striped beetles were winning.

She woke in the morning as exhausted as she'd been the night before. This trying time would end soon, she told herself when her burdens threatened to crush her. Silas would mend and go back to his old ways. Her strength and patience would return, as would the quiet moments during the day when she was free to enjoy her children.

But one thing would remain—Joseph's image in her thoughts, in her dreams, and in her son's eyes. She and Joseph had gone their separate ways. He would live his life, marry, and have more children. But wrong as it might be, the memory of his protecting arms and tender kiss was branded on her soul.

Silas had never mentioned being rescued by Joseph. Had he forgotten or was he holding back the memory to use as a weapon against her? The uncertainty had kept her on edge all week.

Silas was sitting on the front porch, having a smoke in the rocking chair, when his two friends showed up. Annabeth knew them, and she didn't trust them. The bigger man, especially, had a way of looking at her that made her skin crawl.

She stayed in the house with her children while the three men talked on the porch. The front door was closed, but she could hear most of their conversation through the open window.

"We brung your car back. Here's the keys." It was Culley, the small, dark man, who spoke. "We figured you'd be up to drivin' again soon."

"Thanks," Silas said. "I'm still pretty sore, but I should be fit to drive again next week."

"We made a few local deliveries in it." The speaker was Buck, the big man. "But we're gonna need a new truck for the big orders. The old one's still out there by the road. We might be able to salvage the engine, but the cab is riddled with bullet holes. Looks like a damned cheese grater. You're lucky to be alive, man."

"My wife is a good nurse," Silas said. "She dug that bullet out by herself, with a spoon. Hurt like hell, but here I am, sound as a dollar."

Knowing what the next question would be, Annabeth held her breath.

"So how did you get home, all shot up like you was?" Culley asked.

"The memory's still foggy. But some stranger picked me up and took me home. Just dropped me on the porch and left. Never did get his name."

A cold knot twisted in the pit of Annabeth's stomach. Silas was playing a game with her. He knew about Joseph. He had to know.

"I made a delivery to the lady who owns Jake's," Buck said. "She asked about you, wondering why you hadn't been around. When I told her you were laid up, she said to give you her best. Have you got somethin' goin' with that gal?"

"Shut up, Buck." Silas had probably noticed the open window.

"There's more," Buck said. "When I told her what happened to the truck, she made me an offer. She'll bankroll a used truck in exchange for a cut of our business. She's a smart woman, and we need the truck. What do you think?"

"I think she's getting the best of the deal," Silas said. "We'll want an old truck that won't attract attention. We can probably find one in a junkyard and fix it up."

"But we'll need a truck that can outrun the feds and the thugs that shot up the old one," Buck said. "That means good tires and a first-class engine. That won't come cheap."

Silas hesitated, then sighed. "Fine. But don't let her take advantage of us. Find out how much of a cut she's expecting."

"There's more she can do," Buck said. "She can sell out of her basement. Our customers will come to her. We can deliver there and won't have to be running small orders all over the county."

"Can we trust her not to cheat us?"

"She keeps books and says she'll account for every crate."

There was a brief silence as Silas deliberated. "All right," he said. "Get everything in writing and hold her to it. Tell her I'll be back in action in a few days."

"She'll be happy to hear that." Buck's voice dripped with innuendo.

"Meanwhile, we'll start scouting for a truck," Culley said. "With luck, we'll find a good one in Miles City."

"Keep me posted," Silas said. "I'll be ordering a telephone for the house when I can get to town. That'll make it easier to keep in touch. And find out what you can about the bastards who shot me. We need to make sure that doesn't happen again."

As the two men said their goodbyes and drove away in the extra car they'd brought, Annabeth hurried to the kitchen and began pounding down the batch of risen bread dough she'd mixed earlier. Silas meandered into the kitchen and stood watching her. He probably knew she'd overheard the conversation on the porch, but what did it matter? What could she do, report it?

Lucas and Ellie had gone out the back door with a basket to hunt for eggs, with the dog tagging behind them. Annabeth and Silas were alone in the kitchen.

"I see you got the car back," she said, breaking the awkward silence. "When you're strong enough to drive, I'll need to go into town for kitchen supplies. We're running low on sugar and vinegar, among other things."

His eyes narrowed. "We'll see if I have time," he said. "The potato field is probably half dead by now. Why didn't you keep ahead of those damn beetles while I was laid up?"

"You know why. I was busy taking care of you."

"You could've sent the boy out. He knows what to do."

"Lucas is about five years old. I took the children out there with me when I went, but I'm not sending him out there alone."

"I'm raising him to be a man, not a little sissy."

Holding back her anger, Annabeth reshaped the ball of dough, returned it to the bread pan, and covered the pan with a clean towel. "Let's not fight, Silas," she said. "I don't have the energy for it, and neither do you. But if you're too busy to take me to town, I have a suggestion. You could teach me to drive the car. That way, if we needed something, I could take myself to town. I've been watching you drive for years. How hard can it be?"

The naked rage that flashed across his face told her she'd said the wrong thing.

"You'd like that, wouldn't you?" He spoke through clenched teeth. "Cut loose and go whenever the fancy strikes you—maybe even meet somebody in town. I'm going to do you a favor, Annabeth. I'm going to forget you asked me. And you're going to forget it, too. Women don't drive. That's the end of it."

He stalked out of the kitchen. Annabeth turned toward the counter and began peeling potatoes for the rabbit stew she was making. This time Silas had let her off without losing his temper. But there would be other times and other reasons to set him off—including the one she knew he was holding back.

There had been days when she wanted to take her children and leave. But she had no place to go. Lucas and Ellie needed a home and a family. She had no choice except to stay, attend to her wifely duties, and try to ignore the feeling that she was sitting on a keg of dynamite, waiting for it to explode.

And there was one more reality she'd forced herself to accept. Joseph was gone from her life. He was not going to ride in like a knight on a white horse and save her.

* * *

Joseph had spent the morning at the sawmill, seeing to the installation of the large blade and other parts that had finally arrived from the factory in Detroit. Mounting the blade on the shaft had been a delicate process. The slightest degree of tilt would ruin the cut and could break or warp the new wheel as well as the gears and the motor that turned it. Joseph was grateful for the skill of his workers, some of whom had been employed there for more than twenty years. He needed to remember that the mill was more than machinery, lumber, sawdust, and noise. It was people.

With the new saw blade operating smoothly, Joseph left the foreman in charge and drove back to the house to pick up Forrest for his third reading lesson with Francine. The boy had already devoured the first-grade and second-grade readers Francine had lent him from among the books in the classroom. But Forrest wasn't satisfied.

"These stories are stupid!" he'd declared after the last lesson. "Just listen. 'See Bess. See Bob. Bess and Bob see the dog.'" He pulled a disgusted face. "I want to read real stories! Cowboy stories!"

Francine had laughed, showing her small, perfect teeth. "There are plenty of cowboy stories out there, Forrest. But first you'll need to be a better reader. Keep learning."

When Joseph arrived home, Forrest was waiting on the porch with the books, ready to go. Joseph looked forward to sitting in on the lesson as well. The more time he spent with Francine, the more impressed he became, not only with her beauty but also with her intelligence, her charm, and her patience with the headstrong boy.

The last time Joseph had spoken with her, she'd agreed to have dinner with him at Jake's. Their date was set for tonight. With luck, he'd be able to move their relationship beyond polite conversation. Francine was every inch a lady. But he wanted to know her as a woman.

"Your father wants to see you before we go," Forrest said as Joseph came up onto the porch. "He's inside."

"Thanks. Wait here."

Joseph walked into the house. Blake, in his wheelchair, was sitting next to the open liquor cabinet with a glass of bourbon in his hand. The Dollarhides had saved a small supply of good liquor from pre-prohibition days, which they kept under lock and key. For most of his life, Blake had rarely drunk alcohol. But the accident had changed that. Now, if a few sips helped ease his physical pain and mental anguish, Joseph could hardly begrudge him. But there was a risk that, given free access, he might drink too much. As a precaution, the key to the cabinet was kept above the doorframe in the ranch office. When Blake wanted a drink, Joseph would get the key and unlock the cabinet. But he hadn't unlocked the cabinet today.

"Dad, how did you get into the cabinet?" Joseph asked.

"I got the boy to help me." Blake emptied the glass and poured himself another two fingers from the bottle. "Told him where the key was, and he stood on a chair to get it. See, no harm done. I've only had a little. But damn blast it, I get sick of being babysat. I should be able to drink when I want to."

"Where's the key, Dad?" With the passing days, Joseph was becoming the stern parent. Sometimes it was necessary, but he knew how much his father hated it.

Blake's hand shook as he fished the key out of his shirt pocket and handed it to Joseph. His strength was ebbing day by day. Was the decline related to his injuries, or was it simply caused by his broken heart? Joseph could only wonder and worry.

After locking the cabinet, Joseph took the key and put it back above the office door. Returning to the parlor, he watched his father finish the drink he'd poured. "We got the big blade installed," he said, changing the subject. "It's working fine. We should be back on our old delivery schedule in the next couple of weeks."

"That's good. It's about time." Blake sounded oddly disinterested. "What about your search for a wife? The boy tells me you've got a date with the new schoolmarm tonight."

"That's right. And the boy's name is Forrest. I'm glad to hear you're finally making friends with him."

"Yes. I'm finding him . . . useful. He says that your schoolmarm is beautiful and very nice. I think he has a crush on the lady. If I were you, I'd move fast, before some other man snatches her away."

"I'll bear that in mind." The same thought had occurred to Joseph. He found Francine enchanting and wanted to know her better. But it was too soon for a proposal.

And shouldn't love be part of the package? Blake had married the young, pregnant Hannah at his father's insistence. Only later had a tender, passionate, lifelong love blossomed between them.

But that wasn't always what happened. Joseph thought of Annabeth, the sadness in her lovely eyes, and the way Silas had talked about her son. The helpless anger he'd felt was still burning inside him, even though there was nothing he could do.

He wouldn't wish such a marriage on anyone. Love first, then the wedding. That would be the way for him, even with Francine.

"Listen to me, Son," Blake said. "You know my brother, Mason, has just one child, a little girl. From what I gather, his wife can't have more. The Dollarhides need a male heir. If you know what's good for you, you'll get a ring on that woman's finger and a baby in her belly before it's too late. Everything else will work out over time. You'll see."

Joseph sighed. The fact that Mason was actually his father was not to be mentioned in the family.

"It worked out for you, Dad. That doesn't mean it would work out for me. If I move too fast, the lady could say no. Or she could say yes to somebody else, like Chase Calder."

"That skirt chaser? He'd make her life miserable. If she'd take him over you, she hasn't got the sense of a plucked chicken."

Joseph shook his head. There was no arguing with the man. "I've got to go, Dad," he said. "Forrest is waiting for a ride to his reading lesson. When that's done, I'll need to spend some time at the mill and check on the cattle. Patches will be here if you need anything."

"Remember what I said. When I'm gone, it'll be your duty to carry on the Dollarhide bloodline. The sooner you get on with it, the better."

His words followed Joseph out the door as he beckoned to Forrest and went down the steps to his car. What Blake would never know was that the Dollarhide bloodline had already been carried on. But not the Dollarhide name.

For Joseph, the reading lesson had been a pleasant interlude in an otherwise hectic day. Watching Francine go over the new words with Forrest, he could see that the boy adored her. It seemed to be a rite of passage for boys, falling for an older woman. But when Joseph tried to recall his own crush at that age, no name or face came to mind.

At the end of the lesson, Francine brought out a well-worn dime novel, which she presented to Forrest. "This is for you to keep. I know you can't read it yet. But you can look for words you know. When you know enough of them, you'll be reading the story."

Forrest gazed at the cover, his grin almost splitting his face. "Wow! See that gunslinger behind the rocks? Now, that's a real cowboy story."

"Look at the title," Francine said. "Can you sound it out?"

The boy's face was a study in concentration. "$T \ldots O \ldots M \ldots$ That's Tom!"

"Right. Now try the other name."

"$M \ldots I \ldots X$! Oh, boy howdy, that's Tom Mix! My favorite cowboy! Thank you, Miss Francine! I never had my own book before. This one is the best!"

He looked as if he wanted to kiss her. Joseph had to chuckle. It was easy to see how a man—or a thirteen-year-old boy—could fall in love with this woman.

"I think you should marry Miss Francine," Forrest remarked on the way home in the car. "She's pretty. She's nice. And you need a wife."

"Maybe Miss Francine doesn't want me." Joseph drove past Jake's Place, thinking of the evening ahead. He wouldn't be fool enough to propose. But he planned to get a kiss from the lady. That would tell him a lot.

"Why wouldn't she want you?" Forrest fingered his paperback

book as if it were a rare treasure. "You're rich. And I can tell she likes you. That's why she offered to give me lessons, so you would have to bring me."

"Aren't you the smart one?" Joseph had thought of that but couldn't be sure. Maybe Francine was just being helpful. "Actually, I could use your help tonight," he said. "When I take Miss Francine out to dinner, I'll be leaving my father alone. Could you stay with him and make sure he's all right?"

"Sure. He's teaching me to play checkers. Maybe we'll have a couple of games."

This was good news. Joseph had hoped that the boy would provide some company for his father. "I'll probably be home before his bedtime," he told Forrest, "but if he wants to go to sleep and I'm not there, he might need a little help."

"I can help him. I'm stronger than I look."

"Good. If he's too heavy for you, you can get Patches out of his cabin. One more thing, and this is important," Joseph said. "No more liquor tonight. Not even if he asks you for the key. You can tell him I said no. Understood?"

"Understood." Forrest was leafing through the pages in his book, probably looking for more pictures. "When can I be a cowboy? I want to ride horses and sleep in the bunkhouse and do cowboy work."

"We'll see about that when you're older, if you're still around here then." The three cowboys, one a part-time bunkhouse cook, chewed tobacco and used language that would make a prostitute blush. They wouldn't be the best influence on a young boy. For now, Joseph would keep Forrest apart from them.

Before going back to the mill, Joseph gave Forrest tools, nails, and slabs of wood and put him to work mending the walls of the chicken coop. The ranch had lost two hens to a crafty weasel whose fluid body could squeeze through the smallest opening. The challenge of stopping the varmint should keep the boy busy for the rest of the afternoon.

Joseph found everything running smoothly at the sawmill. But the cattle operation was a different story. A section of fence was down. A spring calf had been caught in the wire and killed by coyotes. Two cows and their calves were missing and needed to be rounded up before the fence could be mended and the calf's partly devoured carcass buried to discourage the coyotes from coming back.

After Joseph had given the cowboys a tongue-lashing, docked their pay, and threatened to fire them, he barely had time to make it back to the house, shower, and dress for his dinner date with Francine.

He left Blake and Forrest sharing a game of checkers. They would be all right, Joseph told himself. Patches would be there until after supper, when he would retire to his cabin. If anything were to go wrong, Forrest could run out back and find him.

His spirits rose as he drove down the switchback road and past the mill, which had shut down for the night. He was looking forward to a juicy steak dinner with a beautiful companion sitting across the table. And he hadn't forgotten about that kiss.

Francine greeted him at the door, dressed in the apricot gown she'd worn to the dance. She gave him a radiant smile and took the arm he offered. Her lilac aroma swam in his senses as she sat close to him in the car for the short ride to the restaurant.

"Thanks again for giving Forrest that book," he said, making conversation. "I think he's got a schoolboy crush on you."

She laughed. "He's a smart boy. Keep him on the right track, and he'll go far in life."

"I don't know about that. All he wants is to be a cowboy."

"I know you got him out of jail. Do you plan on keeping him around?"

"Maybe." Joseph pulled into a parking spot outside Jake's Place. "My dad's taken a shine to him. That's a point in his favor. And I don't know where he'll go if I turn him loose. We'll see how it goes."

He escorted her into the restaurant. Almost all of the tables were occupied; but the most private one, in the corner, was vacant, as if it had been saved for them.

As he held her chair, he could sense the gaze of envious eyes.

Most of the diners were male. Tonight Joseph felt like the luckiest man here.

"Good evening, you two." The woman called Lola had appeared next to the table, her scars partly veiled by the black mantilla she wore. "My, don't you make a lovely pair? What a pity we don't have champagne, or at least a good cabernet." Her sharp eyes darted from Francine to Joseph. Something about those eyes—half hidden by the mantilla—triggered a hair-raising chill, like a cold hand on the back of Joseph's neck.

But this was no time for distraction—not while he was sitting across the table from the woman of his dreams.

"So, what's your pleasure this evening?" Lola asked. "Is this a special occasion?"

It was Francine who answered. "No, just a lovely dinner between friends. For now." She gave Joseph a mysterious glance, as if to suggest that things could change. "I'll have the roast chicken, please."

"And you, Mr. Dollarhide?" There was an edge to her gravelly voice. Did her tone carry a hidden meaning? But he was imagining things. Until a few weeks ago, he had never met the lady.

Joseph ordered a steak, medium rare. The Dollarhide Ranch raised good beef, but it was never as tender or flavorful as the meat that was served here. The smartest thing Lola had done was to keep Jake's cook, Smitty, along with his secret recipes.

As the woman turned to go, the movement brushed aside the edge of her mantilla. Joseph glimpsed a twisted smile, directed not at him but at Francine. Francine didn't respond, but as Lola disappeared into the kitchen, her hand crept across the table and found Joseph's. The touch of her satiny palm sent a pleasing tingle up Joseph's arm. His pulse quickened, and his fingers closed around hers and lingered. The evening was off to a good start.

On the far side of the room, three men in ranch clothes sat around a table finishing their meal. Coming in, Joseph hadn't paid them much attention. But now, one man got up and left the table for the restroom, giving Joseph a full view of Chase Calder sitting with his back to the wall.

From where he sat, Chase had a clear view of Francine and Joseph. His gaze appeared casual, almost indifferent. But Joseph sensed that he was watching them intently.

Francine appeared not to notice him. She kept her hand in Joseph's, her bewitching eyes focused on his face.

"Tell me about your ranch, Joseph," she said. "I know about that awful accident and what happened to your father, of course. Is he still running things, or has he turned that over to you?"

"A little of both," Joseph said. "I'm doing the work, but he's still giving the orders."

"Doesn't that annoy you?"

"It might, if I let it. But he needs to be the one in charge. If I were to step in and push him aside, making him feel useless, that would be the cruelest thing I could do. His life would be over."

"But you could take over if you had to?"

"Of course. I've learned a lot since Dad's accident. But I'm not in a hurry to be the big boss. If running the operation gives meaning to his life, then, for the time he has left, I'm all for it. Not that I know everything. I still have questions for him."

"You're a good man, Joseph," she said. "Maybe too good. The wrong people might find it easy to take advantage of you."

Chase was still seated, still watching them. That was when Joseph realized he didn't like where the conversation was going. Was that what she saw in Chase—that ruthless, fire-in-the-belly ambition that was part of being a Calder? Was that what she wanted in a man?

Was that what he wanted for himself—to be another Chase Calder?

What if he were to tell her that all he really wanted was to breed, break, and train beautiful horses, like his grandfather had done?

The tension eased when a waiter brought their meals. Chase and his companions got up and left the restaurant. Joseph willed himself to relax and enjoy the rest of the evening. When he encouraged Francine to talk, she told him about her sheltered childhood in a small Indiana town.

"I always wanted to become a teacher," she said. "But when my mother passed away, I had to stay home and take care of my father, who was an invalid. By the time he died, I was already an old maid by society's standards. I could have married the bank president. He was a widower, wealthy, and very respectable. But that wasn't the life for me. I wanted to follow my dream. So when I read a newspaper notice about a teaching job in the wilds of Montana, I applied—and here I am."

"So you followed your dream," Joseph said. "But there must be more to the dream than teaching school. What do you see for yourself in the years ahead?"

"Oh, a family, of course. Isn't that what most women want? But I'm enjoying my freedom. I'm in no hurry to settle down."

"That sounds like a sensible plan—for a sensible woman." They had finished their meals, including apple pie for dessert. Joseph paid the check, escorted Francine to the car, and drove her home. By now it was night. In the east, the moon was showing a golden edge above the peaks. The setting was romantic enough for what Joseph hoped would come next.

After a moment's hesitation, when she showed no sign of moving toward him, he got out of the car and walked her to her doorstep.

"Thank you for a lovely dinner," she said. "I'd invite you in, but I need to start working on my lesson plans tomorrow, and I want to get an early start."

"I understand. Sleep well, Francine."

He was bracing for disappointment when she came to him, melting into his arms, raising her face for his kiss—a kiss that became everything he'd hoped it might be.

The taste of apple pie lingered on her warm lips. They were satin smooth and cushion soft, molding to his with a teasing flick of tongue that set him ablaze. The fragrance of lilacs swam in his senses as her arms crept around his neck, pulling him closer, deepening the sweet, sensual contact of their mouths. Joseph's fantasies went wild. His tongue met hers in a playful, erotic dance that brought him to an aching arousal. For the price of a chewing gum pack, he could have swept her up in his arms, carried her inside to the bed, and explored all the places where she'd dabbed that maddening lilac scent of hers.

But he wasn't looking for a meaningless tumble between the sheets. Francine was a proper lady. Winning her would take respect and restraint. Reluctantly, he eased away from her. She stepped back, smiling up at him.

"I had a wonderful time, Joseph. I'd love to do this again, but I don't want to rush anything. Do you understand?"

"I do." Catching her hand, he brushed a playful kiss across her knuckles. "Goodnight, Francine."

She was watching his taillights vanish up the street when Chase came around the corner of the house and walked up to the porch. Fury blazed in his eyes—exactly what Francine wanted to see.

"Damn it, woman! I thought he'd never leave. And that kiss! Good God, did you have to let him go that far? Watching you almost drove me crazy!"

"So what are you going to do about it?" she asked with a mischievous glance.

"Guess." He seized her roughly and swept her into the house.

CHAPTER TEN

As Joseph drove out of Blue Moon, the memory of Francine's kiss lingered like a pleasant buzz in his brain. But with the lights of Main Street fading behind him, his hot blood began to cool, allowing him to think.

He'd kissed his share of girls and women—enough to learn a thing or two. Experience had taught him that some kisses were polite, some playful. Some were lustful and some, the most precious kind, came from genuine love. Then there was another kind of kiss—cold, calculating, and manipulative.

Which kind of kiss had he experienced tonight?

Francine's kiss had been expertly delivered. His response had been pure male nature. He'd enjoyed the pulse-pounding rush. But the pleasure had been purely physical—as much for her as for him, Joseph suspected.

Blake was pushing him to marry and continue the dynasty. But an urgent choice could lead to lifelong misery. He thought of Annabeth and the marriage she tolerated for the sake of her children. He ached for her, knowing he was partly to blame for her choice. But there was nothing he could do to change her situation. He could only try to make a better decision for himself.

Francine was beautiful, cultured, and gracious. Falling in love with her could still happen. But he wouldn't be rushed by his father or by anyone else. If Francine was agreeable, he would continue to enjoy her company. But he would put off anything like a proposal until he was sure of his feelings and hers.

Joseph was still lost in thought when he heard an ominous thump and felt the car sag toward the right rear wheel. He groaned out loud as he pulled onto the roadside and turned off the engine. There was no such thing as a good time to get a flat tire. But at least he had a spare bolted onto the back of the car and a jack in the trunk.

He found the flashlight in the glove box and turned it on. The switch clicked, but there was no light from the bulb. Joseph shook the flashlight, whacked it on his knee, and tried the switch again. Nothing.

How long had it been since he'd changed the batteries? The last time he'd used the flashlight was the night he'd found Silas in the bullet-riddled truck. The light had worked then. But it wasn't working now.

Grumbling, he climbed out of the car and walked around to the other side. Clouds had drifted across the crescent moon. In the near pitch darkness, his eyes could make out the tire. It was so badly blown that the rim rested on the ground.

He could try changing the tire in the dark. But he'd be working blind. And if he happened to drop something, like a nut or a bolt, it could be lost for good.

By his reckoning, he was about three miles from the house, an easy distance on foot. The wise course of action would be to walk home and have Patches, or one of the mill workers, drive him back to the car in the morning. Otherwise, he could be here all night. And that wouldn't be a good idea. He needed to be home to look after his father.

After taking the keys and locking the doors—not that anyone would steal the disabled auto—he set off walking along the familiar road. Even with the steep climb up the switchbacks at the end, Joseph figured he'd be home in less than an hour.

The night was cool, the breeze a fragrant whisper in the pines. An owl swooped past his head and landed a stone's toss away. There was a flurry of sound as it closed on its prey in the dark.

From the switchback road that zigzagged up the bluff, he looked down on the security lights at the sawmill. In the dark distance beyond, a pinpoint of light moved along the back road. Moonshiners again. Was Silas Mosby already back in action? Maybe he should have taken the man to the doctor and gotten him reported. With Silas in jail, at least he could have given Annabeth some money. But that hadn't been his call to make.

By the time the road leveled off at the top of the bluff, Joseph was breathing hard. The house was a welcome sight. The porch light was on. Otherwise, the place was quiet, the windows dark. He'd almost forgotten how late it was. By now, everyone was probably in bed.

He mounted the porch and opened the front door. As soon as he stepped across the threshold, he sensed that something was wrong. Was it the smell of stale air or just the feeling that the room was out of order? Reaching for the switch, he turned on the light.

His eyes made a sweep of the room. The first thing he noticed was the open liquor cabinet with the key hanging out of the lock. The checkerboard lay on the floor with the game pieces scattered around it.

An empty Jack Daniel's bottle stood on the coffee table, the glass beside it tipped onto its side, spilling a thin stream on the tabletop. Sprawled face up on the sofa, eyes closed, mouth open in a snore, was Forrest.

Joseph crossed the room in three long strides. Seizing the boy by the shoulders, he shook him hard. Forrest's eyes opened. "Hullo," he muttered, his breath reeking of alcohol.

"You're drunk!" Joseph slapped his face, more to wake him than to punish him, although he deserved that and more. "What have you done? Where's my father?"

"He's fine," Forrest mumbled. "Me and Patches helped him to bed, and he went to sleep. I did what you said. I didn't give him nothin' to drink."

Joseph could imagine the rest of the story. After the cook had gone and Blake was asleep, Forrest had climbed onto a chair, taken the key, and opened the liquor cabinet. The young fool had sampled freely until he passed out.

"Sit up!" Joseph jerked him upright. "You're in a heap of trouble. But right now, I'm going to make you some coffee. You'll drink it and go to bed. We'll deal with what you've done in the morning, when you're sober."

"What . . . what are you going to do to me?" The boy's voice shook. He shrank against the back of the couch.

"I don't know yet. But taking that key and the liquor was stealing. That was one of the rules we made, and you just broke it. If I can't trust you when I'm gone, you don't belong here." Joseph rose, looming above the quaking boy. "Stay right here while I make the coffee. Drink it, and you can go to your room. But you can count on a reckoning tomorrow."

In the kitchen, Joseph put ground coffee and water in the percolator and set it on the electric burner. While he waited for it to boil, he checked the parlor. Forrest was still on the couch, curled on his side with his knees drawn up toward his chest.

Damn kid. Joseph had grown fond of him. He'd imagined giving the boy a future as a cowboy on the ranch. But he'd laid down the law—no stealing. If Forrest thought he could weasel his way out of trouble, that lesson would shape his character for life. There was only one way to resolve this—the tough way. Tomorrow he would drive Forrest back to Miles City and turn the boy over to the sheriff.

The coffee was done. Joseph poured it into a mug, added a little milk to cool it, and carried it back to the parlor. "Here." He thrust the mug toward Forrest. "Take it to your room. I don't want to talk to you or even look at you until tomorrow morning."

Forrest stood, took the mug, and shuffled off through the kitchen to the storeroom, where he had his bed. Joseph took a few minutes to straighten the room, clean up the spilled whiskey, and throw away the empty bottle. Then, as he did every night before going to bed, he went to check on his father.

Blake slept in a room down the hall, in the bed he'd shared with his wife. Since his accident, the room had been rigged with grips and pulleys. With the aid of his powerful chest and arms, he was able to transfer from the bed to his chair and back, dress himself, and even make it to the bathroom. He was proud of his independence and grumbled when he had to be helped. But lately, Joseph had noticed his father's defiant spirit flagging. He'd been through hell and had yet to talk about his loss. Maybe his unspoken grief was wearing on him. But in case the problem was something physical, Kristin had arranged to come and check her brother first thing tomorrow.

Tonight, Joseph found his father in bed, his eyes closed, his breathing deep and regular. All was well. But the night was chilly. Joseph straightened the rumpled quilt, tucked it around his father, and left the room. He could use some sleep himself, but he didn't expect to get much. Between his date with Francine, his concern for Annabeth and her children, the car, and the coming confrontation with Forrest, he would probably be tossing for hours.

After a restless night, Joseph welcomed the glow of first light through his bedroom window. He rolled out of bed, pulled on his clothes, and braced himself for a hectic day.

Before he could drive Forrest to Miles City, he would need to get to his car and change the tire. But he also wanted to be here when Kristin came to examine his father. If Patches could take him down to the car now, he could have the tire changed and be back before she arrived.

Having one of his mill workers change the tire would save time. But his employees weren't servants. They had their own jobs to do. He might be the boss, but he could change his own tire.

As he descended the stairs, the coffee aroma wafting from the kitchen told him the old cook was already at work. Joseph walked into the kitchen and poured himself a mug of steaming coffee from the percolator. "Good morning, Patches," he said.

The old man looked up from the strips he was slicing off a bacon slab. "The boy's gone," he said.

"Gone?" Joseph choked slightly on his coffee. "What do you mean, he's gone?"

"Gone. Skedaddled. Took his clothes and some food and lit out in the night. I reckon we've seen the last of him."

"Damn. I should've known he'd do that." Joseph took another long sip and felt the scald burning down his throat. He was wide awake now.

"I noticed your car was missing," Patches said. "I hope the kid didn't steal it."

"No. The car's down on the main road with a flat tire. There wasn't enough light to change it last night. I'll need you to drive me down there—it shouldn't take you more than a few minutes. First I need to tell my father we're going and make sure he doesn't try to get up alone."

"Go on." The old man untied his apron and tossed it over a chair. "I'll go out and start up the old Tin Lizzie."

He left by the back door. Joseph walked down the hall to his father's room. Blake had been an early riser all his life, and that habit hadn't changed. Even at this hour, he would usually be awake, pulling himself into his chair and rolling into the kitchen for coffee. But he'd appeared tired last night. Hopefully, he was getting some much needed rest. It almost seemed a shame to wake him.

The bedroom door stood ajar, as Joseph had left it last night. The dawn light, filtering through the windowpane, revealed Blake lying amid the rumpled bedcovers, as if he'd been thrashing around in the bed, trying to get up.

"Dad?" Joseph stepped through the door. "Are you all right? Can I help you?"

There was no answer, no movement.

"Wake up, Dad." Joseph leaned over him, reaching out to shake his shoulder. Blake's skin was cool and rigid. No breathing. No pulse.

A single sob broke from Joseph's throat. He sank to his knees as his world crumbled around him.

Three days later, Blake was laid to rest in the family graveyard, next to his beloved Hannah and their younger daughter, Elsa. As one of Blue Moon's leading citizens, he was widely known and respected. A long procession of autos trailed up the switchback road as friends, business associates, and likely a few enemies came to pay respects and witness the simple ceremony.

Never one to show off his wealth or station, Blake was laid out in a plain pine casket lined with a patchwork quilt that his late mother, Sarah, had made for him as a boy. The only speech was a string of homilies and a prayer from a local minister, a man who'd barely known him. But that was all right. Everyone who'd come had their own memories of Blake—his honesty, his kindness, his work ethic, and his plain, straightforward way of speaking.

Joseph, his Aunt Kristin, and his married sister, Annie, stood beside the grave as the casket was lowered into the earth.

Weeks from giving birth, Annie sobbed as her husband supported her from behind. Kristin, who'd examined her brother's body and found no sign of foul play, stood stoic and silent. She'd witnessed countless deaths in the Great War. But this one had struck closest to her heart.

Numb with grief, Joseph kept his emotions under tight control. He would mourn in private. Now, as he took his place at the head of the Dollarhide family, his father would expect him to be strong.

But why had his time come so soon? Blake had wanted to see the family continue, with a daughter-in-law and grandchildren giving new life to the big log home. Joseph had been too intent on his own happiness to give him that wish. Now it was too late—for that and for so many other things.

As the first clods of dirt thudded onto the lid of the casket, Joseph stepped back and surveyed the crowd. Most of the faces he recognized—the mayor and his wife, the sheriff, the president of the Miles City Bank, and the owners of the ranches around Blue Moon. With the sawmill shut down for the day, a number of the workers had chosen to come and honor the man they called the big boss.

Francine was nowhere in sight. Not that Joseph had expected

her. She hadn't known his family, and she had no easy way to get here. But Chase was here, looking like a matinee idol in a fashionable three-piece suit. It would fall to Joseph to greet everyone and thank them for coming. That would include Chase, the boyhood friend who had become his lifelong rival.

The funeral guests had begun to flow toward the house, where a light buffet of sandwiches, donated casseroles, and desserts was set up on the porch. Only as the crowd cleared did Joseph see the tall man standing a dozen yards away, on the far side of the grave. Joseph's throat jerked tight as he recognized the chestnut hair, chiseled features, and confident stance of the one family member he had neither invited nor expected—Blake's half-brother, Mason Dollarhide.

Joseph had broken off all contact with the man who'd fathered him when Mason went to prison ten years ago. Now, as their gazes met and locked across the distance, he found himself at a loss. He'd glimpsed Mason in town and on the road, but they hadn't met face-to-face in ten long years.

What was he supposed to do?

It was Kristin who resolved the situation. With a little cry, she ran to Mason and flung her arms around his neck. He hugged her. "Hello, little sister," Joseph heard him say. "It's good to see you. I'm sorry it took something like this to get me back to the family." Mason's voice broke slightly. "All those lost years. I'm hoping maybe . . ." The words trailed off, as if he feared he might have said too much.

Kristin released him and turned back toward Joseph. He read her message in the stern look she gave him. Forcing himself to move, he walked to where she stood with Mason. He looked older than Joseph remembered, his face etched with lines, his hair threaded with silver. But his eyes were the same. Green like Joseph's. Green like Lucas's.

Joseph gave Kristin a warning shake of his head. Given Mason's impulsive nature, it might be best if he never found out about Lucas, who was his grandson.

Mason's striking eyes took Joseph's measure. "By God, you've grown into the image of your grandfather, Joseph. Joe Dollarhide in the flesh. And now you've stepped up as head of the family—what's left of us."

"I'm still trying to get my head around that, sir," Joseph said.

At the word "sir," Mason raised an eyebrow but didn't respond. What was he to be called? Joseph wondered. Not father. Not really uncle. Mr. Dollarhide seemed too formal, Mason too familiar. Not that he expected to be spending much time with the man. Relationships didn't heal overnight.

"My wife would have come," Mason said. "But our little girl, Grace, has the croup. Ruby didn't want to leave her."

"We can get together another time," Kristin said. "Bring them to our ranch when she's well. My boys would love to meet their cousin. And Britta has girls, too. They could have a grand time together."

"We'll do that." Mason stood for a moment gazing down at the graves—his father's, worn flat by time and weather, his half-brother's, newly covered in fresh earth, and beside it, the grave of Hannah, the pretty farm girl he'd seduced and left to raise his child. Did he have any regrets? But why wonder? He had his own family now. And Joseph had grown to be a man.

He turned to face Joseph. "I won't be staying," he said. "I realize you might not be ready to forgive me. But I want you to know that the door is open. Any time you want to come and visit, you'll be welcome."

He extended his hand. After a beat of hesitation, Joseph accepted the brief handshake. His world, and his role in it, was changing. He would have to get used to that.

"I'll need some time," he said.

"I understand." Mason took his leave of Kristin and headed back to his car. Kristin's husband, Logan, appeared at her side to escort her up to the house, where most of the guests had gathered. Joseph trailed behind them.

Chase, who was heading back to his car, met him on the path.

The two of them stopped for a moment, standing face-to-face. Remembering his manners, Joseph thanked him for coming.

"I'm sorry about your father, Joseph," Chase said. "My dad never thought much of your family, but he respected Blake Dollarhide. Everybody did. He was a good man."

"Thanks, Chase. I know you lost your father, too, just a few months ago."

"That's right. In a truck accident. It was sudden and all too soon. I still miss him every day." Chase's piercing brown eyes met Joseph's. "The two great enemies are gone," he said. "Now it's just you and me." He offered a handshake, which Joseph accepted. "Good luck, Joseph. I imagine you're going to need it."

He turned away and strode to his car.

One week later

Lola sank onto a wooden chair, kicked off her high-heeled shoes, and hoisted her feet to a tabletop. She sighed as the feeling returned to her swollen toes. Her eyes surveyed the basement room—the empty glasses and scattered playing cards, the overflowing ashtrays, the pleasant disorder of abandoned tables and chairs. She thought of the cash she'd just locked away in a strongbox on the bar.

Her speakeasy was doing even better than she'd hoped, the moonshine flowing and the poker games keeping customers at the tables. With the money coming in, she'd even managed to fancy the place up a little, with bigger tables, more solid chairs, and some nice glassware from an estate sale in Miles City. The sheet that had separated the speakeasy from the basement storage area had been replaced by an old velvet drape from a theater. Lola liked the classy look of it.

Her new sales partnership with Silas and his friends was bringing in even more income. But her businesses couldn't run themselves. Between the restaurant, the speakeasy, and the liquor selling, she had no time for what she jokingly called her beauty sleep.

And with Silas's wound still tender, her love life wasn't even worth a comment.

The strain was beginning to wear on her. And then there were the other worries. Her fool sister was mindlessly giddy over Chase Calder, who took his pleasure in her bed but had yet to propose. Why should he, when he was already getting what he wanted?

Maybe it was time Francine took a closer look at Joseph Dollarhide, whose status had gone up since his father's death. He was a decent man—handsome, virile, and probably more intelligent than Chase. He had everything to offer a woman except the Calder name and the cachet that went with it. But with his new responsibilities as head of the Dollarhide empire, Joseph, too, seemed to have lost interest in seeking marriage.

Damn fool girl. Lola had a mind to ship her back to St. Joseph, where she'd at least made money selling what Chase was getting for free. But then Lola's dreams of power and influence would be scuttled. She would have to settle for running a restaurant with a speakeasy downstairs and moonshine coming in the back door. And when prohibition ended, as was bound to happen, she would be left with nothing but a restaurant in a nowhere horse-piddle town.

Now there was a new problem, not a big one, but annoying all the same. For the past few days, food had been disappearing from the kitchen—not raw meat and eggs, but bread, slabs of pie and cake, fruit, and slices of ham and cheese.

The kitchen staff knew better than to steal from her. Lola kept track of every morsel. If they so much as nibbled, they'd be fired. But this thief was bold, probably getting in somehow at night and leaving with enough food to make a good meal. She'd thought of calling the sheriff, but that was out of the question. There were too many things she didn't want a lawman to find.

With a sigh, she lowered her feet to the floor and slipped them into her shoes. Tired as she was, she needed to clean up the speakeasy and get it ready for tomorrow night. With no one else she trusted to do the job, it fell to her to play janitor.

The broom, mop, and cleaning rags she used were kept behind the curtain. Pushing the heavy drape aside, she stepped into the storage area, which was piled ceiling high with unused and broken furniture, kitchen supplies, and crates of moonshine packed in mason jars, both full and empty. More crates were stored in a small room behind the clutter.

The yellow velvet chaise longue sat in front of the pile. For a moment, Lola was tempted to stretch out on it and close her eyes. But that wouldn't do. If she fell asleep, she could be here all night.

That was when she noticed something new. Lying on the chaise longue was a well-thumbed dime novel, spread face down, as if to mark the page. Her heart began to pound as she picked it up and read the title on the cover.

TOM MIX TO THE RESCUE

Someone wasn't just sneaking in. They were here, making themselves at home.

Lola carried a tiny derringer in a holster, strapped to her thigh. Drawing it, she spoke. "Whoever you are, I know you can hear me. Come on out, and we'll talk."

There was no answer, but as she waited in the silence, the prickling sensation that crept over her skin told her she was being watched. Maybe her unseen intruder was afraid of the gun. She decided to try something else.

Putting the weapon aside, she held up the thin paperback novel. "I'm going to count to three," she said. "If you don't come out, I'll rip this book to shreds. And then I'll come after you." She paused for effect. "Ready? One . . . two . . ."

"No!" A boyish voice cried out. "Don't hurt my book! I'm coming out!"

The stacked furniture quivered. A spindly wooden chair toppled to the floor as a skinny, bedraggled boy in his early teens crawled into sight and stood before her. Lola recognized the youth that Joseph Dollarhide had brought into the restaurant for a meal a few weeks ago.

He stood with his head hanging down. His hair had been recently cut. His clothes appeared new but were rumpled and dirty. He looked as if he'd been living in her basement for days, with nowhere to wash.

Lola fixed him with a stern glare. "Stealing food is against the law, young man. I've a good mind to call the sheriff on you. Look at me! What have you got to say for yourself?"

The boy raised his eyes—dark with lashes as long as a girl's. He'd be a heartthrob in a few years. "I'm sorry, ma'am. I was starving. With so much good food, I didn't think you'd miss a little bit."

"And you've been sleeping here, too?"

"Yes, ma'am. I was doing you a favor, guarding what you've got here. If anybody had come in, I would've raised a ruckus. I can help you, ma'am. I'm good at lots of things. I've watched you clean this place every night. It's no kind of work for a fine lady. I could do it for you."

"Whoa, not so fast," Lola said. The kid was not only a skillful thief, he also was an accomplished con artist. It took one to know one, and she recognized talent. But she was not about to be taken in.

"I thought you were staying with the Dollarhides," she said. "What are you doing here? Did something happen?"

"They worked me like a slave," he said. "If I stopped to rest or even asked for water, they beat me. They never gave me enough to eat. And the way that old man looked at me—I could tell what he was thinking. It was that way when I was in the orphanage. I didn't even dare go outside. They said if they caught me out of the house, they'd send me back there."

Lola recognized hogwash when she heard it, but she had to give the kid credit for a colorful story. So what was she going to do with him? He was probably in some kind of trouble. But the boy had seen everything she was trying to hide. She couldn't just let him go. And even though she might be tempted, she knew better than to murder a child.

The little stinker had her right where he wanted her.

"All right," she said. "You've got yourself a job. I'll explain my rules to you. If you'll swear a blood oath to follow them, you'll be bound to me." She drew a small, sharp knife from her stocking. "Are you ready?"

"Ready." The boy was wide-eyed and shaking, but he held out his hand for the ritual that all boys understood. A blood oath was for life.

"Smart boy. First, I'll explain what this means. Once it's done, you can start by cleaning this messy room."

CHAPTER ELEVEN

THE POTATO CROP WAS DYING IN THE FIELD, A CASUALTY OF SUMMER drought, depleted soil, and more hungry striped beetles than Lucas's small hands could pull off the plants, even with his mother doing most of the work.

Annabeth stood on the back porch, gazing out at the wilting vines, knowing that the potatoes below ground wouldn't be worth harvesting. She'd been counting on the sale of that crop to help her family through the winter. Now their future depended on whatever Silas could provide.

The trouble was, Silas didn't seem to care.

Since his recovery from the bullet wounds, he'd been gone most nights, chasing around with his friends, running moonshine, coming home in the small hours, and sleeping long past chore time. Except for the eggs the hens laid, the children barely had enough to eat. They were growing out of their clothes. And Silas was bringing home nothing. If the family was to survive, something had to change.

For the past few days, she'd been working herself up to a confrontation. Now, at ten in the morning, she could hear him stirring in the bedroom. She had sent the children outside to play with the dog. It was time.

As he came down the hall, Annabeth steeled herself. Silas was bound to be defensive. He could easily become violent. But for the sake of her children, she had to stand up to him.

Hastily dressed, with his shirt buttoned wrong, he shuffled into the kitchen and stared at the table, which he'd expected to find set for his breakfast. "Where's my bacon and eggs, woman? Why aren't you doing your job?"

Annabeth squared her shoulders and set her jaw. "Maybe you should try doing *your* job first. We're out of bacon and down to the last of the flour for bread. I had to scrape the barrel to make flapjacks for the children this morning. The last supper we had was stew from the garden and a rabbit that I snared. The bills for the lights and the new phone haven't been paid because there's no money to pay them. We're down to a few sticks of kindling for the stove, and with the potato crop dead in the field, we'll have nothing to sell at harvest time."

His eyes narrowed. Annabeth could imagine barriers sliding into place. "Well, whose fault is that? Maybe you should learn to be a better manager. Besides, I was counting on you to take care of the potato crop. If you'd paid more attention—"

"This isn't about the potato crop, Silas." She spoke calmly, aware that an angry outburst could turn the discussion into a fight. "I know what you're doing at night with your so-called friends. And I know I can't talk you out of it. Even getting shot and almost dying didn't stop you."

Silas didn't respond, but the anger smoldering in his eyes told her she was walking a fine line. Would he choose this time to bring up Joseph?

But she couldn't let him derail her words and turn them against her. She had to remain in control.

"It would serve you right if you got caught," she said. "But you're my husband, the head of the family. If you were to go to jail, the children and I would have nothing. So I have no choice except to ask you, Where's the money you're making? Why don't we have enough to pay our bills and support our children?"

He scuffed his work boot against a broken floorboard. "The money's in a safe place," he said. "I'm saving it for a better life. Do you think I want to go on living like this? In this old cracker box of a house, grubbing in the dirt for every nickel? When I get enough, I'll pull up stakes here and buy me—us—a decent place. Until then, we're not touching that money. If we start spending it, we'll never have enough."

Annabeth's smoldering anger flared like tinder. "Do you think I'm asking on a whim? My family was poor, but they were honest. They raised us to be the same. If I had a choice, I wouldn't touch a cent of that illegal money. But I won't stand for my children going hungry and dressing in rags. So I'm asking—for them. Please, Silas. If you care about us at all—"

"And why should I care?" His voice was cold. "Another man's bastard, along with a useless girl who'll probably run off as soon as she's old enough. And a tramp who'd already spread her legs when I married her and would do it again, with the same man if she had the chance. At least you could've given me a son of my own. As it is, what the hell use to me are you—any of you? I could throw you out tomorrow, all three of you, and not give a damn."

The words slammed into Annabeth with the force of a gun blast. Silas had said some hurtful things to her, but never as cruel as this. It was as if she'd been cut down and left bleeding. It was bad enough that he didn't care about her. But what he'd said about the children—that was unconscionable.

It was time to fight back.

Choking on rage, she drew herself up and riveted him with her gaze. "Here are my terms, Silas," she said. "It's your duty to provide for your family. If you won't do that, you might as well be in jail. I know what you've been doing and who your friends are. Give me what I need for the children, and I won't say a word to anyone. Otherwise, I'll go straight to the sheriff and tell him everything."

He looked stunned but swiftly countered. "That's blackmail! Damn it, woman, I could kill you just for saying that."

"You'd hang for it."

"...ld take your brats and send them where you'd never see ...."

"Then I'd have nothing to lose, would I? You can't imagine what I'd do to you then. How hard could it be to just give me what I'm asking? Then you'd be safe, I'd be satisfied, and the children would have what they needed. I need an answer, Silas."

In part, she was bluffing. Silas could lock her up, rip out the phone, and she'd be trapped with no way out. She could only hope he'd see the sense in what she was asking.

"I'm waiting," she said. "All you need to do is get me enough cash for a good shopping trip and take me and the children to town. And later on, when we need it again—"

"All right, I got the message." He mouthed a curse. "How much are you talking about?"

Her pulse leapt. "Enough to stock the house with a month's staple groceries and buy new shoes and some plain clothes for the children. I won't be spending a cent on myself. How soon can you get me the money?"

"How soon do you want it?"

"Now would be a good time."

"And you can expect to pay me back in bed tonight."

"Of course. I'm your wife." There was no love involved in Silas's lovemaking, only control and humiliation, but it was a small price to pay for peace.

"Fine. I'm going. You stay right here in the kitchen till I get back." He turned and strode across the kitchen. As he reached the door, he suddenly halted and wheeled to face her again. Without a word, he stalked back to her, raised his fist, and slammed it into the side of her face.

Sparks of light flashed through Annabeth's vision. She felt the crushing blow and the bruising of flesh against bone. She forced back a cry as he left by the kitchen door. She had won what she needed from him. But at what cost? Suddenly, she was afraid, not only for herself but also for her children.

After finding a pencil and a pad of scratch paper in a drawer, she sat down at the kitchen table. With a shaking hand, she began to write.

* * *

Joseph had spent the past few days going over the records for the Dollarhide Ranch and Sawmill. He'd been managing the day-to-day mill and cattle operations since Blake's accident. But now he felt the need to know everything—from the time his grandfather, Joe Dollarhide, had acquired the property, constructed the big log house with his own hands, and started the ranch and sawmill to the transitional years when Blake had expanded the ranch's holdings and built the mill into a serious money-making operation.

Now, far sooner than he'd planned, it was Joseph's turn. If he was to plan the ranch's future, he needed to understand the past. Only now, as he closed the last ledger book, did he realize how much he owed that past.

When Blake had talked about the family legacy, Joseph had listened with half an ear, dismissing anything he didn't agree with as the ramblings of a man out of touch with the times. He'd spun selfish fantasies about how, when his turn came, he would do things his way—sell off the sawmill and turn the pastures into a horse operation in partnership with Logan Hunter.

Now his turn had come, and when he walked this house and this land, he could feel the people who'd given their sweat, blood, tears, and lives walking with him. He carried their burdens and their blessings.

Blake had urged him to marry. He was no longer in any rush. But when he finally took a wife, he would need her to be a strong woman like his grandmother, Sarah, and his mother, Hannah. A woman who would stand at his side, work with him, and love him as he loved her. Would Francine be that woman? Joseph was still looking for answers.

As he walked through the parlor on his way outside, he paused before the portrait of his grandfather that hung next to the fireplace. Joe Dollarhide had never been one to fuss. He'd protested when his children had arranged to have his picture painted. At his insistence, he had worn his cowboy clothes, a battered Stetson in one hand and a sweat-stained bandana around his neck. He'd been fifty years old when the portrait was done.

For Joseph, seeing the image was like looking at an older version of himself—like him, but tougher, grittier, and wiser, as he hoped to be someday.

What would the old man have to say if he could be here now?

Joseph walked outside. The day was clear, the torrid weather cooled by an early breath of Montana autumn. It would feel good to get out of the house for a while. He would check on the sawmill and the cattle, then head into town to gas the Ford, check the mail at the post office, and pick up some supplies at the Feed and Hardware store.

Maybe he would pay a call on Francine if she was at home. He might even suggest lunch if she didn't bridle at accepting a last-minute invitation. She was a lovely, charming young woman who would make any man a suitable wife. He owed himself the chance to know her better.

At the sawmill, he found the replacement wheel standing idle and Seamus O'Brien, the shift foreman, oiling the gears. "Is everything all right?" Joseph asked.

"Everything's fine, Boss," the Irishman said. "We're just makin' sure she stays that way. If we're to fill that order for the new warehouse, we've got to run steady all day. We can't have the engine breakin' down." He took a clipboard from its place on a nearby hook. "This here's a list of the sizes and grades for the order that's due at the end of the month. This column shows the output for each day. This one shows how much we've delivered. We got behind when the blade broke, but now that it's runnin', we're almost caught up. I give the gears a few drops of oil at the start of every shift and a good going over every week, which is what I'm doing now. Your dad trained us well, God rest his soul."

Those last words stayed with Joseph as he drove away and headed for the bunkhouse. As the new man at the helm of the Dollarhide empire, he couldn't be everywhere at once. He needed to start delegating. Tomorrow, he would promote Seamus O'Brien to be production boss at the mill, reporting directly to him. He would also give the man a well-deserved raise and look into promoting other valued employees.

The cattle operation was another story. The four cowhands, hired by Blake, were decent boys, but with no one to give them direction, they tended to overlook things that needed to be done. Today Joseph found that one of the water troughs hadn't been filled, and a fence post on the far pasture was about to topple and bring the fence down with it.

More than once, he'd been tempted to fire the lot of them, but that would mean hiring others who might not be any better. What the young cowboys really needed was someone there full time to tell them what to do. That would mean hiring a new man, an experienced cowboy who knew the job and could put fear in any slackers. He would put up a notice in town today or, better yet, run an ad in the Miles City paper and hope the right person would respond.

The fall roundup was a couple of months off. Joseph had been working cattle since he was old enough to sit a horse. But this would be his first year as roundup boss. Having a well-trained crew could cut days off the job of gathering, sorting, branding, and processing the herd—but only if he could find the right man to work the boys into shape.

He added the item to his mental list as he drove into town. Blue Moon was bustling with activity this morning, with folks taking advantage of the cooler weather to run their errands. Passing the school attached to Francine's house, he noticed that the door and windows had been opened to let in the fresh air. He parked in the schoolyard and crossed the porch. Through the open doorway, he could see Francine on her knees arranging books on a low shelf.

For a long moment, he stood watching her, admiring her graceful movements as she wiped each book with a cloth and replaced it on the shelf. When she failed to notice him, he knocked lightly on the doorframe.

As she glanced up, the startled look on her face melted into a smile. "Hello, Joseph," she said. "You caught me working. This classroom is covered with a year's worth of dust. Since there's no one else around, cleaning it appears to be part of my job."

She stood and walked toward him. Her hair was twisted up and pinned with loose curls framing her flushed face. One rosy cheek was smudged with coal dust. The effect was enchanting. "I don't suppose you've come to offer your help, have you?" She gave him a wistful look.

Joseph was tempted for a moment. But she appeared to have the simple job well in hand, and this wasn't how he'd planned to spend his day. "Maybe another time," he said. "This morning, I've got some errands to run. But I was hoping to take you to lunch later, if you'd do me the honor."

She raised an eyebrow, giving him a look of mild displeasure. "I'll think about it. Come back after your errands and ask me again. Maybe by then I'll be hungry."

Joseph could tell that she was peeved. But he wasn't about to change his plans on a whim. "I'll do that," he said. "Think it over. I'll stop by on my way out of town."

"Fine." She flounced away. Joseph was about to leave when she suddenly turned around and walked back to him. "This is so you won't forget me," she whispered, and planted a firm kiss on his mouth.

Before Joseph could react, she backed away from him, laughing at his surprise. "In case you're wondering, that was an apology," she said. "And I'll accept that invitation to lunch."

"Fine. We'll talk then." Joseph took his leave of her, hoping that no one passing by had looked through an open window and seen her kissing him. She could lose her job for that. But Francine didn't seem concerned.

Lost in thought, Joseph climbed into his car and drove the rest of the way downtown. Life with a woman like Francine would never be dull. But would she be satisfied with what he had to offer her? She seemed to thrive on excitement and drama. Where would she find that as the wife of a busy rancher? He would take his time finding out, Joseph resolved. But he couldn't deny that the idea of marriage was already playing in his mind.

At the Feed and Hardware store, he bought a salt block for the cattle, some burlap sacks of oats for the horses, and a roll of barbed wire to replace the weak spots in the fence. After filling the Ford's tank at the gas station and checking the mail, he remembered needing Arbuckle Coffee—the traditional brand that Blake had always favored. Joseph had begun drinking it in his memory. Now the supply was almost gone.

He entered the general store and wove his way among the shoppers to the aisle where the cans of coffee were found. He was about to take what he needed when he heard his name, spoken in a voice that barely rose above a whisper.

"Joseph."

His heart slammed. Annabeth stood beside him, a loaded shopping basket over her arm and her little girl clinging to her skirt. Only when she turned and looked up at him did he see the blackened eye and the wine-colored bruise, still fresh, that covered the side of her face from temple to jaw.

"Annabeth—"

"Don't say anything. I asked for this. It was the price I paid for getting what I needed. I'll be all right."

"Until he does it again. Damn it, Annabeth—" Her calm resignation only fueled Joseph's rage. *I should've left the sonofabitch to die*, he thought. *I could've taken care of her. I could've claimed my son.*

"You deserve better than this," he said. "Leave him. Take the children. I'll help you."

She shook her head. "You know things don't work that way. The law would be on his side. I could lose my children." She glanced around nervously. "Listen. We don't have much time. I need to give you something." She slipped a tightly folded sheet of paper out of her bodice. "I didn't expect to see you here. I was looking for someone I could trust to get this to the right place. But you're the one who should have it." She thrust the paper toward him. "Don't look at it here. Put it in your pocket before someone sees."

He did as she'd asked, tucking the paper into the chest pocket of his shirt. As he did so, he felt a tug at his pants leg. He glanced down to find Ellie grinning up at him. As he gave her a smile, the little girl reached up, clearly wanting to be lifted into his arms.

"She remembers you," Annabeth said. "But you mustn't pick her up. People might be watching."

"Sorry, sweetheart." Joseph gave the small hand a gentle squeeze. "Is she all right?" he asked Annabeth. "Does Silas ever hurt your children, or even threaten to?"

"No. Never. If he were to do that . . ." She took a breath. "If he were to do that, I would kill him."

"Where's Lucas?" Joseph asked.

"Outside in the car with Silas. They're waiting for me. I still have things to buy. You'd better go."

Joseph knew he should leave now—preferably by a discreet back door. He could buy coffee another time or have Patches pick it up. But as he gazed down into Annabeth's beautiful, battered face, he felt as if his feet were rooted to the floor. How could he leave her like this, at the mercy of a brutal man, with nothing to sustain her but her courage and her love for her little ones?

He wanted to cup her face between his hands and kiss her with healing tenderness. He wanted to take her in his arms and promise to keep her and her children safe forever. But not everything he wished for could be made to happen.

"Go," she whispered. "Please, Joseph."

"Be safe, Annabeth." He forced himself to turn away and walk out of the front door.

The boardwalk was crowded. He could see Silas's Model T parked around the corner from the store. Silas, in the driver's seat, appeared to be dozing. Lucas, in the back, was looking out through the window. At the sight of his son, Joseph felt the familiar tug at his heart. He knew enough to keep his distance. He had no claim on the boy.

But the thought of Silas's fist crunching into Annabeth's soft, lovely face had ignited a blazing fire inside him. He couldn't just get in his car, drive off, and let this go. He strode up to the car. Silas looked up as he approached. His eyes glittered with hatred.

"Get out of the car, Mosby," Joseph said. "I've got something to say to you, and I don't want to say it in front of the boy."

After exchanging a word with Lucas, presumably telling him to stay put, Silas climbed out of the car, a hulk of a man, looming over Joseph with murder in his gaze. Joseph was six feet tall with an athlete's lean, muscular body. Silas had bested him in their first encounter at the dance. Still, in his present frame of mind, Joseph wouldn't have hesitated to tear into the big man with his fists and do enough damage to hurt. But there were plenty of people around. Nothing like that was going to happen here.

Silas spoke first. "Leave my wife alone, Dollarhide," he growled. "Stay away, or you're a dead man."

"Shut up and listen to me, Mosby," Joseph said. "There's nothing going on between your wife and me. She's a good woman, a lot better than you deserve. I saw her in the store. I saw her face. I didn't have to ask her what happened. Are you proud of yourself, battering a defenseless woman who only wants to take care of her family?"

"She tried to blackmail me. I gave her what she deserved. But that's none of your business."

"Maybe not. I'm only here to tell you one thing. If you ever hurt her again, and I hear about it, you'll be one sorry sonofabitch."

"Oh?" Silas sneered. "What are you going to do?"

"Think about it," Joseph said. "I know enough about your side business to put you behind bars. I've kept quiet for the sake of your family, but that could change. Remember that the next time you're tempted to lay a hand on your wife."

Silas's lip curled. "You think you've got the best of me. You and her both. But you're the one who'll be sorry. Leave us alone. And don't tell me how to treat my woman. You'll only be making trouble."

Joseph chose to ignore the threat. "If you're smart, you'll learn something from this," he said. "Any minute now, your wife will be coming out of the store with one arm holding your daughter and the other carrying a heavy basket. Maybe you should get off your rear end and help her to the car—if you're man enough."

With that, Joseph walked away and crossed the street to where he'd left his car. When he looked back, Annabeth had come out of the store. Just as he'd described her to Silas, she was holding onto Ellie with one hand and struggling to balance the overloaded basket with the other. Silas leaned against the hood of the car. With a mocking glance toward Joseph, he rolled a cigarette.

Joseph cursed, knowing that interfering would only make the situation worse. Maybe he should have left well enough alone. Somebody needed to stand up to the bully. But his actions and the threat he'd made would do nothing to help Annabeth.

The reckless part of him wanted to cross the street again, challenge Silas, and ram the big man in the gut where the bullet had struck him. The healing wound would still be tender. A solid blow would leave him writhing in agony.

But what would that do to the boy who looked up to Silas as a father—and to the woman who'd have to deal with his rage when she got him home? Joseph was out of options. All he could do was leave.

Joseph drove away with his emotions in turmoil. He would have given anything to help Annabeth and her children. But aside from keeping his distance, there was nothing he could do without making things harder for them.

He'd left Blue Moon behind by the time he remembered his lunch date with Francine. For a moment, he weighed the idea of turning around but decided against it. Francine would be peeved at him, but he was in no mood to enjoy a chatty lunch. Gazing across the table at his charming companion, he would have found himself remembering Annabeth's haunting, battered face and how the sight of her had crushed his heart.

Joseph kept on driving. He had almost reached the turnoff to the ranch when he remembered the paper that Annabeth had given him in the store. It was still in his pocket. He needed to see it now.

He swung the car onto the cutoff road and parked on the shoulder. The paper, torn from a blue-lined dime-store notepad, had been folded and creased multiple times. The writing, hastily scribbled in pencil, was hard to read, but as Joseph studied it, the message became clear.

> *I, Annabeth Coleman Mosby, being of sound mind, do declare this to be my last will and testament. I have no worldly goods to leave, but I request that in the event of my inability to keep them, due to death or other cause, my children, Lucas and Elinor, be given into the custody of Joseph Dollarhide, to care for and raise as he sees fit.*
> *Signed:*
> *Annabeth Coleman Mosby, August 4, 1929*

The breath had left Joseph's body. He read the makeshift document again, then again, his throat swelling with emotion. That Annabeth would trust him, above all others, to care for her children, and that she would give him his son, moved him beyond any possible words.

But he was also terrified for her. Why would she write a will unless she thought she might need it? And why did she assume Silas wouldn't get the children?

The reasons were self-evident—and they left him cold with fear.

There had to be something he could do. But short of taking her and the children by force, his hands were tied. Aside from some ugly bruises, he had no proof that Silas had threatened her life. And he knew that she would never leave him without her little ones.

Joseph could report Silas to the law for his moonshining activity. But if Silas suspected Annabeth had done it, that would put her in even more danger. He could even challenge Silas himself. But any outcome would be risky for everyone involved, including the children.

Worry twisted his gut. He read the will again, imagining the desperate courage it had taken for her to write it. He pictured her hands and her beautiful, bruised face.

Annabeth. She was his first sweetheart and the mother of his son.

He loved her.

CHAPTER TWELVE

By the time Silas drove the truck through the broken gate of the O'Rourke Ranch, the moon had journeyed across the sky to hang above the western hills. With a yawn, he parked behind the dilapidated barn, picked up the envelope of cash that he'd collected, and climbed out of the cab.

The smell of fermenting mash drifted down to him on the wind. It became stronger as he took the winding trail to the hillside cave. His partners were running the still day and night to meet the demand for quality moonshine. After Lola's 25 percent cut, the money Silas carried would be divided three equal ways—even though Silas believed privately that he should get more because of the risk he was taking.

Tonight's loaded run to Miles City had gone well. The new truck didn't look like much, but the engine was fast and powerful. Silas had floored the gas pedal on the way home and gotten the speed up to almost seventy miles an hour.

But Silas knew better than to assume he'd be safe. He'd nearly been killed once, and the thugs who'd hunted him down were still out there. So were the feds. It was only a matter of time until he would have to run for his life again.

He could see the glow of lantern light through the trees. Culley looked up from tending the still as Silas came into the cave. He grinned, showing his missing front tooth. "How did it go? Any trouble on the road?"

"No. Everything went fine. And don't worry, I've got your money."

"Did somebody say money?" Buck came out from the back of the cave, where he'd been loading crates—a job any fool could do, Silas reflected sourly. Yet, for that, Buck was getting an equal share. It didn't seem right.

Silas counted out the bills and gave each man his share. "I suppose you'll be taking care of Lola's share," Buck said with a grin. "And she'll be taking care of you."

"Shut up, Buck. I'm too tired for your comments. Maybe you need to find a woman who'll have you."

"I can get a woman when I want one," Buck said. "But I still don't understand what you see in Lola. If I had a lady at home like that wife of yours—"

"I said shut up, Buck. I'm going now. I'll be making another delivery to Lola tomorrow. Make sure the truck's loaded and ready."

"Be careful," Culley said. "I hear the feds are on the prowl again. And those goons who shot you could be anywhere."

"Thanks. I'll keep my eyes open." Silas went back down the hill to where he'd left his Model T when he took the truck. As he drove toward home, he took a mental count of the cash he had hidden in the potato cellar behind the barn. He was making good money, but it wasn't yet enough to pull up stakes and make a new start. He'd hoped to be ready before winter set in. But he needed more.

He was still debating whether to take Annabeth and the brats with him or leave them behind. They'd be a drag financially and socially in the new life he'd planned. But if he left them here, Joseph Dollarhide would probably get his hands on them. The thought of Annabeth in the arms of the man he hated made Silas grind his teeth. He would rather see her dead than with that bastard.

He could always take them now and leave them somewhere else. That might be the best solution. He would think on it while he saved the money for his freedom.

write this will and give it to me, unless she was afraid he was going to kill her?"

"You love her, don't you?"

Joseph's silence answered her question.

"I feel so damned helpless," he said. "At least, I need to let her know I'm there for her and her children. But I don't even know if this will is legal. It's written in pencil, and the signature isn't even witnessed."

"The handwriting is fine—in fact, it strengthens the credibility of the will. The lack of a witness may or may not be a problem if the will's contested. But Joseph, nothing's happened yet. She's just letting you know that this is what she wants. Right now, all you can do is reassure her that if the worst happens, you'll fight to your last breath to protect those children."

"I hope she knows that," Joseph said. "I'd give my life for them, the little girl as well as Lucas. The same for Annabeth. But she won't leave her husband if there's any chance of losing her children. If the case goes to court, you know who will win. Not that he cares about Lucas and Ellie. He'd take them away just to punish her."

"Yes. I keep hoping that someday things will change and the law will give women more rights. But that won't help you now."

"I could turn him in for running moonshine. I've threatened to if he hurts her again."

"He's a small-time criminal," Kristin said. "The courts and jails are overflowing with people like him. If he goes to trial, he could get a fine, maybe a very short sentence, or nothing but a slap on the wrist. And what would he do after that? Probably take out his anger on Annabeth and the children. Leave it, Joseph. There's nothing you can do that won't make things worse."

"But Lucas is my—"

"Don't even say it. Annabeth was already married when Lucas was born. Not unlike your mother when you were born. If you want to spend the time and money, you can talk to a lawyer. But he'll tell you the same thing. You can't change the past. Silas Mosby is Lucas's legal father."

Kristin rose at the sound of footsteps on the front porch. "That'll be my next appointment. Keep the will in a safe place and pray you'll never need it. I care about your problem, Joseph. I really do. But that's the best advice I can give you."

Joseph drove home, lost in thought. Kristin's advice had been sound. But how could he stand back and let Annabeth be abused? He had threatened to report Silas to the law. But as Kristin had pointed out, it was an empty threat.

For now, all he could do was hold himself back, keep an eye on Annabeth and her children, and try to be there in case of trouble.

He'd driven partway up the switchback road when he noticed that another car—a beat-up Model T—was following him. His first thought was that it might be Silas. But he swiftly realized that this was a different vehicle, one whose driver he couldn't identify, although he could see the vague outline of a cowboy hat through the dusty windshield.

There was no safe place to stop on the steep, narrow road until he got to the top. Then Joseph pulled off to one side, giving the Model T room to park. Before getting out of his car, he opened the glove box, took out the loaded pistol, and cocked it. When it came to strangers, he couldn't be too careful.

The man who stepped out of the old car was dressed in ragged cowboy clothes. He was tall but stoop-shouldered, as if from long years in the saddle. Joseph guessed him to be in his late fifties. In one hand, he held a folded newspaper that appeared to be a recent edition of the *Miles City Star*.

His free hand lifted off his Stetson, revealing a face that was tanned and wrinkled like an old leather glove. His thick hair, which wanted cutting, was iron gray. Joseph could see that the man was unarmed. He released the hammer on the pistol and laid the weapon aside.

"Do I have the pleasure of speaking with Mr. Joseph Dollarhide?" The man's speech was flat, with a slight midwestern twang.

"You do, sir."

"Hiram Hatch is the name. When I asked folks in town how to

find you, they pointed out your car, so I just followed you. I'm here about the advertisement you placed." He made a gesture with the newspaper. "Are you still looking for an experienced cowhand?"

"The job's still open. It remains to be seen whether you're the right man. Come sit on the porch and we'll talk. I can get you something to drink. Cider?"

"No thanks." Hatch settled himself on the top step, his skinny knees jutting upward. "Your ad called for an experienced cowhand. One look at me should put that concern to rest. You can ask me anything you want. I've long since outlived any secrets."

He spoke as if he'd had some education, which piqued Joseph's curiosity. "You don't talk like most cowboys I know," he said.

He chuckled. "So it shows, does it?" My father was a history professor at Brigham Young University in Utah. I was brought up to follow in his footsteps. But I was the black sheep of the family. They put up with my rebellious ways for a while, but they finally cast me out. I haven't been home in more than forty years."

"Your family cast you out? What did you do to deserve that?"

"I killed a man in an Ogden bar fight. Didn't mean to do it, just hit him too hard. I served six years for manslaughter. When I got out, the letter that was waiting for me said I wouldn't be welcomed at home. So I took to cowboying—a profession that's lasted me the rest of my life."

He laughed at Joseph's stunned expression. "See? I told you I'd outlived my secrets. Wouldn't want you to find out later and think I'd hidden something from you. You need to know you can trust me. But if it's experience you want, I've worked on ranches in Wyoming, Colorado, Texas, and Missouri."

"Is there some reason you moved around so much?" Joseph asked.

"Just restless. Things change. And people change. On my last job, I was foreman of a sweet little Missouri ranch. Great people. But they had a run of bad luck and lost the place to the bank. So

I decided to try my luck here in Montana." He shifted his bony haunches on the step. "So tell me about the job, and we can decide if I'm suitable."

"It's pretty much regular cowboy work," Joseph said. "But I've got four young cowhands who need whipping into shape. They're good boys, but they need a boss to give them orders and keep them working, maybe put a little fear in them as well. Does that sound like something you could do?"

"You've heard my story. What do you think?"

"I think you might be just the man for the job," Joseph said. "You'd need to start right away. We'll be getting a new bull shipped in next week. He's arriving by train, so I'll be picking him up in Miles City. Before he gets here, we'll need the pasture fences shored up and the heifers gathered. When the breeding's done, we'll be getting ready for the fall roundup."

"Sounds like the kind of work I've been doing most of my life," Hiram said.

"But you'll also be riding herd on four youngsters who've got a lot to learn. And you'll be reporting everything to me. If you're agreeable to that, follow me down to see the cattle operation and meet the boys. If everything still looks good, we'll talk about your wages, and you can unload your gear in the bunkhouse."

With Hiram following in his Model T, Joseph drove back down the road and took the turnoff to the bunkhouse. With luck, he would end the day with some issues resolved. Francine was engaged and no longer a concern of his. And now, hopefully, he'd found a good man to oversee the cowboys and the cattle.

Annabeth's will was still tucked in his pocket. For now, he would file the will away and keep a distant watch on Annabeth and her children. But what would he do if Silas hurt her again? How could he manage to restrain himself?

Things change. And people change. Hiram's words surfaced in his thoughts. Nothing was settled. Nothing was certain. He could only brace for whatever was to come and try to be ready.

* * *

* * *

Francine clung to Chase as he finished. Then, he rolled off her and lay back in the bed with a murmur of satisfaction. Any minute now, he would become restless, his body stirring, his thoughts leaping ahead to matters that had nothing to do with her. Then he would be up, dressed, and gone. But for these fleeting moments, he was still hers. She had to make use of the time.

Pressing close, she nuzzled his ear. "I have something to tell you, Chase," she said. "Joseph Dollarhide has asked me to marry him. I'm thinking of saying yes."

"What?" His body tensed. "When did all this happen?"

"It's been happening all along. You just haven't been paying attention."

"But why?" he demanded, turning to prop himself on one elbow. "What about us?"

"Us?" She gave a bitter laugh. "This has been fun, Chase. But I want a home. I want a family. And I want the respect that comes from marriage to a good, honorable man. Joseph has offered me all those things. You've never offered me more than *this*. And as much as I enjoy what we do in bed, it isn't enough. I won't settle for being a man's . . . mistress."

His expression reminded Francine of a child who's just been told there's no Santa Claus. "But, damn it, do you love him, Francine?" he demanded.

"Love can be learned," she said.

"But what happens to us?"

"What do you think will happen? If I agree to marry him, that will be the end of us."

He lay back in the bed. "Have you and he . . . ?"

"No. Only you. But I suppose if I agree to marry him, it will happen."

"You're hardly a virgin. Not that it matters to me. But Joseph might question that."

"I'll come up with a good story. And I trust you won't destroy my future by telling him about us. You're a better man than that."

Chase sat up and swung his legs off the bed. "Can't you ask him for more time? I need to think about this."

Her pulse skipped. "Chase, you've never once said you loved me, let alone proposed. Unless that's about to change, I don't have a choice. Joseph wants my decision tomorrow. It's now or never."

Chase gazed down at his bare feet in silence. Francine held her breath, her heart pounding. She had just played her cards in a desperate gamble. If she won, she would become Mrs. Chase Calder, wife to the wealthiest rancher in the state. If she lost, she could only hope that Joseph would still be interested. Otherwise, she would be at her sister's mercy.

"Do you love me, Francine? I've never asked."

She took his hand, interlocking her fingers with his. "Of course I do. That's why I've put up with this arrangement. But I can't go on with things as they are."

"I understand." He drew a long breath. Francine could feel her hopes crashing.

"Well, then," he said, without turning to look at her. "I guess we'd better make things legal, hadn't we?"

Joseph got the news of Francine's engagement when he dropped by Jake's for coffee and apple pie and found her there with Lola.

"Look!" She showed him her diamond engagement ring, moving it this way and that to catch the sunlight that fell through the window blinds. "It belonged to Chase's mother. He was a baby when she died, so he doesn't remember her. But I've seen her picture. She was beautiful."

"And so is the ring. My congratulations. Chase is a lucky man. You can tell him I said so." Joseph was surprised but not displeased. His own heart belonged, however hopelessly, to Annabeth. He could be sincerely glad that Francine had found the happiness she deserved.

"So, have you set a date for the wedding?" he asked.

"Not yet," Francine said. "But it'll be soon. Chase needs everything done and settled before the roundup. Neither of us wants a fancy affair. Just a simple ceremony in the parlor with the judge from Miles City and a few friends."

"Then I don't suppose I'll be included," Joseph teased. "Dang, I was looking forward to kissing the bride."

"You can kiss her at the engagement party I'm throwing for the happy couple next Saturday afternoon." Lola set Joseph's coffee and pie on the bar and added a fork. "It'll be an open house, so anybody can drop by and toast the bride and groom with cider, since we aren't allowed champagne."

Joseph speared a forkful of delicious pie. Why did he have the sense that he was being watched? His gaze scanned the restaurant, the tables and chairs, the shadowed doorway to the kitchen. Nothing. Maybe his imagination was working overtime.

"What about your teaching job, Francine?" he asked. "How can you live on the ranch and teach at the school—especially when you won't be needing the job?"

"That's taken care of," Francine said. "I've already informed the folks on the town council that they'll need to hire a new teacher. Of course, I'll have to move out of the house right away, but I can stay at the Triple C before the wedding."

"So she'll be all settled by the time she says 'I do.' " Lola added. "Won't that be nice?"

It occurred to Joseph that Lola appeared unduly involved in Francine's wedding plans. But on second thought, it seemed fine. Neither of the women had family or close friends in town. It was natural that they'd formed a bond.

Joseph finished his pie and coffee and went outside. He'd come into town on several errands. One of them involved buying new batteries for the flashlights at the ranch. He'd picked up three packs at the Feed and Hardware before stopping by the restaurant. Now, as he climbed into the car, he realized something was wrong. He shook his head as he realized what it was.

He had left three battery packs on the passenger seat. Now there were only two.

An ironic smile tugged at Joseph's mouth as he drove away. Damn fool kid. At least he was all right and probably getting great food. It wasn't worth going after him for a pack of flashlight batteries. Forrest was Lola's problem now. Joseph had more pressing matters on his mind.

With his other business done, he went to pay a call on his aunt. Kristin would be in her town office today. If she wasn't too busy with patients, she might have a few minutes to talk. He needed advice, and she was the only one in a position to give it.

Kristin had remodeled a small house for her medical practice in town. The parlor had become her reception area and the kitchen her surgery. The two bedrooms were used for consultations and patient recovery.

Her appointment schedule was usually full, but today Joseph was in luck. He found her taking a break on the sofa in the reception room, her feet resting on the edge of the coffee table. She looked up as he walked in.

"Joseph, is everything all right?" she asked, reading his concerned expression.

"There's no emergency. But if you have a few minutes to spare, I could use your advice."

"You're in luck." She moved over to make room for him. "My next appointment just cancelled, so we've got a little time. Sit down."

Joseph took his place beside her. "Take a look at this," he said, handing her the will. "Annabeth slipped it to me in town when her husband wasn't looking."

Kristin read the document. "Oh, Joseph," she murmured as she handed it back to him. "Tell me what you're thinking."

"First of all, her husband's a brute. He hits her. I've seen the bruises on her face. She puts up with it because he's threatened to take the children if she tries to leave—or if she has anything to do with me."

"Does he know the boy is yours?"

Joseph nodded. "That only makes things worse. Annabeth claims he's never hurt the children, but I've heard the way he talks about them. If he puts those words into actions, they won't be safe. Neither will she, and she knows it. Why else would she

Francine lay in Chase's arms, watching the play of reflected moonlight on her diamond engagement ring. This would be her last night in the small house attached to the school. Tomorrow she would be moving to the majestic, pillared house known as the Homestead, on the Triple C Ranch.

She had done it. She had won her dream.

And once she was Mrs. Chase Calder, her sister could go to hell.

Chase pulled her closer. She nestled against him. His bare chest was warm, with a dusting of crisp, dark hair. He smelled of sagebrush and leather. "Once you've moved into the house, we'll need to behave ourselves until the wedding," he murmured in her ear. "We won't be alone. There'll be servants. I want them to respect you as a proper lady. If we're fooling around, they'll know it. They'll talk, and the gossip will spread. I won't stand for any whispering behind your back. Understand?"

"Certainly, I do," she said. "But I don't have to like sleeping apart from you. The sooner we can be married the better."

He stretched, moving away from her a little. "Do I really need to go to that engagement party Lola is planning? I've got work to do on Saturday. And people are coming to meet *you*. They already know me."

"Are you asking me to meet them by myself? I need you there, Chase. If I'm to be accepted as your wife, people will need to see us as a couple. Your work can wait."

He sighed, preparing to get up and leave. "All right. Anything for my beautiful bride. I'll send a car and driver tomorrow to pick up your things and take you to the ranch. Ruth, the housekeeper, will be there to meet you and show you around."

"Not you?"

"It's breeding time. I'll be out with the cattle. Get used to it, sweetheart. Ranching is a full-time job. And you're going to be a rancher's wife."

A wealthy rancher's wife, Francine reminded herself.

"I'll be a good rancher's wife," she said. "You'll see."

"I know you will." Chase rolled onto his side and leaned on his elbow, looking down at her. "But there's one thing I want you to promise, cross your heart."

"What's that?" she murmured.

"I want complete trust between us. No lies. Not from me and not from you. Ever. Will you promise me that?"

"Of course, I will," Francine said. "I would never lie to you, Chase. And I hope you'll never lie to me. It would break my poor, crossed, little heart." She traced an *X* on her chest, then pulled his head down to hers for a long kiss.

The night was still dark when Silas drove away from the back of the restaurant. He'd delivered his cargo and stayed for some fun. His wound was still tender, but the romp with Lola on the yellow velvet chaise longue had been worth the pain. Now all he needed to do was drive the truck back to the O'Rourke place, split up the cash with his partners, climb into his Model T, and head home.

Earlier that night, when he carried cargo, he'd driven with the truck's headlights doused. Progress had been slow in the dark, over the rutted back road. But he hadn't wanted to be spotted and caught with a truckload of white lightning. Now the truck was empty, and he was tired. Running with lights would get him back to the O'Rourke place in half the time. And even if he were to get stopped, there was no law against driving an empty truck.

Silas had been driving for about fifteen minutes when he noticed the headlights in his rearview mirror. Emerging out of the darkness, they kept their distance without appearing to gain on him.

He fought the urge to turn off the lights and hit the gas pedal. That behavior had gotten him shot the last time he was followed on this road. He would just mosey along like a man minding his own business. If it was the feds and they stopped him, he would play the part of a married farmer visiting a lady friend in town—not so far from the truth.

Maybe the vehicle wasn't following him at all. But at this hour, whoever it was, they wouldn't be out for a pleasure drive. Maybe somebody else was running moonshine or had a girlfriend in town. If so, they would want nothing to do with him. But what if he was wrong?

As a test, he pressed the gas pedal. As his truck surged ahead, the lights behind him sped up, too, not gaining but staying even. A chill passed through Silas's body. He was being followed.

His hands cramped on the wheel as the memory crashed in on him—the old truck careening off the road, the rattle of submachine gun fire, bullets punching through metal, shattering glass, and ripping into his body, blood spreading like the petals of a flower, then nothing.

Seized by a panic that overrode common sense, he killed the lights and stomped the gas pedal to the floor. He knew this part of the road blindfolded. Just ahead was the cutoff to the O'Rourke Ranch. He swung onto it at full speed, feeling the side wheels leave the ground as he made the turn.

There was no time to check the mirror to see if the other vehicle was coming after him. The truck flew over the ruts and potholes, past broken fences and ghostly, dying pastures. Overshooting the last turn, it smashed through the scrub and came to rest in a grove of scraggly box elders.

The engine sputtered and died. Heart pounding, Silas cocked his pistol and waited in the darkness. He saw no lights, but that didn't mean his pursuers weren't out there, sneaking up behind the truck to attack him.

Seconds stretched into minutes. Little by little, Silas's pulse slowed. He allowed himself to take deep breaths. Cautiously, he rolled down the window and listened to the darkness. He heard only the whisper of the wind and the cry of a night bird—closer than it would be if danger was near.

Shaking with relief, Silas sagged over the wheel. If he wanted to survive, he couldn't keep doing this much longer. This past week, he had taken out a loan on the farm. The money, along with what he'd earned delivering moonshine, was stashed in a burlap gunny sack, buried under a pile of similar sacks in the back of the potato cellar. The place was one where Annabeth would never think to look. He didn't plan to tell her about the money. She'd done nothing to earn it. It was all his. And when the time came, he would take it and run.

He was still of two minds on the question of whether to take her and the kids along. He would make that decision when the time came. But it needed to come soon. No amount of money was worth dying for.

CHAPTER THIRTEEN

THE NEXT SATURDAY MORNING, JOSEPH DROVE DOWN TO THE CATTLE pastures. For the past few days, after delivering Hiram to the bunkhouse, he had purposely stayed away, giving the old cowboy a few days to take charge. Would he find conditions as slipshod as they'd been when Blake was bossing the ranch? That remained to be seen.

There was no one at the bunkhouse to meet him. But when he stepped inside, he found the bunks made, the trash cleared out, the floor swept, and the dirty clothes waiting for the laundry service in a basket by the door.

In the stable, the stalls had been cleaned, the feeders filled with hay, and the floors covered with a layer of clean sawdust from the mill.

Outside, he shaded his eyes and scanned the pastures. At first he saw only distant grazing cattle. After a few minutes, he spotted a rider. He beckoned with his hat. The rider waved and turned his horse to head in. As he came closer, Joseph recognized Andy, the youngest of the cowboys.

As the young man came within speaking distance, Joseph walked out to meet him.

"Boss." Andy touched his hat.

"How's it going with the new man?" Joseph asked.

"Okay, I guess."

"Just okay?"

Andy laughed and shook his head. "Hell, it's like bein' in the army. Out of bed afore sunup, chores done, bunkhouse clean. Stable mucked out. Check every animal and every inch of that damned fence. If you run out of work, find somethin' else that needs doin'. And boy howdy, you don't talk back to the old man, or you'll wish you hadn't."

"It's called a job, Andy. I'm not paying you to sit around when there's work to be done. If you don't like it, you can pack your gear."

Andy sighed and nodded. "Got it, Boss. And the place does look a whole lot better. The old man's even helped me with my ropin'. Says he wants me sharp by roundup time."

"Speaking of Hiram, where is he now?"

"Out in the east pasture with the heifers. You want me to get him?"

"Yes. Now."

Andy kicked his buckskin horse and headed off at a gallop. A few minutes later, Hiram rode up and swung out of the saddle with the ease of a younger man.

"Is everything all right, Boss?" he asked.

"It looks that way. But I'm going to need extra help today. Is everything ready for the new bull?"

"The pasture fence is sound. The heifers are ready, and the older gals are waiting for their turn. When do we pick up the big stud?"

"Today, I hope. But there's been some confusion about the shipping arrangements. The station agent in Miles City can't find the records of when he was loaded. So the bull may or may not come in today. The agent will phone me if he learns anything more. But I have another problem."

"A problem?" Hiram raised an eyebrow in question.

"Not really a problem," Joseph said. "But the woman who owns Jake's is throwing an engagement party for some friends of mine this afternoon. I need to make an appearance to show goodwill."

"So how can I help?"

"The trailer for the bull is hitched behind the truck, ready to go. If the call comes while I'm gone, and the bull's going to be on the afternoon train, I'll need you to drive the rig to the restaurant and pick me up. From there, we can go straight to Miles City."

"So should I wait for the call at the house?"

"If you've got time. Otherwise, Patches can take the call, but then he'll need to get word to you."

"I've got it, Boss. I'll plan to be at the house."

"Fine. I shouldn't be gone more than an hour."

After a stop at the sawmill, Joseph returned to the house in good spirits. He'd been wanting to improve the herd's bloodline; and the new Hereford bull, which he'd bought from a big ranch out of Missoula, was the offspring of champions. The cost for such an animal was five times what his father would have paid. But Joseph was in charge now, and he wanted the ranch to be more than a moneymaker. He wanted quality. If he was going to raise Dollarhide cattle, they would be the best.

After a light lunch, he left Hiram to wait for the phone call and set out for Jake's. By the time he arrived, the parking lot was crowded with vehicles. People were going in and out of the door. Francine had kept to herself and wasn't well-known in the town, but everybody knew Chase Calder and wanted to meet his future bride.

Joseph saw an opening and slipped inside. He hadn't been keen on coming to the open house. But it was a gesture of goodwill to the couple. And since people knew he'd been courting Francine, staying away would have given the impression that he was sulking.

Francine and Chase were greeting guests at the end of the bar. Radiant in the apricot silk gown she'd worn at the dance, Francine was basking in the role of the future Mrs. Calder—smiling, shaking hands, repeating the names of people who appeared important enough to be remembered. Chase looked as if he wanted to be somewhere else, but he was doing his best to be gracious.

Joseph congratulated them both and moved on. Plates of spice cake with brown sugar icing and glasses of cider were set out on a buffet table. Joseph had picked up a glass and taken a sip when Hiram walked in through the open door. Joseph caught his attention and beckoned him over.

"We got the phone call," Hiram said. "The bull's on the 3:15. If we're not there before the train pulls out, he'll be unloaded into one of the stock pens. The rig's outside, ready to go." He eyed the plates of cake arranged on the buffet table. "My, but that cake does look good."

"Help yourself," Joseph said, glancing at his watch. "We've got a few minutes to spare, enough time for you to enjoy a piece of cake and some cider."

"Don't mind if I do." Hiram selected a plate of cake and a fork. "I suppose, since I'm here, I should congratulate the happy couple. Could you point them out for me?"

"Over there, by the far end of the bar," Joseph said. "You've doubtless heard of the Triple C Ranch. That man is Chase Calder. He owns it. And his lady—"

The words broke off as Joseph saw the frozen expression on Hiram's face. He was staring at Francine as she stood next to Chase.

"Is something wrong?" Joseph asked.

"Lord help me," Hiram muttered. "I know her."

He set the plate of cake back on the table. Francine had clearly seen him. Her eyes widened. Her smile vanished. She turned swiftly away.

"Come outside with me," Hiram said in a low voice. "I need to tell you something, and I don't want to do it in here."

Joseph followed Hiram outside. They stepped off the porch and moved around the corner of the restaurant.

"You say you know her?" Joseph asked.

"From St. Joseph. A bunch of us cowboys would go into town after we got paid. There was a dance hall there—fancy front for a whorehouse. High prices, but the girls were young, pretty, and clean."

"And she was there?"

"She went by Sally. Prettiest one of all."

Joseph shook his head in shocked disbelief. "You're sure?"

"Hell, I paid top dollar for her services a couple of times. With that little mole by her mouth and some other things I won't even mention, I'd know her anywhere. Do you think her intended knows?"

"I'll bet the bank he doesn't," Joseph said. "Damn, I've got to tell him. Chase is no friend of mine, but he doesn't deserve this."

"Please." Lola stepped around the corner of the building, her black mantilla shadowing her ravaged face. Her hand seized Joseph's arm, the fingers gripping like claws. "Can't you let the past be the past?" she pleaded. "I brought my sister here to give her a chance at a new life. Now she's found love. Please don't ruin her happiness."

"So she's your sister." Joseph loosened her grip and lifted away her hand. "At least now I understand why you care so much. But you're talking to the wrong man, Lola. The only one who can decide whether to put Francine's past aside is Chase. He needs to be told."

"Please! I'll pay you—both of you—to keep the secret. How much do you want?"

Joseph glanced at Hiram before he spoke. "What good would that do, Lola? One man's already recognized her. There are bound to be more. You can't buy all of them."

Lola glared up at Joseph. "Damn you to hell, Joseph Dollarhide," she muttered, defeated.

"Nobody wants to make a scene," Joseph said. "Do you want to send Chase out here, or do I have to get him myself?"

"I'll send him out." Lola pivoted and went back into the restaurant.

"I'll be in the truck," Hiram said. "Having to look at me won't make it any easier on the man."

Chase stepped outside moments later. "Lola says something's wrong," he said. "Tell me."

Joseph knew better than to be gentle with the news. Chase took it without flinching. He was a proud man. There was no other way. But Joseph could see the subtle signs—a glint in his eye, the twinge of a muscle in his cheek. The truth had hit him hard.

Had he loved Francine, or was it his pride that was crushed? Either way, Joseph didn't relish seeing his rival brought low. Chase wasn't a man to give his heart easily. He deserved better.

"I'm sorry, Chase, but you needed to be told," Joseph said.

"Yes. You'll understand why I'm not thanking you. I'll take it from here." His voice, like his face, was expressionless.

Having nothing more to say, Joseph climbed into the truck, started the engine, and headed for Miles City to pick up the new bull.

"Tough break for a man," Hiram said. "How did he take it?"

"About like I expected," Joseph said. "Like a Calder."

One of the hardest things Francine had ever done was to stand next to Chase while the party played out—smiling and chatting with guests, knowing all the while that he must hate her.

She'd known she was in trouble when that older cowboy had stepped through the door. She couldn't recall his name, but she'd remembered him as a customer who'd treated her well and given her generous tips. When he'd caught her eye and immediately stepped outside, she'd known that he remembered her as well.

Chase hadn't said a word to her when he came back inside. But his coldness told the story. He knew. He knew everything. And when the last guest had gone, she would face the storm.

If this were a fairy tale, he would forgive her. They would marry and live happily ever after. But this was no fairy tale. And Chase Calder wasn't a forgiving man.

Lola had stayed behind the scenes during the open house. But once the party was over, she came out to close the front door and direct the kitchen staff at clearing out the trash, sweeping the floor, and rearranging the tables for the dinner meal. She averted her gaze from Chase and Francine. If her own guilt wasn't already known, it soon would be.

It was Chase who broke the awkward silence as he took Francine's arm. "Let's go," he said in an icy voice.

He walked her out to his Packard and held the door for her. "Where are we going?" she dared to ask as they drove out of the parking lot.

"We're going back to the Homestead," he said. "You'll have a few minutes to pack your things. Then I'll have one of my men drive you to Miles City. He'll give you enough money for a hotel room and buy you a train ticket to wherever you want to go. After that, I never want to hear from you again."

Her eyes flooded with tears. "Chase, I can't change my past and what I did to survive. But I fell in love with you. That part was—and is—real."

"Then you should have told me the truth. It's not your past that I can't forgive. It's the fact that you lied about it—lied when you swore you wouldn't. And you planned to hide the truth forever—or at least until it was too late for me to change my mind." He cast her a stony glance. "Before I forget, give me my mother's ring. There's no more reason for you to wear it."

Anger rising, she twisted the ring off her finger and thrust it toward him. He took it from her and dropped it into his vest pocket.

Francine settled back in her seat, her arms folded across her chest. She was through talking. And she was finished with this podunk town, its dowdy, backward women, and its tobacco-chewing, manure-smelling cowboys. While she still had her youth, her looks, and her talent for charming men, she would move on and move up. San Francisco sounded like a good idea. She could change her name, dye her hair, find herself a rich husband, and settle down to living the good life.

As for her sister, Lucy—or Lola, as she called herself now—she had made her own bed. For all Francine cared, the woman could stay in Blue Moon and rot.

Joseph stood by the pasture fence, watching Major, the new bull, prove that he was worth every dollar Joseph had paid for him. He wasn't as big as some Hereford studs, but he was a perfect animal—solid, muscular, and vigorous. And he loved the ladies. His final measure would be taken in the calves he sired. But so far, Joseph had every reason to be pleased.

"He knows his job, I'll say that for him," Hiram commented with a grin.

"Keep an eye on him," Joseph said. "Have the boys separate him if there's a problem. I'll be at the house if you need me."

He drove back up the bluff, planning to spend a couple of hours in the office, paying bills and updating the ranch books. Leaving the car in the front yard, he walked into a silent house. Even Patches was gone, probably buying groceries in town.

Most of the time, Joseph didn't mind the stillness. Even with his family around, he'd been a loner, taking refuge in books and horses. Now, in the cool shadows of the old log house, he felt a deep emptiness. He passed into the parlor, the empty rocking chair still in its place by the hearth. Joseph could picture his mother there, rocking and humming to the click of her knitting needles. The novel his sister had been reading lay on a side table, bookmarked where she'd left it to ride to town with her parents. After the accident, Blake had refused to let these things be moved. For now, Joseph had left them alone.

His grandfather's portrait gazed down at him from the wall, his stern presence as real as the memory of those so recently passed. What would the old man say if his spirit could speak? If he let his thoughts flow, Joseph could almost imagine hearing Joe Dollarhide's stentorian voice.

The ranch is yours now, Joseph. But you can't keep it on your own. Hard times are coming, with enemies closing in. If you want to survive, you're going to need allies. You're going to need strong family on your side.

Joseph could feel his resistance mounting. He had family—two aunts, their husbands, and their children, who would stand with him if trouble came.

He sensed what the next words would be. But he couldn't stop what the voice in his thoughts was telling him.

I had two sons, Joseph. Two, not one. It's time to make the family whole again.

Joseph had been a boy of fourteen when Mason had gone to prison. Hurt and betrayed by the man he'd idolized, Joseph had cut off all connections with his natural father. Even after Mason had served his sentence and settled into a respectable new life on his ranch, Joseph had kept his distance, refusing to forgive him.

At Blake's grave, Mason had extended the hand of friendship. Still, Joseph was hesitant to trust him. Now he forced himself to ask what was holding him back. Was it fear? Or could it be his own self-righteous pride?

Joseph had made mistakes of his own. He thought of Annabeth and Lucas, sentenced to life with a brutal man. And he remembered the reckless act that had cost a sheriff the use of his legs. Jake, who was married to Joseph's aunt Britta, had never held the tragedy against him. But Joseph would always blame himself. How could he presume to judge another man?

It was time.

After letting Hiram know that he was leaving, Joseph drove to the main road and turned south toward the Hollister Ranch. Mason, the son of Joe Dollarhide's first wife, Amelia, had inherited the ranch from his late mother. Modest in size, it was one of the choicest parcels in the county, its rolling green hills blessed with virgin soil and abundant well water, its cattle fat and contented.

He remembered going there for the first time in his early teens, crawling under the thorny hedge with his friends, Buck and Culley, to be met by a terrifying figure of a woman with a whip in her hands and two massive dogs at her side.

The woman and her dogs would be gone now. But as he drove the familiar road, Joseph felt a shadow of the same trepidation. Maybe he should have telephoned before leaving the house—the operator would have given him the number. But it was too late for that now. Hating Mason Dollarhide had become a habit over the years. The prospect of change was daunting. But it was time to face the emotions that had held him back.

The stately house, one of the few brick homes in the timber-rich county, was much as he remembered it. But the rusted wrought iron gate had been replaced, and the yard was well tended. Sunlight gleamed on the polished leaded windows.

Joseph left the car at the side of the road, opened the gate, and strode up the walk to the porch. After a beat of hesitation, he knocked on the door. He heard a light patter of footsteps before the door swung open.

"Joseph! It's really you!" The khaki-clad woman in the doorway was petite, pretty, and vaguely familiar. Her auburn hair was tied back with a scarf. One hand held a feather duster. "You look puzzled," she said, smiling. "Don't you remember me? My father gave you an airplane ride. I'm Ruby, Mason's wife."

Joseph's memory cleared. "Sure, I remember you. I had a free ticket. You took it and helped me strap on my helmet. I knew Mason was married, but I had no idea it was to you."

"Yes, there's a long story behind that. But I suppose you've come to see Mason. He's been so hopeful that you would." She laid the feather duster on the arm of a chair, the silence becoming awkward.

"You were so excited about flying," she said. "Did you ever become a pilot?"

"No. At the time it was all I wanted to do. But my father had other ideas. And now I've got a ranch to run," Joseph said.

"Yes, I know. I was sorry about your father and that I couldn't make it to the service."

"I understood. Mason explained that your little girl was sick. I hope she's doing better."

"Grace is fine now. She's out in the stable, watching her father fix a horse's loose shoe. Follow me. I'll take you to him."

She led Joseph around the house and down the slope of the yard. As the barn and stable came into sight, Joseph felt a stab of memory—the dark night, the canvas-covered trucks, and the crates of Canadian whiskey that he and his friends had unloaded for more money than they'd ever seen in their lives. But the past was the past. It was time to let it go.

As they approached the stable, he could hear the faint, metallic ping of a hammer. Upon entering, he saw Mason bent over the raised hoof of a big bay horse, hammering a shoe into place. A few more blows finished the job. He released the hoof, straightened, and turned around. Only then did he see Joseph.

"Is everything all right?" He masked his surprise.

"Everything's fine. You invited me over. I hope this isn't a bad time."

"It's a good time." Mason extended his hand. Joseph accepted the handshake, his gaze meeting the green eyes that were so like his own. This man was his father. But Joseph would always be the son of Blake Dollarhide.

"Daddy, who is this man?" The child tugged at Mason's free hand. She was a lively little thing with coppery curls and a spill of freckles across her nose. Her eyes were as green as Joseph's.

Good Lord, she's my little sister. Joseph's knees weakened as the realization struck him. The child looked nothing like a Dollarhide. She appeared to be made in the image of Mason's red-headed, strong-willed mother, Amelia Hollister. The child would be Lucas's aunt. But why was he wasting thoughts on his disconnected kin? He had no claim on them.

"Who is he, Daddy?" the little girl demanded again.

Mason gave her a smile. "This is Joseph, Grace. He's a friend who's come to visit us. Say hello to him."

"Hello." With no trace of shyness, Grace held out her small hand.

"Hello, Grace." Emotions surged in Joseph as his palm enclosed her fingers. Maybe he should have stayed away. He wasn't prepared for what he was feeling.

His father. His stepmother. His half-sister. Family.

"Let's go back to the house, Grace." Ruby beckoned her daughter to her side. "You can help make some lemonade to go with the cookies we baked this morning."

Hand in hand, the two of them headed up the path, Grace dancing with each step. Joseph watched them go. "I don't have to tell you who she reminds me of," he said to Mason.

"My mother was a hellion," Mason said. "She took over the ranch when her father died and ran it for years. She even outfoxed both Benteen Calder and Joe Dollarhide to buy the parcel that almost doubled the ranch's size. Time will tell whether Grace inherited her determination as well as her looks." Mason released the horse and turned it into the paddock. "Let's walk," he said.

Joseph fell into step beside him, their strides matching as they walked along the paddock fence. The silence between them was awkward but not as uncomfortable as Joseph had feared it might be.

"You've got the ranch looking good," Joseph said.

"Thanks. My mother had to let things go in her later years, when I should have been here for her. Getting the place back into shape has taken a lot of work, as much for Ruby as for me.

Mason paused to watch a pair of leggy spring colts romp across the paddock. "I've been hoping you'd come, and I couldn't be more pleased to see you. But what made you choose today? Is something going on?"

"Not really. It was just a day when the house felt too big and empty. Nobody to talk to except my grandpa's picture." Joseph gazed out across the pastures to the distant hills. "This might sound strange to you, but I had a premonition that there could be hard times ahead. If they come, I don't want to face them alone. We'll be stronger as one family—you, me, Kristin, and our people. Does that sound crazy to you?"

Mason shook his head. "When I was in prison, I did a lot of reading—newspapers, magazines, books on history and economics. I kept it up after I got back here, and I've figured out some things. It's like the country's on this carnival wheel, going faster and faster. Stocks climbing, more and more people investing, banks overextending credit, surplus grain that nobody wants . . . It's complicated as hell, but if that wheel keeps spinning, things are going to start flying off. Pretty soon, the country will be in the worst depression you ever saw—banks closing, people losing their savings and jobs. It won't be a pretty situation, not even for you and me, with nobody buying beef or lumber."

"You really think it'll be that bad?"

"We can always hope it won't be. But I'd say if you've got money in the stock market or even the bank, don't wait too long to get it out. And yes, you're right about the family needing to stick together. Right now, I'm just grateful to have this ranch, a good woman by my side, and a daughter who makes me smile. After the things I've done, it's more than I deserve."

"I have a son," Joseph said.

Mason didn't reply. He began walking again. Joseph fell into step.

"I was nineteen when I got his mother pregnant. She married another man without telling me. I just found out. The boy's name is Lucas."

Mason cleared his throat. "You didn't ask me for advice. But leaving your mother to marry Blake was the only good thing I ever did for you. My brother was a far better father than I would have been. And you turned out fine. All you can do is hope the same for your boy. You've got no claim on him."

"That's the problem," Joseph said. "Annabeth's husband is a brute. They're dirt poor, he hits her, and he's liable to get arrested any day for moonshining. She won't leave him because he's threatened to take her children away."

"Children?"

"Lucas and a little girl. They're her world. He doesn't care about them—he even calls Lucas a bastard—but he uses them to control her."

Mason shook his head. "It sounds like you're already involved with them."

"I didn't plan it that way, but yes. She's even given me a handwritten will, asking that I take her children if anything happens to her. It's almost as if she's afraid he's going to kill her."

Mason stopped walking and turned to fix Joseph with a piercing look. "Listen to me and listen good. Your situation has all the elements of a tragedy in the making. Take my word for it, Joseph. Give the will to a lawyer. Then back off as far and as fast as you can. I know you care about the woman and your boy. But there's nothing you can do without making things more difficult for them.

"If Annabeth decides to leave her marriage, that's on her. But you need to walk away now. If you continue to meddle, I can almost guarantee you one thing. Somebody is going to die."

CHAPTER FOURTEEN

SILAS'S CLOSE ENCOUNTER ON THE ROAD HAD LEFT HIM SHAKEN. He'd begun to dread the nighttime runs, with the constant fear of headlights appearing in his rearview mirror. Only the lure of money—and the reward of his trysts with Lola—kept him climbing behind the wheel of the truck every few nights.

Still, the urge to take the cash from its hiding place in the potato cellar and leave Montana for a new life was a burning hunger in his gut. To find a new place that was warm like California or Mexico, to take a new name, live high, and have all the women he wanted—that dream was the only thing that made his miserable life worth living.

How much money would be enough? Silas asked himself that question as he drove toward the O'Rourke place, where the loaded truck would be waiting. The loan he'd taken on the farm, which he never planned to repay, had almost doubled what he'd put aside from the moonshine runs. He wasn't rich, but he had enough to get him where he wanted to go, especially if he didn't take Annabeth and the brats along.

Tonight's run should pay decently. After that, he would arrange for one more. Once it was scheduled, he planned to take his money out of the hiding place, pick up that last run of moonshine, and hit the road. When he didn't show up, his partners and his wife would assume he'd been hijacked and killed. No one would bother to look for the vehicle or his body.

There were a few details left to work out, but the plan was a good one. Once it was carried out, he'd be free.

As he drove through the broken gate, Silas could tell that something was wrong. The first thing he noticed was that the truck, which should have been loaded and waiting, was gone.

His pulse lurched into a gallop as he pulled into the shadow of the trees, parked, and climbed out of the car. The smart course of action would have been to leave at once. But he needed to know what was going on.

Heart in his throat, he crept up the hill. The way was dark, with no lantern light from the cave to guide him. He could hear nothing but the familiar sounds of night. But he could smell the smoky aroma of the fire and the fruity stench of fermenting mash. As he climbed, he steeled himself for what he would find.

Seeing no sign of movement, Silas stepped into the clearing. In the scant light from the waning moon and the glowing coals of the fire, he could make out the debris scattered on the ground—broken glass, crushed copper vessels and copper tubing, and shattered wooden crates. There was more of the same in the mouth of the cave. The still had been totally and wantonly destroyed.

Had the feds made a move on the place? Busting up a still was something they would do. But where were Buck and Culley? Had they been arrested and taken away?

Silas heard an agonized groan from the underbrush a few yards up the slope. He followed the sound.

Concealed by a clump of sage, Culley lay with his legs curled against his belly. His face was a mass of bloodied bruises. His nose was partly flattened, and his purpled eyes were swollen almost shut. One arm lay at a jutting angle.

Silas leaned over his partner. "Who did this, Culley?" he demanded. "Was it the feds?"

Culley moved his head to indicate no. So it had been the mob, probably the same ones who'd shot Silas earlier and stolen his cargo.

Culley's lips moved. His words emerged as a hoarse whisper. "Get me to the house."

"Can you walk?"

"Don't know."

Silas worked his arms under Culley's body. Culley was a small man, but so broken that getting him upright was like lifting a sack of loose kindling. He bit back cries of pain. The breath whistled through his teeth as Silas supported him down the hill to the dilapidated house, inside through the back door, and onto the rumpled bed. The stained china pitcher on the kitchen sink had likely seen better days. Silas filled it with water and gave him a drink. Then, using two straight kindling sticks and a ragged shirt he found, Silas set the broken arm and fashioned a splint.

White with pain beneath his bruises, the tough little man endured Silas's none too gentle doctoring. Some probing revealed two broken ribs, which Silas wrapped before he sponged the blood from Culley's face. Except for some ugly bruises, his legs appeared sound. But he could have internal injuries—like a punctured lung or a ruptured spleen. Silas knew of a man who'd been kicked by a horse and died from something like that. There was still a chance Culley wouldn't survive.

Culley drank a little more water. His breathing had eased. He appeared to be more comfortable. Silas pulled a chair close to the bed and sat down.

"Can you tell me what happened, Culley?" he asked.

Culley drew a painful breath. "Buck and me was loadin' the truck when they just showed up. They tried to make me tell them where my money was. I wouldn't, so they beat me. I crawled away while they was bustin' up the still or I'd most likely be dead."

"What happened to Buck?"

"I guess he lit out. You know Buck. He never had much stomach for a fight." He released a long breath. "Will you stay with me a while, Silas?"

"Sure." Silas was itching to leave, but Culley had mentioned something about money. His share from the moonshine would be equal to Silas's. If Culley were to die and that money could be found, it would double what Silas had put away. The least he could do was keep watch for a while.

"There's some laudanum in the cabinet over the sink," Culley said. "It's been there since before my ma passed, so it might not be any good. But maybe you could find it for me."

Silas found the small brown glass bottle at the back of a cluttered shelf. There was a finger of liquid in the bottom. He tipped it to Culley's mouth, giving him all of it.

"Thanks..." Culley closed his eyes. His breathing was shallow, his sleep broken by restless muttering. Would he rally or die? Silas thought of the money. He sat down again to wait.

An hour passed, then another. Culley was still sleeping, but his breathing was deeper and more regular. He'd stopped thrashing and appeared to be resting peacefully. Maybe he wasn't going to die after all. Silas got up and did some casual looking. The money wasn't in the cupboard or under the bed. Maybe it was hidden in the mattress. But he couldn't look there without waking Culley up.

Frustrated, he sat down to think. Silas had never killed a man. But when he thought of the money, he was tempted. All he would have to do was press a pillow over Culley's face for a minute or two. Then he'd be free to search the house, take the money, and leave.

Culley groaned in his sleep. It was now or never. Silas rose to his feet, flexed his hands, and took a deep breath, working up his courage.

"Hey, is anybody here?" A familiar voice called from the kitchen door.

Silas felt the breath leave his chest as Buck walked into the room. Culley opened his eyes. "Damn you, Buck, where'd you run off to?"

"There was nothing I could do, partner," Buck said. "But I'm here now. Just glad you're alive."

"I found him up the slope, half dead, no thanks to you," Silas said. "The still's nothing but trash, and the truck's gone. I'd say we're out of business for now. As long as you're here, maybe you can play nursemaid for a while. I need to get home to my family."

"Sure, Silas," Buck said. "Honest, there was nothing we could've done. Those bastards showed up out of nowhere, like they had a map. There were four of them. They had guns and sledgehammers."

Silas remembered the recent night when he'd been followed. The thugs could have marked the road he'd taken to get away. But he wasn't about to mention that.

"I'm going," he said, and walked out the door to his car. It was a shame about the money, but at least Buck hadn't caught him putting Culley out of his misery.

All the way home, he thought about the stacks of bills he'd stashed in the potato cellar. He'd lost track of the amount he'd stuffed into the gunny sack. He could plan his getaway better if he knew exactly how much cash was there. It was still dark out. His family would be fast asleep. Counting the money shouldn't take more than a few minutes.

As he approached the house, he turned off the headlights, then parked on the far side of the barnyard so Annabeth wouldn't know he'd come home. The potato cellar, dug in a wide trench and covered by a hill of earth supported by boards, was about twenty yards from the house. The heavy wooden door, installed at an angle over the entrance, had to be lifted on the open side and laid back on its hinges.

After a glance toward the house to make sure no one was up, he turned on the flashlight he kept in the car, unlatched the door, and hefted it open. The cellar was less than a third full, and the potatoes that remained were beginning to sprout. They would need to be thrown out before the next harvest—which wasn't his worry anymore.

The empty sacks were piled four feet high in the back of the cellar. Kneeling, Silas worked the one with the money out from the bottom of the pile, untied the knotted top, and spread the bills on the dirt floor. He wouldn't need an exact count, just a rough idea of how much there was.

After sorting the bills into hundreds, twenties, tens, and a few smaller dominations, he began a quick count. As the numbers grew, Silas began to sweat. With the loan on the farm thrown in, he had almost $60,000—not a fortune, but more money than he'd ever dreamed of having in his life. It would be more than enough to get him off to a new start.

He would leave tomorrow night if he could get away. Annabeth and her brats would have to fend for themselves.

Suddenly, he felt exhausted. After replacing the money in the sack, he knotted the top and shoved his treasure back under the pile, where it would be waiting for him tomorrow night.

Dragging his feet, he tossed the flashlight into the car and shuffled across the yard into the house. Annabeth was still in bed. If she'd heard or seen anything, she would know better than to ask. For now, what he craved most was sleep.

Lola sat at a table in the speakeasy, sipping a glass of homemade burgundy and waiting for the sound of Silas's truck. The boy had cleaned up the room and gone to his bed in the storage room off the kitchen. She was alone in the basement now.

Tonight she was tired. Her head ached. Her feet were swollen in their new, red pumps. Worse, she was almost out of moonshine whiskey for tomorrow night. Business was booming. But she couldn't keep her customers happy if she didn't have anything to serve them. If Silas didn't come through with a shipment tonight, there was going to be trouble.

Her spirits rose as she heard the familiar rumble of the truck backing up to the door. She stood on her swollen feet, tottered to the door, and raised the bar on the inside. The door swung open.

Two strangers in suits stood before her. They weren't pointing guns at her, but she could see the bulge of holstered pistols beneath their jackets.

Lola was quaking inside. But she stood her ground, knowing she couldn't show fear. "Who the hell are you two?" she demanded.

The shorter of the pair, a pudgy fellow with a mean-looking face, grinned. "We're your new partners, Miss De Marco. Would you be so kind as to invite us in?"

Not having a choice, she stepped out of the way. The two men strolled inside, surveying the tables and the makeshift bar.

Through the open doorway, Lola could see the canvas-covered truck outside—the same truck Silas had used for his deliveries. With her sister's prospect of a Calder marriage gone, this restaurant and the speakeasy were all the prospects she had. If she wanted to keep them, she needed to take a stand.

"What's going on? Where's my driver? How did you get my truck?" Lola expected to be shot any minute, but the pudgy stranger smiled again.

"Your old partners are out of business. Oh, they're alive. Don't worry your pretty head about that. But they won't be making any more product for you to sell. You'll be buying from us. The first truckload is outside. Once we've made a new contract, I'll have our driver unload it."

Lola gave him a bold look and bluffed for all she was worth. "I had a good deal going with those partners," she said. "Fifty percent discount on the product and a one-third share of the net. And the truck is mine. If you want my business, mister, sit down and make me an offer. If it sounds fair, I'll think about it."

Lucas was never allowed to go into the potato cellar. But this morning, his father was snoring behind the closed bedroom door. His mother was on the front porch, doing her mending in the rocker, with Ellie and the dog for company. He was alone in the backyard.

And for the first time in his young memory, he saw that the heavy cellar door had been left open.

His first thought was that the situation could be dangerous and he should run and tell his mother. She was strong enough to pick the door up by its edge and swing it safely shut. But the shadowy space beyond the opening beckoned him like a treasure cave in an explorer's dream.

Lucas took a few steps closer, imagining what the forbidden place might hold. Could it be a treasure? A dangerous animal? A skeleton? Edging forward now, he could see partway inside. What he saw was mostly potatoes sprouting hairy, white roots that reached up like ghostly fingers into the dim light.

But there was nothing scary about potatoes. Lucas had watched his mother peel off their brown skins. He ate them almost every day. Emboldened, he stepped through the doorway and into the pit. As the shadows closed around him, the odors of rot and damp earth penetrated his senses. His eyes, adjusting to the dim light, could make out a pile of empty sacks in the darkness at the back of the pit. Aside from that, there was just potatoes. No surprise at all.

Mildly disappointed, Lucas turned to leave. He had taken a few steps when he heard an ominous-sounding buzz at his feet. He jumped back in time to avoid the rattlesnake that had been coiled where he was about to step.

Lucas's mother had taught him about rattlesnakes, and he knew enough to stay clear of them. But this one was in a dangerous place. He had heard the warning and jumped away. But the snake could still bite anyone who came into the pit—his father, his mother, or Ellie if she happened to wander in. Even Freckles could get curious and be bitten.

The snake, of medium size, was still coiled where he'd found it. He could go and tell his mother, but he'd likely get a scolding, and meanwhile, the snake could go back into hiding. Maybe he could kill the snake himself. The more he thought about that idea, the more adventurous it sounded.

He looked around for a weapon, something like a shovel or even a big stick. There was nothing within reach but potatoes. Lucas selected the biggest potato in sight, took aim, and lobbed it at the snake.

The throw missed, but it startled the snake enough to send it slithering toward the dark end of the pit. Lucas had raised his arm to throw another potato when the reptile vanished beneath the pile of gunny sacks.

Lucas lowered his arm and let the potato drop to the ground. For a long moment, he stood at a safe distance, thinking. The snake was as dangerous as ever, but moving the sacks could get him bitten. Telling his mother would only get him into trouble. But he couldn't just leave the creature to crawl out and bite somebody.

Suddenly, he had an idea.

Breaking into a sprint, he raced out of the pit and into the kitchen. His mother was still outside on the porch, but he knew where she kept the box of matches she used to light the stove. With a chair slid against the counter, he climbed up, opened the cupboard, and took several matches out of the box.

Clutching the matches and a stick of kindling from the woodpile, he ran back to the potato pit.

Was the snake still there? Lucas tossed a small potato at the pile of sacks and saw a slight movement. Still keeping his distance, he struck a match on a rock and held it to the kindling as he'd seen his parents do. It took several tries to get the fire to catch, but finally, the end of the stick began to smolder, then to burn.

His plan was a daring one. Either the snake would die in the fire or it would be driven out where he could kill it.

With the burning stick held in front of him, he walked closer to the pile, reached out, and touched the flame to one of the sacks. The dry, frayed burlap caught fire at once and began to blaze. Lucas glimpsed a flicker of movement as the snake streaked out from under the pile and disappeared among the potatoes. The creature was too fast for him. And now the fire was getting bigger.

He backed off as sparks popped and flew from the burning fabric. Too late, Lucas realized that he should have given his plan more thought. Now he was in big trouble.

With the crackling blaze growing by the second, he wheeled and ran for his life.

Annabeth had finished darning two of Silas's socks and had started on a third when she smelled smoke. Standing, she could see a dark trail billowing skyward from the far corner of the yard. Her first thought was of Lucas. He'd gone around there to play.

"Get in the house, Ellie!" She shooed the little girl inside. "Sit down and stay put till I come back."

With the dog at her heels, she raced around the house and came to a dead stop. Her knees went liquid, threatening to give way beneath her.

Clouds of smoke poured from the opening of the potato cellar. Through the sooty haze, Annabeth glimpsed tongues of leaping flame.

There was no sign of Lucas.

"Lucas!" The name ripped from her throat. With no thought for herself, she raced toward the cellar. If her boy was in there, she would fight through walls of fire to reach him.

Smoke swam around her as she neared the entrance, stinging her eyes and throat. A spark fell on her dress, burning a small hole. Another spark fell on her arm. Ignoring the pain and the heat that singed her hair, she pushed forward.

Now, through the roiling smoke, she could see the blaze at the far end of the pit where the empty sacks had been piled. The potatoes wouldn't burn much, but the fire had climbed partway up the timbers that braced the low roof. If it burned far enough, the supports would weaken. The whole structure would cave in. It could happen anytime.

An expanse of dirt floor lay between Annabeth and the fire. That was where Lucas would likely be. Maybe he'd been overcome by smoke. Covering her nose and mouth with her apron, she crouched low, where the air was safest. Now she could see the floor, all the way to the fire. She could see small footprints in the soft dirt. She could even see several dropped, burnt matches. Her heart sank as she guessed what the boy might have done. But she couldn't see Lucas anywhere. Maybe he'd gotten out.

She coughed hard, feeling the smoke burn all the way to her lungs. She had to get out now or she would die in there. But if there was any chance that she'd be leaving her son, she would never forgive herself.

From somewhere outside, the dog was barking. Maybe he'd found Lucas. With a silent prayer, Annabeth turned and stumbled out of the cellar.

The air was a life-giving blast of freshness. Coughing, she gulped it into her lungs. As her eyes adjusted to the blinding sunlight, she saw the brown-and-white dog outside the barn. He was running back and forth as he barked, as if trying to get her attention.

She hurried toward him. When he saw her coming, the scruffy collie mix raced into the barn. She found him pawing and whining at the closed gate of an empty stall where hay and feed were stored.

"Lucas, are you there?" She paused, hushing the dog and straining to hear. At first there was only the creak of old wood and the chirp of sparrows nesting on a roof beam. Then she heard it through the stall gate—the muffled sound of sobbing.

She flung open the gate and strode inside. Lucas was huddled behind a stack of hay bales. His face, as he looked up at her, was streaked with crusted tears. "I'm sorry, Mama," he said in a small voice. "I didn't mean to do it."

Overcome, Annabeth knelt, caught him in her arms, and crushed him against her. "You could have died," she muttered against his damp hair. "Don't you ever, ever do anything like that again! Promise."

"I promise. Please don't be mad." Lucas was still crying.

"Just tell me what happened," Annabeth said. "Everything. The whole truth."

The story spooled out between bouts of sobbing—the open cellar, the snake, the matches, and the fire. It sounded almost too far-fetched for Annabeth to believe. But her son's tears told her it was true.

"So, tell me what you did wrong, Lucas," she said. "I need to know you understand."

Lucas wiped his nose on his sleeve. "I wasn't supposed to go in the potato cellar, but I did."

"And what else?"

"I stole the matches, and I started the fire. I really didn't mean to, Mama. I only wanted to kill the snake so it wouldn't bite you or Ellie or Dad." He gasped. "Oh, no! Dad is going to be so mad at me!"

Standing, Annabeth took his hand. "Let's go back to the house.

We mustn't leave Ellie alone too long. We'll talk more about this later."

Lucas fell into step beside her. "I'm in trouble, aren't I?"

"Yes," Annabeth said, "you certainly are. And you can expect to be punished. But that doesn't mean we don't love you."

As they crossed the yard with the dog at their heels, Annabeth tried to imagine how her husband would react when he woke up. Silas had abandoned all hope of this year's potato crop, so the cellar shouldn't be needed. Maybe he would shrug off Lucas's misadventure or even find it amusing. But he was just as likely to be angry. And an angry Silas was as unpredictable as a wild boar. Silas was Silas. And Annabeth was worried—more than worried. She was terrified for her son.

When Annabeth had returned to the house with Lucas, she had found Silas still asleep. He was bound to wake up soon and discover what had happened outside, but the slight delay had given her time to come up with a plan.

Now, as she stood at the kitchen counter, cutting up a hunk of beef for stew, she could hear him stirring in the bedroom. Willing herself to stay calm, she shooed the children to their room. "Don't come out until you're called, no matter what you hear," she warned them.

After closing the door, she returned to the kitchen and continued her work as if nothing had happened. Glancing out the kitchen window, she could see that the fire was shooting flames through the roof of the pit. The far end had partially caved in.

From the bedroom she shared with Silas, she could hear something hard crashing against the wall, followed by the sounds of shattering glass and screamed curses. Annabeth took a deep breath and kept on preparing the stew she meant to simmer for supper.

Moments later, Silas came pounding down the hallway and burst into the kitchen. He was hurriedly dressed, his shirt unbuttoned and his belt buckle hanging loose from the waist of his trousers. His bootlaces trailed on the floor. His hair stood wildly on end. His expression could only be described as murderous.

Annabeth put down the knife and turned toward him and spoke in a quiet voice. "I can see you're upset, Silas. But I swear, it was an accident. I needed a few good potatoes for the stew, some that hadn't sprouted. Since the door was already open, I took a candle and went down into the pit to look for them. There was a snake. It startled me. I dropped the candle on the stacks. They started to burn . . ."

She gestured toward the charred spots on her dress and arms. "I tried to put it out, but . . ." Annabeth could sense the fury building in him. She forced herself to smile. "At least with the potato crop gone, we won't need the pit this year. There'll be plenty of time to rebuild—"

A savage scream tore from his throat, cutting off her words. "You stupid bitch!" he bellowed, grabbing her arm and twisting it until she felt her shoulder pop out of its socket. "Our money was in that cellar, under the sacks—money for our family! For our future! Now it's gone, damn you to hell!"

Still gripping her arm, he whipped her around and slammed his huge fist into her jaw. "You've ruined me!" he snarled. "I'll kill you for this! Then I'll take the brats to Mexico and sell them!"

Silas had raised his fist to strike her again when a small voice stopped him in midmotion.

"Stop, Daddy! Don't hurt Mama!" Lucas stood at the entrance to the kitchen. "She didn't start the fire. It was me. I did it."

With a muttered oath, Silas flung Annabeth against the counter. As she fell back, struggling to right herself, he turned on her son.

"No, Lucas!" she shouted. "Run!"

But by then Silas had already grabbed the boy's arm.

Hanging on tight while Lucas struggled, Silas whipped the leather belt from the waist of his trousers. Raising the strap high, he brought it down with a resounding whack on the boy's back. Lucas screamed with pain.

With the second blow, the boy was sobbing. Annabeth could see the blood seeping through his thin shirt. Silas was furious enough to beat him to death.

The butcher knife lay behind her on the counter. Her left arm hung painfully from her shoulder, but her right arm was strong. Seizing the knife, she held it in a threatening pose. "Stop, Silas," she shouted. "Let him go, or so help me, I'll use this on you!"

He looked startled. Then his face went mean. He let go of Lucas, who slipped to the floor and lay still. "Try it, bitch," he said.

She stepped back, still gripping the knife as he lumbered toward her. She didn't have a chance against his strength, but maybe her stand would buy Lucas a little time.

"Get up, Lucas! Run!" she urged as Silas's bulk filled her vision. She braced the knife as well as she could manage with both hands. If she was going to die, she would die defending her son.

Silas's face was a mask of rage. Intent on grabbing her weapon, he took a step toward her, then another. Suddenly, he stumbled and seemed to lose his balance. He pitched forward, his weight falling against the knife.

The point entered his chest by the breadth of two fingers. He bellowed with pain, wounded but still dangerous. At that instant, Annabeth caught a glimpse of Lucas on the floor.

He was pulling with all his strength on Silas's trailing bootlaces.

Seizing their only chance to live, Annabeth leaned into the blade and drove it to the hilt.

CHAPTER FIFTEEN

Mason's advice had been sound and well-meant. Annabeth's family life was none of Joseph's business. Trying to interfere would only cause her, and himself, more trouble.

Joseph had tried to follow Mason's counsel. He had even turned Annabeth's handwritten will over to the family lawyer for safekeeping. His intentions had been good. But Annabeth had been in his thoughts day and might.

Whenever he'd gone to town, he'd watched for her and the children. But he'd failed to catch even a glimpse of them. Were they all right? Was Silas caring for his wife and family, or had he become the enemy?

Joseph had even driven the back road within sight of their farm. From a distance, he'd seen nothing out of order. He'd known better than to drive closer or even slow down in his red Model A, which could easily be seen and recognized. But the urge to see and touch her, or at least to know she was safe, had never left him.

He was doing paperwork in the ranch office, thinking of taking a break, when the telephone rang. He answered the call at his desk. His heart lurched as he recognized Annabeth's strained voice.

"Joseph? Is that you?"

"Yes. What's wrong, Annabeth? Are you all right?"

"The doctor gave me your phone number." Her voice quivered. "I'm in trouble, Joseph. I didn't know who else to call."

"It's all right. I'm here for you. What's wrong?"

There was a pause on the line. "Silas is dead," she said in a flat voice. "I killed him."

Joseph forced himself to breathe past the tightness in his chest. "Are you all right? Where are you? What about your children?"

"I'm in the house. The children are in the car, out back where Silas left it. We're safe, but we need help."

"What about Silas?"

"He's in the kitchen. I had to do it. He would have killed Lucas." Her voice broke. "Lucas needs a doctor. I've never driven the car, but I could try."

"No. I'll be right there. Go to your children and wait for me."

"Joseph—"

"We can talk when I get there. Don't worry, I'm coming right now."

He drove at breakneck speed over the back road, wheels flying over the bumps and ruts. The content of Annabeth's phone call was still sinking in. He only knew one thing. Whatever she'd been forced to do, he would be there for her.

At first, he couldn't see the old Model T. But when he pulled around the house, it was there, in a corner of the yard, next to the blackened, caved-in remains of a potato cellar. The children were in the back seat, the dog between them. Annabeth was in the driver's seat. As Joseph stepped out of his car, she flung open the door and ran to meet him.

He caught her close. She was pale with shock, her hands and clothes spattered with burn marks and blood. For a long moment, he held her. She quivered in his arms, shaking but not crying. Something told him she had passed beyond the point of tears.

"Get the children," he said, releasing her. "We can talk in the car."

They loaded Ellie, Lucas, and the dog into the back seat of the Model A. The children were silent. They'd been through an ordeal that no child should suffer. When Joseph saw the strips of dried blood on the back of Lucas's shirt, the anger that rose in him was almost dizzying. Silas Mosby had deserved to die.

Annabeth told him her story as they drove to the Hunter Ranch, where Kristin was scheduled to be at home today. She spoke in a low, emotionless voice that the children couldn't hear from the back seat. Joseph sensed that she might not be telling him everything, but he would let that go for now.

"How many people know about this?" he asked her.

"Just you—and Lucas. He was there. Ellie was in her room. I got her outside before she could see Silas's body."

"So my aunt doesn't know yet?"

"No. I only asked her for your phone number. But of course, she'll have to be told. And the sheriff as well. I can't just leave Silas's body in the house."

"This might not be a good idea, but we could set the house on fire."

"No!" Annabeth shook her head. "A fire to hide the crime, or even hiding the body, would only make me look worse in the eyes of the law. And Lucas knows the truth. He's likely to be questioned. I would never ask him to lie for me."

"It sounds as if you've thought this all out."

"I had time while I was waiting for you. The sheriff will need to be told, even if it means I might be arrested and jailed." She went silent for a moment, as if pondering the weight of her words. "Do you have the will I gave you?"

"My lawyer has it."

"If I go to prison, Joseph, I want you to take my children. Promise me you'll do that."

"I'll do everything I can."

Joseph wanted to promise her. But the lawyer had warned him of roadblocks. The will might not hold up in court. Even with Silas gone, his sister could claim the children. Or they could be taken as wards of the state. Whatever happened, he would look after their welfare and continue fighting in the courts for their custody. But there was still a chance he could lose.

However, there was one thing he could do to strengthen his case. He thought about it as he drove through the gate of the

Hunter ranch. It was the best possible solution—but would Annabeth agree to it?

Annabeth looked on as Kristin applied salve to the bleeding welts on Lucas's back. The boy winced as the healing balm penetrated, but he was making an effort not to cry out.

"You're a brave boy, Lucas," the doctor said. "Your mother must be proud of you."

"Yes, I'm very proud." Annabeth meant every word, even though she hadn't told anyone how truly brave her son was. Not even Joseph knew how Lucas had seized Silas's bootlaces and caused him to stumble into the knife. That would forever remain her secret.

"Would you let me photograph Lucas's back?" Kristin asked. "I'd also like to photograph your face, as well as your shoulder and the bruises on your arms before I work the joint into place. If the worst happens, the pictures could serve as evidence of the abuse the two of you suffered."

"Yes, of course." Annabeth understood. She had killed Silas to defend her son and herself. But without evidence, once the law got involved, she could be charged with murder. It was more important than ever that Joseph be allowed to keep her children safe.

Annabeth exposed her injuries to Kristin's pocket Kodak. The pictures, and those of Lucas's back, would have to be developed in Miles City. But if they could make a difference, she was more than willing to cooperate.

Ellie was with Joseph's Aunt Britta, who lived close by on the ranch with her husband. She'd welcomed the little girl and her dog with open arms. Annabeth was overcome with gratitude for the kindness of Joseph's relatives, who'd accepted her and her children without prejudice.

After working Annabeth's dislocated shoulder back into its socket, Kristin had found Lucas some clean clothes. Her own boys were close to his age, but she knew that Lucas was going to need some quiet time before making new friends.

"I have some spare clothes that should fit you, Annabeth," Kristin said. "I'll get them for you. Then you'll want some private time to shower and dress. Joseph is outside with my husband. When you're ready, we'll have some lunch. With all that's happened, you mustn't forget to take care of yourself."

Alone in the shower, with warm water streaming down her battered body, Annabeth forced herself to face what she'd done. She had killed a man—her own husband. Whatever justice meted out to her, she would live with that truth forever. But that couldn't be allowed to matter. In the days ahead, nothing could be more important than the safety and welfare of her children.

As for Joseph, whom she had never stopped loving, he had promised to be here for her. But she knew that didn't mean forever. She was facing arrest, possibly prison, even hanging if the scales of justice swung that way. And even if she were to be found innocent, she was already a branded woman. The scandal would stain her for the rest of her days. She wouldn't saddle him with that shame.

For now, she needed Joseph. But the man she wanted could never be hers.

The clothes that Kristin had laid out in the guest room were simple in style but finer than anything Annabeth had ever worn. Wearing the pretty blue frock should have lifted her spirits. But one look at her bruised face in the mirror reminded her of who she was and what her lot was to be.

Never mind, Annabeth chided herself. These good people had opened their home to her and her children. The least she could do was stop brooding and show her gratitude. Tomorrow—or sooner if the children were settled—she would contact the sheriff, confess what she'd done, and prepare herself for the consequences. In the meantime, she would make every effort to forget her troubles and be gracious.

After lacing on her old work shoes and fluffing out her damp hair, she squared her shoulders, took a breath, and walked down the hall to meet her hosts.

In the parlor, only one person was waiting to greet her. Joseph stood as she entered. "I checked on the children," he said. "Ellie is playing dolls with Aunt Britta's little girls. Lucas is sleeping. Freckles is keeping him company on the bed. Sit down, Annabeth. We need to talk."

He motioned her to the couch. "Is something wrong?" she asked, sitting. "I mean something new."

He took his seat beside her. "Nothing new. But you're going to need a plan to get through this mess. Do you have one?"

She shrugged, determined to stand alone without involving him. "Here's my plan," she said. "As soon as I know my children are all right, I intend to call the sheriff. I'll tell him the truth and take whatever justice is coming to me."

"No, you're not thinking." His stern gaze riveted hers. "Listen to me, Annabeth. The rest of your life could depend on your doing this right. You're going to need a lawyer. My family retains a good one. Don't talk to the sheriff until you've spoken with him."

"But my children—"

"*Listen.* I'll do all I can to keep them with me. But as things stand, if you're arrested and charged, they could be taken into state custody. There's no guarantee I'll have access to them—or even to you. Only one thing can guarantee that."

She stared at him.

"Marry me, Annabeth," he said. "Now. Today. I mean it. It's the best chance for the children and for you."

She shot to her feet. "Are you mad, Joseph? My husband's only been dead a few hours! And I'm the one who killed him! How would it even be legal?"

"Why wouldn't it be?" He stood to face her. "There's a justice of the peace in Miles City. We could leave this afternoon. Kristin and Britta have offered to tend your children. As your husband, I could legally adopt them. They'd be safe. Lucas, as my son, would be heir to the ranch. And Ellie would become my own daughter."

"What about me?" she asked. "What happens if I go to prison—or what if I'm found innocent?"

His gaze softened. "Either way, you'd be my wife, to have and to hold, to love and to cherish, until death do us part."

"But you don't love me, Joseph!"

Joseph didn't reply. Annabeth's breath caught as his hand cupped her bruise-mottled face. "You're wrong." His voice was husky with emotion. "I thought I'd forgotten you all those years ago. But when I saw you in town, I began to fall in love all over again. Your courage, your loyalty, your tenderness . . . Every time I saw you, I came to love you more. You broke my heart because I couldn't take you in and care for your little family. Give me that chance now, Annabeth."

As he bent to kiss her, a voice shrilled in her head that she couldn't ask him to make this sacrifice, not even for her children. She would only drag him down, and in the end, he would resent her for it. But as his lips claimed hers in a gentle act of possession, she felt the fire spark and grow inside her until she burned with need. She wanted him, not just for her children but also for herself. She responded, stretching on tiptoe to deepen the kiss. Her fingers wove into his hair, pulling him down to her. Her senses swam with the feel of him, the aroma of his sweat and the low rasp of his breathing. The timing was all wrong. This was the most terrible day of her life. But if fate had chosen her for this brief gift of happiness, she would seize it and hold on tight.

He released her, the ghost of a smile playing about his mouth. "Can I take that as a yes?" he asked.

Annabeth found her voice. "I suppose you can. I only hope you don't come to regret it."

Reaching out again, he drew her close, cradling her in his arms. His lips brushed her temple as he spoke. "No regrets," he said. "Not ever."

After a hurried lunch with the family, Annabeth kissed her children, she and Jospeh climbed into the car, and they started for Miles City. Annabeth carried a canvas duffel bag that Kristin had pressed on her as they were leaving the house.

"It's my wedding dress," she'd said. "There won't be time to get it pressed, but if you choose to wear it, may it bring you as much happiness as it's brought me."

Now Annabeth sat in the passenger seat of the red Model A,

cradling the duffel on her lap. There was good reason for haste. Once Silas's body was discovered in the house, everything could change. She could be placed under arrest and taken to jail. The marriage had to take place before it was too late.

There would be talk, of course, although theirs wouldn't be the first marriage scandal to shake Blue Moon. Years ago, Webb Calder, Chase's father, had set his eyes on a beautiful, married immigrant woman. When her older husband had died of cholera, Webb had whisked her away and married her at once. Not long after giving birth to Chase, the woman had died in a shooting. Webb had never remarried.

But that didn't make Annabeth's marriage to Joseph any less shocking.

They planned to return in the morning. Joseph had telephoned ahead to make sure the justice of the peace would be ready for them. Explaining things to the children would have to wait. They were so young. It would take time for them to understand why they suddenly had a new father. In the meantime, they would be safe and cared for among their new family.

Logan Hunter had offered to look after the livestock and chickens left on the farm. How he would manage without rousing suspicion was a worry, but he'd assured Annabeth that everything would be all right. She trusted him. And right now, she had more pressing concerns.

"You've been awfully quiet," Joseph remarked. "I hope you aren't getting cold feet."

"Not a chance," she said. "You've been quiet, too. What are you thinking?"

"I was just wishing I'd married you when I was nineteen. Think of the grief it would have saved us."

"We would've most likely had our own grief," Annabeth said. "And if I'd married you, I wouldn't have my little Ellie. I can't imagine my life without her. There's some good that comes even from a hard situation."

A chill passed through her body. The horror of Silas's death, and the guilt over her part in it, would never stop haunting her.

Today she had Joseph's love. But how long would it last? What would she do when it was gone?

"Spoken like a wise woman," Joseph said. "Ellie stole my heart that day when I found her with her leg full of stickers. I hope you know she'll be as much my daughter as Lucas is my son."

"Then let's make it so." She laid her hand on his knee, trying not to think of the morning's terror or the uncertainty that awaited them back in Blue Moon. With this marriage, she would be providing a future for her children and stealing a few precious, happy hours for herself. That would be all she could ask of heaven.

They arrived in Miles City to find the elderly justice of the peace waiting for them in his home. His wife, chattering and smiling, helped Annabeth into the beautiful silk gown Kristin had lent her. The fabric was so fine that it was hardly wrinkled at all. But there was no way Annabeth could hide the ugly bruises on her face and body.

"Goodness me, dearie," the woman said with a click of her tongue. "What happened to you?"

"An accident. Just being clumsy." Annabeth dismissed the subject.

"Accident, my foot! I've lived a long life and seen a lot of things. I know when a woman's been beaten. I just hope the fellow that done this to you isn't the one you're marrying."

"No. My Joseph is a good man." The simple words brought a mist to her eyes.

"Well, I hope the brute that hurt you got what was coming to him."

"I suppose he did." Closing the subject, Annabeth turned to look in the full-length mirror. The gown, worn with a wisp of a veil, was exquisite. It was a shame she didn't have pretty shoes. But maybe that was all right. The dusty, worn work boots would be there to remind her of who she really was and where she'd come from. The lovely bridal gown was only borrowed.

Joseph, in his everyday clothes, was waiting in the parlor with the justice. His expression warmed when Annabeth walked in. He held out his hand and led her to a small desk, where they signed the legal papers. Then, side by side, they recited the traditional wedding vows and he slipped a plain silver band on her finger. Surrendering to the moment, she gave herself up to his kiss.

This was no time to question whether she was doing the right thing. She was Joseph's wife now. He had gambled his reputation to rescue her and her children. She could only pray that she wasn't about to ruin his life.

As the justice's wife helped Annabeth remove the wedding gown and put it away, she noticed the ring. "Ah, that one," she said. "Yes, it was always one of my favorites. My husband keeps a box of simple rings for couples who show up needing one. This was your groom's choice. Of course, you'll probably want him to replace it with something finer."

"Not at all." Annabeth turned the ring on her finger. The fit was perfect. Her old ring had been taken by Silas long ago to pay a poker debt. "This will be my wedding ring for the rest of my life," she said, loving it.

By the time they left the justice's home, it was late in the day. Joseph took Annabeth to a family clothing store, where he invited her to choose a stack of practical outfits for the children and herself. She even found a pair of nice-looking but serviceable shoes. "Buy the best and plenty of it," he said when he caught her checking prices. "We can afford it. And you're not going back to your old house for anything. That's finished."

They dined discreetly in a small but elegant restaurant down the street from the Olive Hotel. Annabeth had dreaded the idea of eating in the hotel dining room, where Joseph was well-known. The thought of curious eyes and wagging tongues had made her want to shrink away to nothing. Thank heaven he'd understood that she didn't wish to be put on display. She'd done her best to finish the delicious Italian food on her plate, but the memories of the day were catching up with her. She had to force herself to eat.

Joseph had made a reservation at the hotel. Their suite was sumptuous, with velvet furnishings, an oversized bed, and a luxurious bath. But Annabeth was grateful that it wasn't the bridal suite she'd seen advertised in the lobby, with its sentimental décor and special services.

By now it was dark outside. The bedside lamps lent a soft glow to the room. Joseph secured the lock on the door and turned toward Annabeth, who'd sunk onto the edge of the bed, totally exhausted. It was as if the determination that had fed her energy during the day had finally run out, leaving her drained.

Sitting beside her, he laid an arm around her shoulders and drew her against his side. "It's all right, girl," he murmured, cradling her head against his shoulder. "You've been through a hellish time. All I'm asking tonight is that you get some rest."

Tears welled in her eyes, spilling over to trickle down her cheeks. "I'm sorry," she whispered. "If you were expecting the good-time girl you used to meet on moonlit nights, you'll be in for a letdown. There's been a lot of water under the bridge since then."

Tilting her face toward him, he kissed the salty traces of her tears. "We'll have more moonlit nights," he said. "Once this mess is cleared up, we'll have all the time in the world. Now, Mrs. Dollarhide, let's get ready for bed and get some sleep."

All the time in the world.

Joseph's words came back to Annabeth as she lay awake in the warm darkness of the night. Would they really have all the time in the world—time to love, time to raise their family, time to grow old together?

Or had their time already run out?

She drifted in and out of twilight sleep. Finally, lulled by the sound of Joseph's breathing, she sank deep enough to dream. She was back in the kitchen, watching Silas reel sideways with the knife planted below his ribs. His bewildered eyes stared at her as if to ask, *What have you done to me?* Then he toppled to the floor. As his breathing ended in a gasp, she scooped Lucas up in her arms and fled from the room.

She made it to the porch and left him on the steps with the dog while she ran back inside to get Ellie. But when she opened the door to the children's room, she found the room empty.

In a panic, she raced through the house. Silas was lying where she'd left him, in a pool of blood. But there was no sign of her little girl. Maybe she was with Lucas.

She ran for the front porch. When she flung the door open, there was no one outside but the dog. Her children were gone.

No! She jerked awake, her skin cold, her body shaking beneath the thin shift she'd worn to bed. The dream had been so horrifyingly real—as if the loss of her little ones was the price she would have to pay for taking her husband's life.

Joseph's warmth in the bed reassured her that she'd only been dreaming. Earlier, his lingering goodnight kiss had let her know that he would have welcomed more. But Annabeth had nothing of herself left to give. Understanding that, he had stretched out beside her and fallen asleep.

Now he was stirring. He turned on his side to face her. "Are you all right?" he asked.

"Yes. Just a bad dream."

"Do you want to tell me about it?"

"No." Annabeth could feel herself crumbling, as if the day's horrific events were caving in on her like rotted timbers in a mine shaft, crushing her under their awful weight.

Killing Silas had given her everything she'd ever dreamed of: for her children, safety and a loving home; for herself, a life with the only man she'd ever truly wanted. It was more than she deserved. Somehow, there had to be a price to pay.

Reaching out, he laid a hand on her shoulder. "You're shaking, Annabeth. It's all right. I can imagine what you're facing. But you're not alone. I'm your husband. I'll be here for you and our children. We're family now."

Something broke inside her. In all her life, she'd never felt loved and protected. She'd survived by fighting her battles alone. But she couldn't do it any longer.

She moved closer to him. "I'm scared, Joseph," she whispered. "Hold me, please. Just hold me."

He wrapped her in his arms and gathered her close. Annabeth nestled against him, pressing her face into the crisp mat of his chest hair, filling her senses with the manly aroma of his skin. She loved the scent of him, the feel of him, the rich interplay of textures—rough and smooth, warm and cool.

He had worn his cotton briefs to bed, probably to reassure her and make her feel safe—as if she needed to feel safe from him. The tingle between her thighs was already deepening into an ache of need.

His breath stirred her hair. She closed her eyes, remembering soft summer nights, riding his horse up the canyon, lying on the silken grass, gasping with pleasure as he slid inside her for the first time. His strokes had brought her to a sensation that felt like a thousand stars exploding inside her. Still, she'd been mildly disappointed when he'd pulled out and she'd felt the hot spurt of his seed on her belly. After a few times, she'd come to expect it—until the night when she'd decided *no more* and stopped him with her legs. That had been the end of their secret meetings—and the beginning of Lucas.

They'd been little more than children then, innocent of all but the needs of nature and their vital young bodies. Now, tempered by time and sorrow, they were different people. As a young girl, she had fancied herself in love. But she had learned what love was—and what it wasn't.

She was Joseph's wife.

Tonight, nothing else could be allowed to matter.

She could hear the drumming of his heart against her ear, its beat urgent and powerful. The tingle between her thighs had become a pulsing current of heat that surged upward until her womb contracted like a clenched fist.

She stifled a moan, her hips curling forward to move against his hard, swollen erection. She gasped as the light pressure sent a burst of shimmering waves through her body. Her seeking hand fumbled with the waistband of his drawers.

"Joseph," she whispered, "I . . ."

"Hush." His mouth covered hers in bittersweet possession as he stripped off his drawers and moved over her. They were old friends, old lovers, and even with the hard years that had passed between them, he knew the way.

With her body and her soul, she welcomed him home, opening to him, meeting his thrust as he glided into her. This was Joseph—Joseph inside her, filling her, loving her. She closed her eyes and lost herself in the bliss of it as they moved in a well-remembered dance, letting the old hurts and bad memories fall away.

Together, they reached their shuddering climax. As she lay in his arms, he kissed her tears. Tomorrow loomed bleak and frightening, but tonight he was hers and she was his. It was all she could ask.

They left early the next morning after a light breakfast in their room. Joseph drove in silence, his thoughts on the day ahead and what needed to be done. The first thing, after reuniting Annabeth with her children, would be to phone Ezra Dillenbeck, the family lawyer, and get him started on Annabeth's defense as well as the formal adoption of the children.

He would have to check on the sawmill, of course, and the cattle at the ranch, but his first concern would be keeping his new family safe. At least he'd had the foresight to put two good men in charge under him.

With luck, Silas's death would be dismissed as justifiable—a mother protecting her child. But he had to be prepared for anything. The sheriff, Matthew McTeer, was new in town. A short, pugnacious man with few friends, he was hard to read. If he was trying to make a name for himself, there could be trouble. That was why Joseph needed to get Ezra in place right away.

He glanced over at Annabeth. She was visibly nervous, her hands clenched in her lap. He felt that they had bonded as man and wife last night, their trust and love already strong. She had to know that he would do anything for her and their children.

She looked back at him with a faint smile. "I love you, Joseph," she whispered.

"And I love you, Mrs. Dollarhide," Joseph said. "Don't worry, you'll soon be with the children again. Everything's going to be fine."

They were approaching the outskirts of Blue Moon, the forests and meadows giving way to scattered farms. There was no traffic on the road, which seemed a bit strange. But soon they'd be back in town. And soon they would know whether Silas's body had been discovered.

Suddenly, Annabeth gasped. "Up ahead—what's that?"

Joseph followed the direction of her startled gaze.

A quarter mile ahead, three cars were parked sideways across the road, blocking the way.

Standing in front of them, flanked by two deputies and armed with a double-barreled shotgun, was Sheriff Matthew McTeer.

CHAPTER SIXTEEN

JOSEPH SLOWED THE CAR AS THEY APPROACHED THE ROADBLOCK. McTeer could be waiting for somebody else, and they'd be allowed to pass through. But Joseph knew better. Instinct and logic told him that the body had been found and the evidence examined. Anyone could have seen Annabeth leaving town with him, and a call to the hotel would have confirmed that they were on their way back to Blue Moon.

"It's me they want, Joseph." Annabeth's voice was icy calm. "Don't take any action to stop them. I'll need you free and safe to look after the children. Promise me." She gripped his arm hard. "*Promise me!*"

"All right, I promise. But don't tell the sheriff anything. You'll have the right to remain silent and to have your lawyer present for questioning. I'll call Ezra as soon as I can get to a telephone."

"I'll be fine. Just make sure the children are all right. And don't worry them. Just tell them I'll be back soon." Annabeth's voice was calm, but Joseph could read the terror in her eyes as they pulled up to the roadblock and stopped.

"I love you, Annabeth," he said. "We'll get through this."

"Yes, we will," she said as McTeer walked up to the car. "One way or another."

McTeer, with the face and manner of a schoolyard bully, tapped on the driver's side glass. Joseph rolled down the window, which he'd raised protectively as they approached the roadblock.

"Is there a problem, Sheriff?" he asked.

"You're damn right there is, Dollarhide. You and the lady, get out of the car."

"The lady happens to be my wife. And if you lay a hand on her, you'll pay for it."

"Your wife?" McTeer sneered. "Now, isn't that a pretty picture. You'll be interested in knowing that a neighbor found her husband's body on the kitchen floor with a knife in his belly. Lucky thing we stopped you, mister. You could've been next."

With the armed deputies looking on, McTeer walked around the car to Annabeth's side and opened her door. She stepped down, head high, like a queen. Her expression betrayed nothing.

McTeer produced a set of steel cuffs, pulled her hands behind her back, and snapped them on her wrists. Joseph battled the urge to bloody the pompous little man's face. That would buy them nothing.

"Where are you taking my wife?" he demanded.

"To jail. She'll be locked up like any other criminal."

"Damn it, Sheriff, she's not a criminal. And you can't shut a woman in a cell in full view of the men. Let me take her home to her children. There's no chance she'll run. She would have turned herself in today if you'd given her the chance."

"That's not my problem, Dollarhide. Do what you have to. Your wife's going to jail."

Joseph might have said more, but he caught the pleading look in Annabeth's eyes. *Let it be,* her gaze told him. There were other ways to fight. And the children would need him.

Sick with helpless rage, he watched as she was shoved into the back of the sheriff's car and driven away. Then, as the roadblock broke up, he started his car. The tires spat gravel as he headed for the Hunter Ranch to find his children and telephone his lawyer.

Dirty army surplus blankets had been hung from the top of the bars to separate Annabeth's cell from the three next to it. At least for now, the cells were empty. But that could change at any time. The only furnishings in the small space were a bunk with a thin, stained mattress, a jug of water, and a bucket in one corner that she had yet to use. The place smelled of urine, bleach, and other things she didn't want to imagine.

She had tried to put on a brave face while she was with Joseph. Now the mask crumbled away. Perched on the edge of the bunk, she buried her face in her hands. Her shoulders shook with dry sobs.

"Ma'am, you've got a visitor." At least the young deputy on duty was polite. Annabeth arranged her features in the semblance of a smile as the blanket was pulled away from the front of the cell. The door was opened to admit her lawyer.

Joseph had told her about him over dinner the night before. Ezra Dillenbeck was a bespectacled scarecrow of a man, dressed in a brown business suit with a plaid tie. Nearing seventy-five, he had served three generations of Dollarhides. He knew the family, and he knew the law.

He glanced around the cell as the door closed behind him. "Good God, how can they keep a decent woman in here?"

"I'm just hoping it won't be forever." Annabeth rose to greet him. "Thank you for coming, Mr. Dillenbeck."

"You can call me Ezra," he said. "I'll have you out of here as soon as I can, but it'll take a judge's order to set your bail. I'm afraid that might take a day or two."

"Do what you need to. It's my children I'm concerned about. Are they all right?"

"They're fine. For now, they're safe at the Hunter Ranch while Joseph takes care of business."

"And the adoption? Will Joseph be able to take them?"

"Since he's your husband and he can prove that he's the boy's natural father, that shouldn't be a problem. But for the formal adoption, the paperwork has to be signed off by a judge. We're working on that. But that's not why I'm here now."

The lawyer shifted his position on the bunk to face her. "Joseph told me everything he knows about your late husband's death. I'd say it looks like a clear case of self-defense. But the sheriff has other ideas. The fact that you married another man before Mr. Mosby was even cold in his grave casts you in an unfavorable light."

Fear tightened its noose. "We only did it for the children—to make sure Joseph could adopt them. Are you saying that Joseph could be implicated?"

"Not for the physical crime. He can prove that he was at home. But your motive might be called into question. The prosecution could claim you murdered your husband so you could be free to marry your lover."

A chill passed through Annabeth's body.

"Forgive me for asking a personal question," Ezra said. "I need to know. Your marriage to Joseph—was it consummated?"

Heat flooded Annabeth's face. She nodded.

"And before?"

"No. There was nothing. Except, of course, when we were teenagers. Can they really ask me that in court?"

"The prosecution can ask you anything that proves relevant to the case. McTeer is pushing for a speedy trial. He'll be up for re-election this fall. He's not the prosecutor, of course, but a conviction in a sensational case like yours would be a feather in his cap."

Sensational. Annabeth thought of the press, the papers. What kind of monster would they make of her?

"But I never meant to kill Silas!" she insisted. "He would have beaten Lucas to death. That was why I threatened him with the knife. But he was out of control, like a wild animal. When he stumbled into the blade, it wounded him, but he was still strong enough, and mad enough, to kill us both. I stopped him the only way I could."

Annabeth could have claimed that the knife had gone in all the way when Silas stumbled. That might have been ruled an accident. But she knew the truth. And so did Lucas.

"Look at me," she said. "Look at the bruises on my face. The doctor can testify that my shoulder was dislocated. And she treated the bleeding welts on Lucas's back. She even took pictures with her camera."

"Yes, the doctor—a close member of your new husband's family. That could cast her testimony into question. Bruises can heal. And the film for those pictures would have to be sent off to be developed. That could take weeks. The trial will most likely happen sooner."

He studied her through his thick spectacles, his hazel eyes direct and penetrating. "But you have a witness," he said. "An unimpeachable eyewitness who saw everything. His testimony could make all the difference."

"No!" She recoiled from him. "I won't allow Lucas to testify. Having to relive that time, with the questioning and the attention, and all those eyes watching. It would be torture for him! I won't put him through that. There has to be another way."

The lawyer stood, preparing to leave. "I'll see what I can do," he said. "But you'll want to think hard about the situation you're in and what your options are. If you change your mind, let me know. I'll be in touch."

"I won't change my mind," Annabeth said. "But thank you for your help. Tell Joseph I'm all right."

"I'll do that," he said, turning to go. "He'll be fighting for you. So will I."

The next day, after being charged with second degree murder and denied bail, Annabeth was transferred to the jail in Miles City. She had better quarters in a section reserved for women prisoners. But being farther away from Joseph and her children was distressful for her.

Joseph had been allowed a ten-minute visit with her. They'd held hands through the bars, talked about the children, and murmured reassurances that everything was going to be all right. But Joseph had walked out of the jail with rage and frustration eating a hole in his gut.

He'd goaded Ezra into pushing harder for her release. He'd also talked to anyone who might be able to help, including the Miles City sheriff. None of his efforts had made any difference. The judge had ruled against bail. Another trial had been cancelled. Annabeth's trial had been moved to that date with the same jury—just four days from now.

By the time he'd driven back to the Hunter Ranch, night had fallen. Annabeth's children were staying with Joseph's Aunt Britta and her husband, former sheriff Jake Calhoun. They had supper waiting for him, warm from the oven. At his aunt's insistence, Joseph forced himself to eat the tasty meatloaf and fried potatoes Britta had prepared.

"You need to keep your strength up, Joseph," she chided him. "Starving yourself isn't going to help anybody."

"This mess is partly my fault," he said. "I was the one who talked Annabeth into getting married. Now it's come back to make everything worse. I just wish there was something I could do."

"There is." Britta laid a hand on his shoulder. "You can do what she wanted and take care of her children. They're your children now. Be a father to them."

Joseph's breath stopped for an instant as he felt the impact of her words. He had become a father to two precious children who needed him. And he had no idea where to begin. His natural father had deserted him before he was born. His adopted father had been busy with work, leaving most of Joseph's upbringing to his mother. How could he keep his word to Annabeth and become a loving father to her little ones? All he could do was try.

"How have they been?" he asked.

"They've been good but very quiet. I could tell they were worried about their mother, especially Lucas. He was asking questions, and I didn't know what to tell him. They're in bed now. I put them in the guest room. You might want to look in on them."

Joseph left the kitchen and walked down the hall to the bedroom on the right. The door was ajar, the darkness made friendlier by a teddy bear light on the nightstand between two single beds.

For the space of a long breath, he stood looking down at them. Ellie was curled in her quilt, lost in dreams. Lucas lay on his back in the near bed. His eyes were closed, but Joseph could sense his alertness.

How could he show them that, even with their mother absent, they were safe and loved?

As Joseph bent over him, Lucas opened his eyes. Joseph realized his son had probably been awake all along.

"Hello, Lucas," he said, speaking softly.

"Are you our new dad?" the boy asked.

The question caught Joseph by surprise. "How do you know that?"

"People talk. I listen. I learn lots of things that way. I know that you and my mama got married."

"That's right. We did. Is it all right if I sit down?"

"Uh-huh. We can talk that way."

Joseph lowered himself to the edge of the bed, near the foot. The moment was fragile and precious, like having a butterfly pause to rest on his hand. "What would you like to talk about?" he asked.

"Is my mama in jail?" Lucas asked. "I heard that, too. Don't worry, I won't tell Ellie."

"We're doing everything we can to get her out," Joseph said. "We hope she won't be there much longer."

"Is it because she killed my dad?"

"Yes. We know she did it to save you. But some people don't believe that."

"They're wrong."

"Yes, they are. We just have to prove that."

Lucas was silent for a moment. "I should go to jail, too," he said.

"Why would you say that?" Joseph tried to conceal his surprise.

"I helped Mama. He was hurting her. I was on the floor. I made him fall—with his shoelaces."

Joseph spoke carefully. "Who knows about this, Lucas?"

"Just me and Mama." Lucas sat up. "Am I going to jail?"

Joseph wrapped the boy in his arms. Hugging him close, he spoke past the lump in his throat. "No, Son. It sounds like you saved your mother. You're not going to jail. I can promise you that."

The small arms crept around his neck. Heart bursting, Joseph eased Lucas back onto the pillow. "Go to sleep now," he said. "I'll get your mother home as soon as I can. You're a brave boy, and I'm proud of you. Don't forget that."

Before leaving the room, Joseph allowed his gaze to linger on his sleeping children. Being their father was more than he deserved. It was an honor and a blessing.

As he closed the door, leaving it ajar, his thoughts turned to what he would tell Ezra. Lucas's testimony could save his mother from prison. But something told Joseph there was going to be a problem. Annabeth would protect her children at any cost. She would never allow her son to take the stand.

Lola was waiting when the truck arrived with her shipment of moonshine whiskey. There were two men in the cab, a driver in work clothes and the pudgy man she'd met earlier, known only as the Boss.

The driver had backed the truck up to the basement door. He climbed out and began unloading. Forrest came out to help him. Thanks to good food and hard work, the boy had put on muscle. He carried the heavy crates with ease.

The Boss took a seat at one of the tables and beckoned Lola to join him. The new partnership was earning her more money than ever. The product was good, but the partners involved, especially this man, made her nervous.

She took a chair across the table from him and waited while he took a Havana cigar out of his vest, lit it, inhaled, and took a leisurely puff.

"I guess you heard the news about your former partner." The bastard had eyes and ears everywhere.

"You mean that his wife stabbed him to death with a butcher knife? Sure. The whole town knows by now. His sister put him in the ground this morning. With his wife out of the way, I'm betting she'll be trying to get her hands on that farm." Lola had shed a few tears over her lost lover. They'd had some good times together. Maybe his prim little wife had found out. Maybe that was why she'd murdered him.

"If that's what you think, you don't know everything," the Boss said. "Joseph Dollarhide has married the widow. He's adopting her two kids. If anybody gets that farm, it'll be him. Not that the place is worth much. The land is pretty well played out."

"Joseph Dollarhide. I'll be damned." Lola had picked Joseph as a backup match for her sister before that plan went south. Now

Francine was gone, Joseph was married, and Lola was stuck here with nowhere to go.

"So why are you telling me this?" she asked the Boss. "What's any of it got to do with you?"

The Boss took a long drag on his cigar. "Your partners made good money off their moonshine business. The little weasel who was brewing the hooch let himself get beat to pieces because he wouldn't tell my associates where his stash was. What do you think? How much did Silas Mosby have put away?"

Lola shrugged. "I never asked Silas how much he made before I came on board or what he made on the side. I take it you want to get your hands on that money."

"As I see it, that money belongs to the partnership. If anyone dies or leaves, we're entitled to take their share."

"I see." Lola knew the Boss's claim about the partnership was bullshit. But she was in no position to argue.

"We can't get to the big cowboy—Buck they called him," the Boss said. "He's safe on the Calder Ranch. But now that your friend Silas Mosby is six feet under, we figure, as your partners, his cash should be ours for the taking."

"Don't look at me," Lola said. "I don't know where it is. Maybe his wife took it, or Joseph."

"Now you're thinking," the Boss said. "If the new Mr. and Mrs. Dollarhide have the money, what would make them give it to us?"

Lola read the evil glint in his eye. "Oh, no!" she said. "Running a speakeasy is one thing—hell, the sheriff is one of my best customers. But kidnapping? That's a major crime. And too many things can go wrong. Count me out."

"But that's just it, my dear." The Boss stubbed out his cigar in a heavy glass ashtray. "You can't count yourself out. We need you—not to do the snatch, we can manage that. But we need you to act as a go-between. Joseph Dollarhide knows you, maybe even trusts you. He'll believe what you tell him." He made a show of examining his manicured nails, giving Lola time to think. "Of course, I wouldn't ask you to do it for nothing," he said. "You'll be getting your share of the money."

Seeing no way out, Lola leaned toward him. "How much of a share?" she asked in a sly voice.

Joseph was back in Miles City to visit Annabeth the next day. The sight of her, looking drawn and weary in her drab prisoner garb, tore at his heart.

"The children?" she asked. "How are they?"

"They're all right. Aunt Britta's taking good care of them." Joseph reached through the bars and clasped her hand. "I talked to Lucas last night after Ellie was asleep. He seems to understand most of what's going on. He claims he learned it by listening."

She managed a wan smile. "That's our Lucas for you. I don't have to tell him much."

"Ezra wants to put him on the stand."

"I already told him no. I won't put him through that ordeal."

"He could save you, Annabeth. He saw everything that happened, and I know he wants to help. He's stronger than you seem to think he is."

"It's still a no," she said. "At least, I would need to talk with him first, and I can't let him see me like this."

"Blast it, Annabeth!" Frustration made his words harsh. "Your family needs you. *I* need you. You have to let yourself be saved."

"I know." She opened his hand and pressed her lips to his palm. "But there has to be another way."

"Then pray that we can find it."

Seething, he left the jail and took the road back to Blue Moon. How could he convince her to let Lucas testify? The boy was willing, and he would make the perfect witness—innocent and clearheaded. His testimony, along with the still-healing wounds on his back, would prove to any jury that Annabeth had acted in defense of her son and herself.

By now, it was late afternoon. Joseph had spent last night at home in his own bed. That morning, he'd checked on the ranch and sawmill, then had a long visit with Ezra before leaving for Miles City. Now he planned to stop by the Hunter Ranch and spend some time with his children. They would be worried and wanting their mother. He would do his best to be there for them.

Driving through the ranch gate, he could see Britta's house. The front yard, with swings for the children, was empty. He could see Britta's tall figure on the porch with the dog. She was pacing in agitation. As he came up the drive, she plunged off the porch and raced toward him. Even from a distance he could see her anguished expression.

Dread clawed at him as he climbed out of the car and ran to meet her.

Out of breath, she collapsed against him, then caught her balance. "The children," she gasped. "Lucas and Ellie. They're gone! They've been taken!"

CHAPTER SEVENTEEN

REELING BETWEEN PANIC AND RAGE, JOSEPH STEADIED HIMSELF AS Britta gasped out the story of what had happened.

"The children—Lucas, Ellie, and my girls—they were playing on the swings in the front yard. I was busy in the kitchen and didn't see anything. But my daughter told me later that a man drove up in a big, fancy black car. He got out and said that he'd been sent by their mother. She wanted to see them right away."

Joseph groaned, imagining Lucas and Ellie, in their happy excitement, running to get in the car. It would have been so easy for someone to take them. How terrified they must be now.

"When did it happen? How long ago?" Joseph demanded.

"Half an hour maybe," Britta said. "I came to check on the children and found out just a few minutes after it happened. Then I tried to call you—at your house and at the jail. I talked to a deputy. He said you'd been there and gone."

"How much did you tell him?"

"Nothing. I was afraid he might tell Annabeth."

Joseph breathed his thanks. Annabeth would be frantic if she knew her children had been stolen.

"I tried calling the sheriff when I couldn't reach you," Britta said. "But there was no answer. I know you don't think much of him."

"Try him again," Joseph said. "We need all the help we can get."

While Britta went back inside to use the telephone, Joseph examined the scene to learn as much as he could.

It was surprising that the kidnapper had managed to approach the house without being seen by an adult. But it wouldn't have been impossible. Once they knew where the children were staying—which would have been easy enough—they could have watched the place from the road, maybe with binoculars, waiting for the right moment.

Joseph studied the tire tracks in the dust, looking for anything that might help him identify the vehicle. The depth of the tread suggested that the car, or at least the tires, were fairly new. The pattern looked ordinary. But as Joseph bent closer, he could see the imprint of something stuck in the tread—a bit of gravel, maybe, or a shard of glass. If he were to see it again, it might help him track the car. But what were the chances of that? Heaven save him, he had never felt more helpless in his life. But he took a moment to memorize the exact shape and location of the tiny object.

Why would two children be kidnapped? They and their mother had no enemies. But what about Silas? Joseph remembered pulling the wounded man from the bullet-riddled truck. Silas had had enemies, dangerous ones. And he'd had money—the cash that Lucas had burned when he started the fire in the potato pit.

If the kidnappers were after Silas's money and didn't know it had been burned, Joseph might expect to get a ransom demand. What then? He would willingly pay the ransom himself. But he knew what happened to most kidnap victims, even after the ransom was paid. The urgency of the situation screamed in his head. He had to find his children before it was too late.

Britta came out of the house. "I tried the sheriff again. Still no answer." Her hands twisted the hem of her apron. "Why would anybody do that—take two innocent children?"

"My guess is, it's about money," Joseph said. "If I'm right, we should be getting a ransom message. I'm going home to wait. If there's a message, it's likely to come there. Or it could come here. Stay close to the phone and keep your eyes open. Call me if anything changes."

"Of course, I will," Britta said. "And I'll do something else. I'll pray."

* * *

The room was dark and chilly, with a thin quilt laid over the hard earthen floor. Lucas could hear the sound of footsteps overhead and the occasional mutter of voices. The gray light that filtered under the door allowed him to see the wooden crates stacked around the walls and the porcelain chamber pot in one corner. But he had no idea where he and Ellie were. Two men in the car had wrapped them in blankets so they couldn't see where they were being taken. Lucas only knew that it wasn't to see their mother.

"I'm cold," Ellie whimpered. "I want Mama."

Lucas pulled the thin blanket they'd been given around her. "Be still. Whining won't help. We need to find a way out of here."

Brave talk. But he'd already explored as much of the room as he could. The only way out was the door, and it was locked. The one thing that seemed strange was the aroma of mouthwatering food that drifted down from somewhere above them. The smell reminded him of how hungry he was. Ellie would be hungry, too. But something told him they would get none of the food he could smell. He didn't know much about the men who'd taken them prisoner. But their evil was something he could feel.

Time crawled as Joseph waited in the ranch office. The sunset was fading from the sky when the telephone rang. Answering, he was startled to hear a familiar voice.

"Joseph, this is Lola. Don't talk, just listen, please."

"Where are my children, Lola?" he demanded, almost screaming at her. "So help me—"

"I don't know." Her voice shook. "I didn't take them, and I don't have them. I'm only the messenger. I'm trying to help you."

Joseph took a deep breath, struggling to stay calm. "All right, I'm listening."

"The men who took them, all they want is Silas's money—the money that he saved from his moonshining business. Give them that—I'll tell you where to leave it—and you'll get your little ones back. Otherwise . . ." She left the words unspoken, letting Joseph's imagination fill in the unthinkable.

"The money's gone," Joseph said. "Mosby hid it in the potato cellar, and Lucas set it on fire. It was burned to ashes. The sheriff's men looked for it. That was all they found."

"Do you really think those men are going to believe that?" Lola asked.

"That won't make any difference. I'm prepared to pay whatever they want. How much would they take?"

"You could offer thirty thousand. But they might want more."

"I don't have the cash here. I'd have to take it from the bank in Miles City, and they're closed now. I could get it first thing tomorrow. I would just need to know that Ellie and Lucas are safe."

"I'll pass that on. Meanwhile, you know better than to involve the law—no sheriff and no feds. And don't play hero and try to rescue them yourself. If anything goes wrong, those children will be the first to die."

Her words sent a shudder through Joseph's body. "Damn it, who are those men? Where are my children? You know more than you're telling me, Lola!"

"I don't know enough to help you. As I told you, I'm just the messenger. Stay near the phone. I'll relay your message and get back to you."

The call ended. Sick with dread, he hung up the phone and walked out onto the porch. In the distance, he could see the lights of Blue Moon like an island in the dark. Farms and ranches were scattered here and there across the landscape. Headlights crawled along the roads. Somewhere out there, his precious children were being held hostage. He would pay any amount of money to get them back. But what if their captors got tired of waiting? What if the money came too late?

The Boss faced Lola across the table. Her ravaged face wore a calm smile, but her fingers drummed a nervous rhythm on the tabletop. She had shut down the speakeasy while her partners were here, so no one would be coming downstairs to disturb them. But she'd begun to feel trapped by these men—and scared. For the first time since prison, she sensed that she'd gotten in over her head.

She had just told the Boss about the burned money and Joseph's offer to replace it with his own cash. Now, as she waited for his reaction, she could hear the swish of Forrest's broom as he swept behind the bar. In her head, she counted the strokes, *one . . . two . . . three . . .*

At last the Boss spoke. "I don't like it," he grumbled. "The idea was, we get Silas Mosby's money and hit the road. If there's a question, we can claim that the money was in the partnership and we were just claiming our share. Now we've got Dollarhide offering cash that he can't get his hands on until tomorrow. While we wait, the feds could move in, and we'd all be in trouble. It's too damned risky. I say we bail."

"And the children?" Lola dared to ask. "Surely, it would do no harm to let them go."

"You know better than that. Kids see and hear things. And they talk. They saw Carlos and his pals when he took them. They saw the car. And they've heard our voices. They could point you out in a second, and you'd probably turn the rest of us in to save your hide."

The Boss stood, one hand massaging the small of his back. The motion exposed the shoulder holster with the .38 Special he wore under his jacket. "The world has plenty of kids. It won't miss a couple. Keep Dollarhide dangling. Don't tell him anything. By the time he figures it all out, it'll be too late. Got it?"

"Got it." Lola swallowed her terror. The man could kill her on a whim and would if he had no use for her. She felt sorry for the children, but if she were to cross him, she'd be as good as dead.

Needing a distraction, she listened for the familiar swish of Forrest's broom. But there was nothing to hear. Forrest had finished his work and gone.

It was past midnight, and Lola hadn't called. Joseph knew that there would be no call. For whatever reason, most likely distrust, the kidnappers had withdrawn. There would be no demand for ransom and no more reason to hold the children. Either Ellie and Lucas would be released or they would be killed.

The risk involved in rescuing them no longer mattered. He might have already waited too long. But dwelling on that idea would be as useless as it was heartbreaking. He couldn't think about it. He could only make his move.

Lola's involvement was his only lead. Find her, shake the truth out of her. Maybe the children were at Jake's, with its labyrinth of back rooms. It was his best chance, but what if he was wrong? Or what if he was right and his rush to rescue them cost their precious lives? He had no choice except to take that chance.

Earlier, needing an ally, he had called Mason and told him everything. Mason had promised to help and was on his way. Joseph was waiting for him now.

An urgent knock at the front door sent Joseph rushing to answer it. But it wasn't Mason who stood on the threshold. It was Forrest, looking stronger and more mature than the boy Joseph remembered from a few weeks earlier.

"We don't have much time," he said before Joseph could question him. "Your kids are locked in a storeroom in the basement of Jake's. The man holding them doesn't plan to let them live."

Joseph's heart slammed. "How many men are there?"

"Three with pistols. Then there's Lola, but she won't fight you. The door to the basement is under the back stairs. I'll try to leave it unlocked, but you might have to shoot your way in." He took in Joseph's astonished expression. "I've done some pretty bad things in my time, but you were decent to me. I owe you. And I can't stand back while innocent kids die."

"How did you get here? It's a long walk."

Forrest flashed a cocky grin. "I'm driving Lola's car. Got to go. They'll miss me. Hurry." He sprinted into the darkness. Seconds later, Joseph heard the sound of an engine starting.

There was no time to wait in the house for Mason. Joseph holstered his revolver, ran out to his car, and headed down the switchbacks. At the junction with the main road, he saw distant headlights coming from the direction of the Hollister Ranch. That would be Mason.

Joseph waited for Mason to catch up with him. Then, motioning for him to follow, he gunned the engine. Raising dust clouds, the two of them sped toward town.

Forrest had been caught getting out of Lola's car in the parking lot. The biggest of the thugs, the man called Carlos, had dragged him inside, punched him in the face and gut, then flung him, bruised and bleeding, into the storeroom.

Forrest landed hard on his back. As the door locked behind him, he lay gasping with pain. As his eyes adjusted to the dim light, he became aware of two small faces looking down at him—a somber, dark-haired boy and a little blond princess of a girl. Joseph's children. He had glimpsed them earlier when they were brought in. Now, his fate would be the same as theirs.

"Did you come to save us?" the little girl asked.

How could he tell her the truth—that minutes from now all three of them could die? "I came to help," Forrest said, sitting up. "Your father, Joseph, knows you're here. He's on his way. He'll be here any minute now."

"How will he get in?" the boy asked.

"He might have to fight his way in," Forrest said. "If you hear gunfire, here's something you can do to be safe. Let me show you."

Ignoring the pain of his beaten body, he stretched out face down on the floor. "Like this. Pretend you're a pancake. Spread yourself out as flat as you can and stay that way. Whatever you do, don't sit up. Don't even raise your head to look around. Got it? Show me."

From the other side of the door, Forrest could hear a growing commotion—crashing furniture, shouted curses. "Now!" he said. "Down, like I showed you!"

As the children lay flat, Forrest spread himself over them, bracing his weight with his elbows and knees. So far, he hadn't led a very good life. But if he was going to die now, protecting these kids with his body might earn him a few points at the pearly gates.

* * *

Joseph and Mason parked in a vacant lot, twenty yards from the back of the restaurant. No lights could be seen, but Joseph spotted two cars parked to one side of the open stairway that climbed the back of the building. One was a newer Model T, which Forrest may have driven. The other was a black DeSoto—possibly the car that had taken his children. Below the stairs and off to one side was the door to the basement.

Lucas and Ellie could be behind that door. Joseph could only pray silently that he would find them alive.

Mason had driven his heavy-duty ranch truck, which he used for hauling hay and towing trailers. Joseph had his Model A. They stepped to the ground, leaving the doors ajar. There'd been no chance for them to talk since their phone call, but Mason seemed to know what to do. He'd lived a dangerous life as a smuggler before settling down, Joseph reminded himself.

There was no sign of Forrest. Hopefully, the boy was safe. He'd mentioned that he'd try to leave the door unlocked, but when Joseph crept close and tested it, the latch would not budge.

Joseph glanced back at Mason, who beckoned him to return to the truck. Guessing what Mason had in mind, Joseph climbed into the truck bed and crouched behind the cab with his pistol drawn. Mason climbed into the cab, switched on the bright headlights, and started the truck. The engine roared as he stomped the gas pedal and sent the big vehicle rocketing toward the basement door.

The jarring impact shattered the base of the rickety stairs and tore the door out of its moldering wood frame. They were inside.

A hail of bullets greeted them. Through the clearing cloud of dust, Joseph could see that the tables and chairs had been piled into a barricade. Evidently, the gangsters had heard them drive up and made hasty preparations. Off to his left, he glimpsed a closed door in a side wall. On the chance that his children were behind it, that was the place he needed to protect.

Joseph fired over the back of the cab. He could no longer see Mason through the rear window. Had he been hit or was he just staying low? There was no time to find out, but he didn't seem to be shooting.

Joseph ducked behind the cab long enough to reload. He could hear the loud pop of pistol fire and shattering of glass as bullets hit the windshield of the truck. He was standing up to fire again when he heard a nightmarish sound—the rattle of a Thompson submachine gun shooting ribbons of bullets that fed into the magazine and sprayed a deadly hail, piercing the chassis of the truck and the vital door at the side of the room.

If he stood higher, in full view, he should be able to look down on the shooter. Heedless of the danger, he rose into full view. He could see the man with the machine gun now. The glare of the truck's headlights would blur the shooter's vision, but a spray of bullets could easily hit Joseph. A shot grazed his cheek as he took careful aim and fired.

The machine gun's chatter ceased. The man went down and didn't get up.

Two men remained—a big fellow who looked like a driver had dropped his gun and was clutching his wounded arm. A burly, fat-faced man in a brown suit was still gripping his weapon. Together, they made for the stairs that led up to the kitchen on the next floor.

Let them go, Joseph told himself. All he wanted was his children.

But someone was still here. A table was being pushed aside. Ready for anything, Joseph aimed his pistol.

Lola crawled out from under the debris and stood with her hands raised. "Don't shoot, Joseph," she shouted. "You know me! I'm Lucy! Lucy Merriweather! You loved me once!"

The fat man on the stairs raised his pistol and fired a single shot. The woman dropped to the floor, a patch of crimson blooming over her heart.

Before Joseph could return fire, the two men had vanished up the stairs. Still alert, he jumped down from the truck and opened the cab. Mason lay across the seat, bleeding from a shoulder wound. He was conscious, his jaw clenched in pain as he stanched the blood with a red-soaked handkerchief.

"Is it over?" he asked.

Joseph heard the sound of a car driving away. "It's over," he said. "Let me get you something better to press on that wound."

"I'll be fine," he grumbled. "Damn it, just leave me be and find my grandchildren!"

Joseph made his way through the debris that blocked the door. There were several bullet holes in the thin wood. Would he find anybody alive in there? Bracing for heartbreak, he slid back the bolt and opened the door.

In the darkness of the storeroom, three figures scrambled up from the floor. As the light penetrated the gloom, Joseph recognized them.

"Daddy!" The little girl broke away from the others, ran to Joseph, and flung her arms around his neck. "You found us!"

Holding her with one arm, Joseph reached out to his son and drew him close. Lucas was trembling but silent, as if he'd already decided that he was too old to cry.

Overcome with gratitude, Joseph gazed up at Forrest. "I owe you my children's lives," he said. "Know that you have a home with us forever, Forrest. You can be a cowboy, go to college, or anything you want. It's the least I can do for you."

After clearing a way past the truck, Joseph left the children in his car, then went back to bind Mason's wounded shoulder with a clean tablecloth and help him to the car for the ride to the doctor's home. Kristin would know what to do.

Forrest would follow them in Lola's old car, which he wanted to keep if he could make the arrangements.

As he and Mason drove through the night, with the children already asleep in the back seat, Joseph pondered the challenges that had yet to be faced. First and foremost would be freeing Annabeth. Lucas and Ellie needed their mother, and he needed his wife—her warmth, her wisdom, her strength, and her love. He wanted to be a husband and a father to his new family, to shelter them from the hardship they'd known—to keep them in safety and comfort for the rest of their lives.

What would happen if the trial went the wrong way?

* * *

From the Miles City Star:

The trial of Annabeth Coleman Mosby Dollarhide has attracted spectators from all over the state. As the hours have stretched into two days, it has become clear that this is more than the trial of a woman. It has become a question of a woman's right to protect herself and her children from the husband she vowed to love, honor, and obey.

Witnesses for the prosecution have included the neighbors who found the body, Sheriff McTeer, and Silas Mosby's sister, Nancy, who swore that her brother had been a kind and loving husband who had only wanted to keep his rebellious wife in her place.

Rancher and businessman Joseph Dollarhide, the defendant's new husband, was also called by the prosecution. He testified that he had offered friendship and support but that there had been no improper relationship with the defendant during her marriage to Mosby. He insisted that they had married to protect Mrs. Dollarhide's children. But his admission, under oath, that the marriage had been consummated, threw his entire testimony into question.

The defense called Dr. Kristin Dollarhide, who had failed to produce the photos she claimed to have taken but had described in detail the injuries Mosby had inflicted on his wife and son and supported the claim that there was no improper relationship between the defendant and Mr. Dollarhide, who happens to be her nephew. An advocate from a women's support group also spoke about the unfairness of laws that failed to protect women from spousal abuse.

The final witness for the defense was Mrs. Dollarhide's five-year-old son, Lucas. As the only eyewitness to his father's death, he gave a clear and gripping account of the entire event, including his part in it. When he allowed his shirt to be lifted, showing the brutal scars on his back, the collective gasp could be heard even from the back of the courtroom.

Throughout his testimony, the boy showed remarkable poise and self-control. But when defense attorney Ezra Dillenbeck asked him whether he believed his father had wanted to kill him and his mother, Lucas burst into tears and was led from the courtroom.

Mrs. Dollarhide had to be physically restrained from rushing to her son.

Joseph's stomach clenched as the jury filed into the box. After three hours of deliberation, they'd arrived at a verdict.

From his seat in the first row behind the defense table, he could see his wife's back as she sat next to Ezra. She held herself straight and proud, wearing the blue dress Kristin had given her. Her hair hung down her back in a neat, golden braid. She looked as innocent as a child—as innocent as she surely was.

Joseph wanted to reach out and lay a supporting hand on her shoulder, but that would be out of order. He could only wait, suffering the torments of hell for her as the jurors took their seats.

The verdict could go either way. The prosecution had twisted the facts to make her appear guilty, and Joseph's own testimony, with its painful truths, had only strengthened their case.

On the side of the defense, it was all Lucas.

Annabeth had been prepared to testify on her own behalf, but Ezra had insisted that the boy would make a more credible witness. She had resisted until both Ezra and Joseph had assured her that Lucas understood the situation and wanted to help. Only then had she agreed to let the boy take the stand.

Joseph couldn't imagine that he'd ever feel more proud of his son. Lucas's clear-spoken, brutally honest story had touched hearts. But would it be enough to save his mother?

The children waited with Britta in the front hall. If Annabeth was found guilty and sentenced, she would be given a few heartbreaking minutes with them before being sent to the prison at Deer Lodge.

If that were to happen, Joseph vowed, he would never stop fighting to free her. He would file appeals, write letters, talk to reporters and anyone else who would listen. He would never give up.

Kristin was sitting next to Joseph. As the jury foreman, an elderly man in a shabby suit, stood and faced the judge, she found his hand and squeezed it hard. In the packed courtroom, not a sound could be heard.

"Gentlemen of the jury, have you reached a verdict?" the judge asked.

"We have, your honor."

"Will the defendant please rise?"

Annabeth stood. She was trembling, but she kept her dignity, head high. Joseph's own heart was pounding like a trapped bird against his rib cage.

The foreman handed a slip of paper to the bailiff, who passed it to the judge. The judge read it and nodded, his face expressionless.

"Will the foreman please read the verdict?"

"Yes, your honor." The old man cleared his throat. "We the jury find the defendant, Annabeth Coleman Mosby Dollarhide . . . not guilty."

Not guilty.

Annabeth swayed as her knees buckled beneath her. Reaching over the barrier, Joseph caught her in his arms. For a moment, he held her close. Around them, the tumult of the courtroom seemed to fade into the distance.

She looked up at him. "The children?" she whispered.

"They're waiting for you outside," Joseph said. "Come on, Mrs. Dollarhide. Let's find them and go home. It's over."

Epilogue

Thanksgiving Day, 1929

As Joseph surveyed the Thanksgiving table, laden with traditional food and surrounded by family, gratitude raised a lump in his throat. The past months had been fraught with loss, heartbreak, and danger, but the people at the table had made it through. With the roundup over and the last of the steers shipped off to eastern markets, it was time to celebrate.

The places at the table were filled except for the empty chair on Joseph's right. Annabeth was busy checking last minute details in the kitchen. When she took her seat, the food would be blessed and dinner would begin.

Joseph sat at the head of the table. Mason and his wife, Ruby, sat on Joseph's left. As the oldest living Dollarhide, Mason had deferred to Joseph as host and head of the family. His shoulder still pained him, but he was enjoying his new role as honorary grandfather to Lucas and Ellie. The truth about the complex relationship would be left for the future, when the children were old enough to understand.

Kristin and Logan sat across from them. Logan's offer to include Joseph in the horse business was still open. In the year ahead, Joseph had resolved to make time for the vocation he loved. He could still make it happen. He just had to want it badly enough.

Jake Calhoun sat in his wheelchair next to a glowing Britta, who was weeks away from the birth of their second child. When Joseph had told Jake about the death of Lola—whose perfidy as Lucy Merriweather had led to his losing the use of his legs—he had taken the news with his usual calm acceptance. "It was her boyfriend who pulled the trigger," he said. "I never blamed her. Not any more than I blamed you. And I don't believe her death was any kind of payback for what she did. She had a hard life, she did her best to survive, and now she's gone. To brood on it would only be punishing myself."

The children shared their own low table. Lucas, Ellie, Grace, Kristin's boys, and Britta's little daughter and eight-year-old stepdaughter were squirming with impatience as they waited for the meal to start. Only Forrest, who had volunteered to sit with them, kept the little group from breaking into chaos.

Forrest was now working for Mason, who'd needed the extra help. The boy was learning to be an honest-to-goodness cowboy. Mason had even confided to Joseph that, if Forrest continued to do well, he might adopt him. "Two rogues gone straight," Mason had joked. "We'll understand each other."

The buzz of conversation fell to a hush as Annabeth came out of the kitchen. She was smiling, her lovely face flushed from the heat of the cooking. Joseph stood and held out her chair. She was his queen. His wife. His everything.

The family joined hands around the table while the meal was blessed. Then the happy feast began.

Joseph's grandfather looked down from his portrait on the wall. A scene like this was what he'd foreseen when he built the big log house and when he'd insisted that Blake marry pregnant Hannah to give her son the Dollarhide name. It was the reason Blake had urged Joseph to marry and have children before time ran out. It was about family.

Amid the celebrating, Joseph's thoughts wandered to Chase Calder in his huge house. Today, if he bothered with dinner at all, Chase would likely be eating alone or with a few of his longtime ranch hands. Joseph had always admired Chase, even envied him, with his self-confidence and the air of entitlement that came with the Calder name.

Calder strong. That was Chase. But as Joseph looked around the table, he realized that he had no reason to envy any man on earth. This was his strength—his family, here together.

Dollarhide strong.